W9-CUN-692

It Had to Be You

Center Point
Large Print

**This Large Print Book carries the
Seal of Approval of N.A.V.H.**

It Had to Be You

JILL SHALVIS

CENTER POINT LARGE PRINT
THORNDIKE, MAINE

This Center Point Large Print edition is published
in the year 2013 by arrangement with
Grand Central Publishing, a division of
Hachette Book Group, Inc.

The text of this Large Print edition is unabridged.
In other aspects, this book may vary
from the original edition.
Printed in the United States of America
on permanent paper.
Set in 16-point Times New Roman type.

ISBN: 978-1-61173-928-2

Library of Congress Cataloging-in-Publication Data

Shalvis, Jill.
It had to be you : a Lucky Harbor novel / Jill Shalvis.
pages ; cm. — (Lucky Harbor ; 7)
ISBN 978-1-61173-928-2 (library binding : alk. paper)
1. Lucky Harbor (Wash. : Imaginary place)—Fiction. 2. Love stories.
    3. Large type books. I. Title.
PS3619.H3534I8 2013
813'.6—dc23
                                        2013024169

It Had to Be You

Chapter 1

Some things were set in stone: The sun would rise every morning, the tide would come in and out without fail, and a girl needed to check herself out in the mirror before a date no matter the obstacle. To that end, Ali Winters climbed up on the toilet seat to get a full view of herself in the tiny bathroom mirror of the flower shop where she worked. Ducking so that she didn't hit her head on the low ceiling, she took in her reflection. Not bad from the front, she decided, and carefully spun around to catch the hind view of herself in her vintage—aka thrift store—little black dress.

Also not bad.

She'd closed up Lucky Harbor Flowers thirty minutes ago to get ready for the town's big fundraiser tonight, where they were hopefully going to raise the last of the money for the new community center. Earlier, she'd spent several hours delivering and decorating Town Hall with huge floral arrangements from the shop, as well as setting up a display of her pottery for the auction. She was excited about the night ahead, but Teddy was late.

Nothing unusual. Her boyfriend of four months

was perpetually late but such a charmer it never seemed to matter. He was the town clerk, and on top of being widely beloved by just about everyone who'd ever met him, he was also a very busy guy. He'd been in charge of the funding for the new community center, a huge undertaking, so most likely, he'd just forgotten that he'd promised to pick her up. Hopefully.

Still precariously balanced, she eyed herself again, just as there was a sudden knock on the bathroom door. Jerking upright in surprise, she hit her head on the ceiling and nearly toppled to the floor. Hissing in a breath, she gripped her head and carefully stepped down. Managing that without killing herself, she opened the door to her boss, Russell, the proprietor of Lucky Harbor Flowers.

Russell was in his mid-thirties and reed thin, with spiked blond hair, bringing him to just above her own almost-but-not-quite, five foot five. He was wearing red skinny pants and a half tucked–in red-and-white checkered polo shirt. These were his favorite golf clothes, though he didn't golf, because he objected to sweating. He was holding a ceramic pot filled with an artful array of flowers in each hand.

Ali took in the two arrangements, both colorful and cheerful, and—if she said so herself—every bit as pretty as the pots, which were hers too.

"What's wrong with this picture?" Russell asked.

She let go of the top of her head. "Um, they're all kinds of awesome?"

"Correct," Russell said with an answering smile. "But they're also all kinds of waste. No one ordered these, Ali."

"Yes, but they'll look fantastic in the window display." An age-old argument. "They'll draw people in," she said, "and *then* someone will order them."

Russell sighed with dramatic flair. The flower shop had been his sister Mindy's until two years ago, when he'd bought it from her so that she could move to Los Angeles with her new boyfriend. "Sweetkins, I pay you to make floral arrangements because no one in Lucky Harbor does it better. I love your ceramic-ware and think you're a creative genius. I also think that genius is completely wasted on the volunteer classes you give at the senior center, but that's another matter entirely. You already know that I think you give too much of yourself to others. Regardless of that big, warm heart of yours, *you* make the arrangements. *I* run the business."

Ali bit her tongue so she wouldn't say what she wanted to. If he would listen to her ideas, they'd increase business. She was sure of it.

"And speaking of the shop," he went on, "we need to talk sometime soon. Um, you might want to fix your hair."

She turned her neck and glanced in the mirror.

Eek. Her wildly wavy hair did need some taming. She quickly worked on that. "Better?"

"Some," Russell said with a smile, and put the flowers down to fix her hair himself. "Where's your cutie-pie, live-in boyfriend?"

Two months ago, her apartment building had been scheduled for lengthy renovations, and Ali had needed a place to stay. Teddy had generously offered to share his place. He was like that, open and warm and generous. And fun. There hadn't been a lot of that in her life. And then there was the pride of being in a real, adult relationship.

So she'd happily moved into his beach house rental, and suddenly everything she'd ever dreamed of growing up—safety, security, and stability—was right there. Her three favorite S's. "Teddy's late," she said. "I'll just meet him there."

Russell peered at her over the top of his square, black-rimmed glasses. "Don't tell me that Hot Stuff stood you up again."

"Okay, I won't tell you."

"Dammit." He sighed. "The sexy ones are all such unreliable bitches." He hugged her. "Forgive me for my complaint about the fabulous arrangements?"

"Of course. What did you want to talk about?"

A shadow passed over Russell's face but he quickly plastered on a smile. "It can wait. Come on, I'll take you to the auction myself. I want to get there before all the good appetizers are gone."

"How do you know there'll be good appetizers?"

"Tara's cooking."

Tara Daniels Walker ran the local B&B with her sisters, and she was the best chef in the county. Definitely worth rushing for.

Russell drove them in his Prius. Lucky Harbor was a picturesque little Washington beach town nestled in a rocky cove with the Olympic Mountains at its back and the Pacific Ocean at its front. The town itself was a quirky, eclectic mix of the old and new. The main drag was lined with Victorian buildings painted in bright colors, housing cute shops and a bar and grill called The Love Shack, along with the requisite grocery store, post office, gas station, and hardware store. A long pier jutted out into the water, and lining the beach was a café named Eat Me, an arcade, an ice cream shop, and a huge Ferris wheel.

People came to Lucky Harbor looking for something, some to start over and some for the gorgeous scenery of the Olympic Mountains and the Pacific Ocean. Ali was one of those looking for a new start. The locals were hardy, resilient, and, as a rule, stubborn as hell. She had all three of these characteristics in spades, especially the stubborn as hell part.

They parked at the Town Hall building at the end of the commercial row, and found the place filled to capacity.

"Look at all the finery," Russell said as they walked in, sounding amused. "For that matter, look at us. We're smoking hot, Cookie."

"That we are."

"Not bad for a pair of trailer park kids, huh?"

Ali had grown up in a rough area of White Center, which was west of Seattle. Russell had done the same but in Vegas, though he'd made himself a more-than-decent living in his wild twenties as an Elvis impersonator. About ten years ago, he moved to Lucky Harbor with his sister. Ali actually hadn't ever lived in a trailer park, but in a series of falling down, post–WWII cracker-box houses that were possibly even worse. Lucky Harbor was a sweet little slice of life that neither of them had imagined for themselves. "Not bad at all," she agreed.

They entered the hall to the tune of laughter and music and the clink of glasses. Ali caught a fleeting glimpse of Teddy working the crowd, gorgeous as ever in a suit and good-old-boy smile, which he flashed often. His light brown hair was sun kissed from weekends golfing, fishing, hiking, and whatever other adventures he chose. Extremely active and fit, he'd try anything that was in the vicinity of fun. It was one of the things that had drawn her to him.

He caught sight of her and smiled, and Ali's heart sighed just looking at him. She called it the Teddy Phenomenon, because it wasn't just her

—everyone seemed to respond to him that way.

But then she realized he was smiling at the pretty server behind her, who then turned and walked into a wall. Ali shook her head and sipped her champagne. She got it. It was his job, pleasing the public. And he did have a way of making a girl feel like the most beautiful woman in a crowded room.

Mayor Tony Medina took the stage and tapped on the mic to get everyone's attention. A financial advisor, he'd been mayor for coming up on two years now, having taken over when the previous mayor, Jax Cullen, had stepped down from the position to concentrate on his first loves—his family and carpentry.

"Good evening, Lucky Harbor!" Tony called out. "Thanks for coming! Let's all raise our glasses to our very own Ted Marshall, who worked incredibly hard at raising the funds for our new community center."

At that, the crowd whooped and hollered, and Russell nudged Ali. "You worked hard too. Where's your credit?"

"I don't need credit," Ali said, and she didn't. She'd assisted by running car washes and other donation drives to help Teddy behind the scenes, where she was content to stay.

"As you know," Tony went on, "the town council promised to match the funds raised tonight. So without further ado, we're adding a total of *fifty thousand dollars* to the pot tonight."

Everyone cheered.

Teddy hopped up onto the stage with the mayor, hoisting a very large aluminum briefcase. He'd worked damn hard at getting this rec center built for the town, and it was within his sights now. Looking right at home, he smiled. "The build is an official go," he said into the mic. He opened the briefcase and showed off the fifty thousand, neatly stacked and wrapped in bill bands. Obviously it'd come straight from the bank for the reveal, but the crowd ate it up anyway.

After the ceremony, Ali went looking for Teddy. She needed a ride home, not to mention it'd be nice to see her boyfriend. She circled the large room twice to no avail, and then finally headed down the hallway to the offices to check there. She could see the light under Teddy's door, but to her surprise it was locked. Lifting a hand to knock, she went shock still at the low, throaty female moan from within. Wait . . . that couldn't be . . .

And then came a deeper, huskier moan.

Teddy.

Ali blinked. No. No, he wouldn't be with someone else . . . in his office . . .

"*Oh, babe,* yeah, just like that . . ."

It was Teddy's sex voice, and Ali got really cold, and then really warm, and she realized she had far bigger problems than finding a ride home.

• • •

Ali woke the next morning, alone. A sympathetic Russell had driven her home. In the dark, she'd paced the big house for a while, steam coming out her ears.

When Teddy hadn't shown up, she'd called her very soon-to-be ex-boyfriend, *twice,* but there hadn't been a return call. She did, however, now have a waiting text:

Babe, this isn't working. It's not you. It's all me. I just need to be alone right now. FYI, our lease ended on 5/31. So no worries, you're free to leave right away.

Ali stared at the words in shock. She hadn't had caffeine yet so her brain wasn't exactly kicking in, but she was pretty sure he'd just broken up with her—by text—and that he'd also rendered her homeless.

Ali pulled up the calendar app on her phone. Yep. Yesterday had been May thirty-first. Flopping back on the bed, she stared up at the ceiling, trying to sort her tumbling emotions.

He'd beaten her to the break up, and after last night, hearing him in the throes and calling someone else "babe," she'd *really* needed to be the dumper not the dumpee. "Damn," she whispered, and sat up.

You're free to leave right away.

Magnanimous of him. And also a vivid reminder. Men came and went. That was the way of it for the Winters women. She'd nearly forgotten that it was a lifetime goal of hers to not perpetuate this pattern, that she needed to be more careful.

She'd remember now. And while she'd like to lie around and plot Teddy's slow, painful death, and maybe wallow with a day in front of the TV and a huge bag of popcorn, she had work to do. She had to get back to Town Hall and take down the floral designs and collect whatever ceramics hadn't sold at the silent auction.

Then she apparently needed to figure out her living situation.

Still stunned, she showered and dressed in jeans and a sweatshirt for loading up boxes and then headed out. The rental house she'd shared with Teddy was high on the cliffs on the far north face of the harbor. It was isolated and not easy to get to, but she didn't mind the narrow road or being off the beaten path. The house itself was old and more than a little creaky, but full of character. Ali loved it and loved the view, and after a childhood of city noises, she loved sleeping to the sound of the waves hitting the rocks.

Normally, early mornings were her favorite part of living in Lucky Harbor. Cool and crisp, the sun was just peeking over the rugged mountains, casting the ocean in a glorious kaleidoscope of light. Beyond the surf, the water was still, a sheet of glass, perfectly reflecting the sky above. A brand new beginning. Every single morning.

Never more so than this morning . . .

She parked in front of the Town Hall. The place was locked, but Gus the janitor let her in. Mumbling something about getting back to his work, he vanished, and Ali began lugging the heavy floral arrangements out of the building, down the steps, and into her truck by herself. Then she carefully packed up the pottery that hadn't been sold and took that out as well. With every pass she made, she had to walk by Teddy's office, and each time her emotions—mostly anger—coiled tighter and tighter. Her mom and sister had the quick fuses in the family. Ali had always been more of a slow burn, but today she'd gone straight to red-hot ticked off.

When she was finally finished, she searched out Gus again, finding him indeed very busy— kicking back in the staff room watching a ball game on his phone. In his thirties, six feet four and big as a tank, Gus hadn't shaved since sometime last year. He looked like a tough mountain man who belonged on a History Channel show hauling logs—except for the tiny kitten in his big palm.

"Aw," Ali said, softening. "So cute."

At her voice, Gus startled, and with a little girl–like squeal, fell right out of the chair. Still carefully cradling the unharmed kitten, he glared at Ali. "Christ Almighty, woman, make some noise next time. You scared Sweetheart here half to death."

Sweetheart had her eyes half closed in ecstasy. "Yes, I can see that," Ali said wryly, reaching out to pet the adorable gray ball of fluff. "I can also see how very hard the two of you are working back here."

She couldn't tell if Gus blushed behind the thick, black beard, but he did have the good grace to at least look a little bit abashed as he lumbered to his feet. "I wanted to help you," he said, "but I had Sweetheart in my pocket, and the boss told me twice already not to bring her here. But she howls when I leave her home, and my roommate said if I didn't take her with me today, she was going to be his Doberman's afternoon snack."

"Sweetheart's secret is safe with me," Ali said. "I just need to get into Teddy's office for a minute."

Gus scratched his beard. "I'm not supposed to let anyone into the offices."

"I know," Ali said, "and I wouldn't ask, except I left something in there." She'd made Teddy a ceramic pot. It was a knotty pine tree trunk that held pens and pencils, and she'd signed it with her initials inside a heart. There was no way she was leaving it in his possession. He didn't deserve it. "Please, Gus? I'll only be a minute."

He sighed. "Okay, but only because you guys are always real nice to me. Teddy knows about Sweetheart, and he didn't rat me out." He set the sweet little kitten on his shoulder, where she happily perched, and then led the way to Teddy's office. There he pulled out a key ring that was bigger around than Ali's head, located the correct key by some mysterious system, and opened the office door. "Lock up behind you."

"Will do," Ali said, and as Gus left her, she went straight to Teddy's desk.

No knotty pine pot with the little heart she'd cut into the bottom. She turned in a slow circle. The office was masculine and projected success, and the few times she'd been here, she'd always felt such pride for Teddy.

That's not what she was feeling now. In fact, she sneezed twice in a row at some unseen dust, annoying herself as she looked for the pot. She finally located it in the credenza behind the desk, shoved in the very bottom beneath a bunch of crap. It was the shape of a Silver Pine tree trunk, every last detail lovingly recreated down to the knots and rings around the base. For a minute, Ali stared at the pot she'd been so proud of, shame and embarrassment clogging her throat. Swallowing both, she grabbed it, locked the door as she'd promised, found and thanked Gus, and left.

In her truck, she drew in a deep breath and drove off. It was a Winters's gift, the ability to shove the bad stuff down deep and keep moving. Teddy wasn't even a five on the bad stuff meter, she told herself.

As always in Lucky Harbor, traffic was light. At night, strings of white lights would make the place look like something straight from a post-card, but now, in the early light, each storefront's windows glinted in the bright sunlight.

Things stayed the same here, could be counted on here. She thought maybe it was that—the sense of stability, security, and safety—that drew her the most.

Her three S's.

At least until last night . . .

She put in her shift at the flower shop, worrying about how light business was. She brought it up to Russell at lunch, gently, that she felt she really had something to offer here, the very least of which was a website. But Russell, equally as gently, rebuked her. Like his sister Mindy before him, he was a technophobe. Hell, even the books were still done by hand, despite their bookkeeper's urging to update their system. Grace Scott, a local bookkeeper, had given up on changing Russell's mind, but Ali was going to bash her head up against his stubbornness, convinced they would make a great partnership.

On her break she used her smartphone to fill out as many online applications for apartments as she could find. By six o'clock, she was back at the beach house, hoping not to run into Teddy. She didn't, which was good for his life expectancy. Even better, the front door key still worked. Bonus. She had a roof over her head for at least one more night.

In the kitchen, she tossed her keys into the little bowl she'd set by the back door to collect Teddy's pocket crap. Out of curiosity, she poked through the stuff there: a button, some change, and . . . two ticket stubs, dated a week ago for a show in Seattle.

A show she hadn't gone to.

She stared at the stubs, then set them down and walked away. Something else niggled at her as she headed into her bedroom, but she couldn't concentrate on that, because she was realizing that Teddy had been working 24/7 for weeks. And before that, he'd been sick and had slept in a spare bedroom. They hadn't actually slept together in . . . she couldn't even remember.

Which meant that Ali had been very late to her own break up.

At this, her heart squeezed a little bit. Not in regret. She tried really hard not to do regrets. It wasn't mourning either, not for Teddy, not after hearing him cheat on her. It was the realization that she'd really loved the *idea* of what they'd had more than the actual reality of it.

Sad.

She stripped down to her panties and bra before

it occurred to her what the niggling feeling from before was. Reversing her tracks, she ran barefoot back to the large living room.

The house had come fully furnished, but Ted had always made the place his own, thanks to the messy, disorganized way he had of leaving everything spread around. Running shoes hastily kicked off by the front door. Suit jacket slung over the back of the couch. Tie hanging askance from a lamp. His laptop, e-reader, tablet, smartphone, and other toys had always been plugged into electrical outlets, and when they weren't, the cords hung lifeless, waiting to be needed.

Not now. Now it was all gone, even his fancy, highfalutin microbrews from the fridge. Everything was gone, including *her* iPod.

How she'd missed that this morning, she had no idea, but facts were facts—Teddy had moved out on her like a thief in the night.

Detective Lieutenant Luke Hanover had been away from the San Francisco Police Department for exactly one day of his three-week leave and already he'd lost his edge, walking into his grandma's Lucky Harbor beach house to find a B&E perp standing in the kitchen.

She sure as hell was the prettiest petty thief he'd ever come across—at least from the back, since she was wearing nothing but a white lace bra and a tiny scrap of matching white lace panties.

"You have some nerve you . . . you *rat fink bastard,*" she said furiously into her cell phone, waving her free hand for emphasis, her long, wildly wavy brown hair flying around her head as she moved.

And that wasn't all that moved. She was a bombshell, all of her sweet, womanly curves barely contained in her undies.

"I want you to know," she went on, still not seeing Luke, "there's no way in hell I'm accepting your breakup message. You hear me, Teddy? I'm not accepting it, because *I'm* breaking up with *you.* And while we're at it, who even does that? Who breaks up with someone by text? I'll tell you who, Teddy, a real jerk, that's who—hello? *Dammit!*"

Pulling the phone from her ear, she stared at the screen and then hit a number before whipping it back up to her ear. "Your voice mail cut me off," she snapped. "You having sex in your office while I was in the building? Totally cliché. But not telling me that you weren't planning to re-sign the lease? That's just rotten to the core, Teddy. And don't bother calling me back on this. Oh, wait, that's right, you don't call—you *text!*"

Hitting END, she tossed the phone to the counter. Hands on hips, steam coming out her ears, she stood there a moment. Then, with a sigh, she thunked her forehead against the refrigerator a few times before pressing it to the cool, steel door.

Had she knocked herself out?

"It's just one bad day," she whispered while standing in the perfect position for him to pat her down for weapons.

Not that she was carrying—well, except for that lethal bod.

"Just one really rotten, badass day," she repeated softly, and Luke had to disagree.

"Not from where I'm standing," he said.

Chapter 2

At the unexpected male voice, Ali's heart leaped into her throat. She whirled and stared in shock at the guy standing in her kitchen. Reacting without thinking, she grabbed the key bowl off the counter and flung it at his head.

He ducked, and the bowl bounced off the wall behind him, shattering into a hundred pieces. As ceramic shards tinkled to the tile floor, he straightened, dominating the kitchen as he turned to her, eyes narrowed.

"Who the hell are you?" she demanded, heart thundering.

"Oh no, you first," he said, arms crossed, looking impenetrable and imposing. "Why are you throwing shit at me?"

Wishing like hell that she had clothes on, she was surreptitiously reaching for the coffee mug on the counter—another of her creations—to pitch at his head when he lunged and wrenched the mug from her hand. "Stop with the target practice," he said, oozing dangerous levels of testosterone.

He was tall—six feet, at least—and built like he was very familiar with a gym or physical labor. And while he stood there in the middle of the kitchen as if he owned the place, she took in other details. Sharp eyes. *All the better to see you with, my dear,* she thought half hysterically, feeling a little bit like Little Red Riding Hood must have when she'd been trapped by the big, bad wolf.

His hair was dark brown and tousled, as if he couldn't be bothered with a comb. His T-shirt was stretched across broad shoulders, his jeans sitting low on lean hips. And his cross-trainers made no noise when he took a step toward her.

All the better to catch you with, my dear . . .

He didn't look like the big, bad wolf, she told her panicky self. Nor did he look like an ax murderer who broke into homes and tortured women in their undies—not that she was sure what an ax murderer might look like. Snatching the dish towel off the counter, she attempted to cover herself since her Victoria's Secrets weren't hiding much of her secrets.

The maybe–ax murderer's gaze wasn't leering, though he was definitely taking in her body, and she forced herself not to squeak as he snatched her sweater off the back of a chair and held it out to her, mouth hard.

All the better to eat you with, my dear . . .

Heart in her throat, she didn't reach for the sweater. She was afraid to. Instead, she eyed the block of knives two feet over on the counter, wondering if she could possibly get to them before . . .

He shoved them farther away.

Dammit. "You're trespassing," she said, proud of her steely voice.

"No, that would be you."

Clutching the towel for all she was worth, she shook her head. "I live here." Although technically, thanks to Teddy, that wasn't quite true anymore. "And if you don't go, I'm going to call the cops."

He didn't go.

Ali knew exactly one self-defense move, and she went for it, risking everything to step into him and jerk her knee up.

But he moved so fast she didn't have to time to get him in the family jewels. She didn't even have time to blink before she was helplessly pinned against the counter by a tough, sinewy body.

"Stop," he said in her ear. Then, as if nothing had happened, he stepped back from her, once again offering her the sweater.

This time she took it, dropping the tiny, ineffective dish towel and diving gratefully into the long garment, wrapping it around herself so that she was covered from her chin to her thighs.

Better.

Or as better as she could be with the stranger watching her carefully. He stepped back a little farther still, giving her some badly needed space. His expression was carefully neutral, but his body language spoke of a deadly tension that she didn't want to further provoke.

"So," he said calmly, propping up the door-

27

jamb with a broad shoulder. "You break in?"

Was he serious? He certainly looked serious. Not to mention stoic and controlled, which set her nerves crackling.

His eyes were blue. Ice blue. She only noticed because she was watching him closely for any sign of aggression. His face might have been classified as devastatingly handsome, but it could also have been carved in stone, his expression dialed to an intimidating pissed off.

But she was pissed off too. And more than a little bit scared. Sure, she'd grown up in a tough neighborhood, but this guy was light-years ahead of her in badass experience. He had attitude written all over him, and a day's worth of stubble darkening his jaw. Though his hair was cut short, some of it managed to fall across his forehead, which didn't soften his appearance. She doubted there was anything soft about this man. "I didn't break in," she said. "I live here."

"That's impossible."

"How would you know?" she asked.

"Because I own the house."

Still leaning against the doorway, Luke gave the woman standing in front of him a long look that usually had bad guys running like hell.

But she wasn't running. Instead she met his gaze with wide, hazel eyes, making him wonder about the glimpse of fierceness he'd seen when she'd been leaving that phone message. He ached for peace and quiet, and she was clearly the opposite of peaceful and quiet—so he needed to show her the door.

"You own this place?" she asked. "You're Luke Hanover?"

"Yes."

She didn't relax. "I'm going to need to see your ID."

That was usually *his* line. And for a woman standing in little more than a lightweight peach sweater, she had balls. Except what she really had was an acre of creamy, smooth skin and that mind-warping sweet, curvy body. He pulled out his wallet and showed her his driver's license. "Now you."

She blinked once like an owl, her hazel eyes not nearly as hostile now as she shoved some of her wild hair from her face. "I'll have to get it out of my truck," she said. "I left my purse out there."

The cop in him winced. But this was Lucky Harbor not San Francisco, and people felt safe here. And yet he knew better than anyone that shit happened everywhere. "I had this place rented out to a single male through a management service," Luke told her. "No B and E experts or half-naked women were on the lease." He'd really counted on finding the place empty and was prepared to facilitate that by whatever means necessary, because he needed that few weeks of peace and quiet in the worst possible way.

"Teddy didn't tell me until a few hours ago that he hadn't re-signed the lease," she said.

"Teddy," he repeated. "The 'rat fink bastard' you were yelling at on the phone?"

She nibbled on her lower lip. "So you heard all that, huh?"

Yeah, he'd heard it and had suddenly appreciated his long dry spell in the women department. "Where's Marshall now?"

"Moved out." Turning from him, she climbed onto the barstool, and for one brief glorious second, the sweater raised, flashing him another quick peek-a-boo shot of those hot, little panties before she settled. She really did have a world-class ass. And a wedgie.

"He never mentioned he wasn't re-signing the lease?" Luke asked.

"No. Hence the rat fink bastard part."

That nearly got a genuine smile out of him. It would have been his first in weeks, but he bit it back. Because in truth, there was nothing funny about this. He'd come to Lucky Harbor to be alone.

He *needed* alone.

It'd been years since he had been here. After inheriting the house from his grandma, he'd kept it rented out. He'd done so purposely, even though he'd spent some of the best times of his life here while growing up. The cliffs and water had been a teenager's haven and so had the pier and arcade. Back then, he hadn't cared that the house was inconvenient to get to or isolated. He cared even less now. In fact, he liked both of those things.

The property included a rickety set of stairs down to the beach and its own small dock. The huge, old house was equally rickety. He hadn't thought of selling it though, not once. He couldn't, not without far more guilt than he was equipped to handle.

He was glad for that now, because he'd needed out of San Francisco after his life had detonated. On his last case, he'd been part of the unit that had been tasked with gathering evidence against Senator Robert Danielson, who was accused of murdering three young women over the course of a year.

From the beginning, the evidence had been shaky at best: a few emails, texts, and phone calls between the senator and the women. A handful of questionable expenses. But Danielson was respected, and, by all accounts, also a decent guy. During four months of investigation, not one person had said a negative thing about him other than the guy worked too hard. Eventually, due to lack of evidence, the case against him had been dropped.

Two days later, the senator's pretty, young aide, Isabel Reyes, had floated in on the tide of the San Francisco Bay.

The senator had been found only an hour after, hanging from the rafters.

The press had gone ape-shit that no one had

31

seen this coming, questioning the integrity of everyone involved with the case, including the judge, the DA, and the entire investigative team —which Luke had led.

He still felt sick about Isabel Reyes's death. He couldn't get past his gut feeling that he *should* have known. Disgusted with the job, the system, and most especially himself, he'd put in for all twenty-one days of the vacation he'd accumulated and left the city, hoping to find his sanity. He'd come here to Lucky Harbor, planning to sleep for at least a week and then maybe have some pizza and catch a few games, and then sleep for another two weeks. He'd wanted to do that free of other people, especially recently dumped-by-text renters.

"Okay," he said, "so Marshall's gone, and you're . . . ?" He paused for her answer, thinking that the only acceptable response would be "leaving now."

"I have a place to move to," Hazel Eyes said. *Thank God.*

"Probably." She paused. "Hopefully. Soon as I hear back from the applications I put in today, I'll know more. Not that this is your problem, of course." She hopped off the barstool, and Luke told himself that the reason his body tightened was relief that she was on the move. He wasn't going to have to forcibly remove the sexy, crazy, naked lady from his house.

But instead of gathering her things and going,

she walked to the refrigerator and pulled out some ingredients. "You like turkey?" she asked.

He blinked at the quick subject change. "Yeah."

"Your stomach's growling." Quick as lightning, she put together a thick turkey sandwich with some fixings and handed it to him.

"Thanks," he said in surprise.

"No problem." Moving to the counter, she stared out the window.

The hem of her sweater covered her ass, even most of her thighs, hugging her curves for all it was worth. Her legs were long, toned. *Bare.* Working at not imagining running his hands up their entire length, he shoved in a big bite.

Still looking out the window, she set one foot on top of the other and cocked a hip, silent.

"I think there are boxes in the garage," he said, trying to be helpful. Hell, he'd even carry her shit out for her, no problem.

More silence, which was normally *his* thing. He was good at it too. But when she finally spoke, the words stabbed him.

"Dumped and made homeless in the same day," she said softly. "That's got to be some kind of record for pathetic, right?"

Luke let out a breath, pushed the now-empty plate away, and tried to harden his already stone heart. That his ex-renter had screwed her over wasn't his problem. He was temporarily off duty from solving other people's problems. Sure, she'd had a tough break, but the cold, hard fact was that lots of good people got screwed over every day of the week. He couldn't care right now. He hadn't slept in days, and he was going to pass out on his feet if he didn't get horizontal in the next five minutes. "Look, stay tonight. It's not that big of a deal."

She didn't move from her perch. "Thank you, but no. I'll be okay."

Luke followed her gaze to the ancient Toyota truck parked at the curb. He'd been a detective long enough to know exactly what she was thinking—she was going to sleep in her truck. "Seriously. Stay one more night."

She turned and looked at him then, eyes bright with pride. "Don't you dare feel sorry for me."

He had a sister. A mom. He knew how to swim through the shark-infested waters of a woman's psyche without getting injured. "Are you kidding?" he asked. "I feel sorry for me. The sandwich was great, and I'm not much in the kitchen. Even if I was, I'm too tired to go to the store for stuff. If you leave now, I'll go hungry tomorrow."

She stared at him for a long moment. Luke didn't have to work at looking genuine, because he'd spoken the utter truth.

"You won't be sorry," she finally said. "Or hungry." And then she vanished down the hall.

Luke didn't like to disagree with a pretty woman, but he had a feeling she was going to be dead wrong on at least one of those points.

Chapter 3

Luke followed his unintentional houseguest to the master bedroom.

His grandma's old room.

Clamping down on the memories, he stopped in the doorway, happy to note that it didn't look like his grandma's room. There were clothes and shoes and bottles and jars of stuff everywhere. It looked like a girl-bomb had gone off.

"Did I tell you that I love your house?" Sexy-Crazy-Nearly-Naked Tenant asked, coming out of the attached bathroom.

But she was no longer nearly naked. She'd buttoned up and added a pair of jeans. Her feet were still bare though. Her toes were painted sky blue, with little daisy decals on the big toe.

And he had no idea why he was checking out her toes.

None.

Twisting up her hair, she sailed by him and out the bedroom door, once again leaving him to follow after her.

"So you filled out some apartment applications?" he asked.

"Yes." She walked into the kitchen, where she

grabbed a watering can from beneath the sink and filled it.

"Any background checks?"

"No. Why?"

"I ran one on Marshall before he moved in here," he said.

She stared at him. "You did?"

He nodded. Being a detective, he often dealt with the dregs of society, the bottom feeders and the ones who'd sell their own mother's soul to the devil. In Luke's world, trust was not a given; it was earned. "If I'd known you were living here, I'd have done one on you too."

"Oh." Her voice was different now, which had him taking another look at her. She'd dropped eye contact and was biting her lower lip.

Ah, shit. She had something to hide. "Would that have been a problem?" he asked.

"No. Nope, not at all."

He raised a brow.

"Really," she said.

"The search program I have on my laptop is pretty intense," he said.

"Intense, like . . . you could see my third grade teacher and when I stopped believing in the Tooth Fairy?" she asked. "Stuff like that?"

"Yeah," he said dryly. "Stuff just like that."

"Fine. Do it."

"What's your name?" he asked.

"Ali Winters. Ali with an 'i.'"

He pulled his laptop out of his duffle bag. "Let's see what comes up."

"Sure." She shifted back and forth on her bare feet while he worked. He hadn't been kidding; this program was pretty damn invasive. It came in handy when he was hunting down suspects. Not so handy for running a background check on cute, hazel-eyed houseguests, because he was bound to find out far more than he needed.

The basics began to spit out, including a list of her previous known addresses, her age, job history, public records, etc. Ali-with-an-i was twenty-six, and her listings for previous addresses were fifteen deep, most in and around White Center and Burien, both just below Seattle. A longer look told him that ten of them had been before the age of eighteen.

She'd been questioned by the police a handful of times, thanks to being related to a Harper Winters —her sister—who'd been arrested for petty theft and assault after stealing a Peeping Tom neighbor's binoculars and beating him over the head with them. And then again when her mother— Mimi Winters—had threatened a lowlife ex's life by chasing him down the street with her car.

Ali herself had steered clear of any arrests. She'd gone to a junior college and worked as a singer in a casino/hotel lounge and at a flower shop.

"Is it bad?" she asked, leaning over his shoulder,

seeming torn between wanting to know and not wanting to know.

He craned his neck and looked at her. "You're a singer?"

"Not even a little bit. I gave up the singing job when I got jumped by a Cher impersonator for forgetting the words to that 'do you believe in life after love' song. But I got to keep my clothes on, and the tips were good. Plus I got my associate's degree with no student loans." She moved into the living room and began to water the plants scattered throughout the big, open space. There were several large ceramic pots on either side of the couch and beneath the picture windows. Several smaller pots were scattered around on shelves and the coffee table.

This was new. Luke's grandma had been warm and funny and bossy as hell, fiercely loving all who crossed her path—except plants. Plants she'd killed with just a look, including the supposedly invincible cacti. "Where did these come from?" he asked.

"Me," Ali said. "This house is so wonderful, all old and filled with character and charm . . ." Her smile was a little wistful. "But it needed . . . life. Besides feeding you, I'll take care of the plants."

"They're your plants."

"Hmm."

Hmm? What did *hmm* mean?

"Your yard's a mess," she noted casually. "You've got smooth douglasia and piper's bell-flower out there, and they're being choked to death by the red willow-herb. And the Indian paint-brush . . . do you have any idea how hard it is to grow that?"

"I'm not looking for a gardener. Or a tenant," he said, seeing where this was going. He rubbed the ache between his brows. "I'm not looking for anything or anyone, just some peace and quiet." Which wasn't to say that he didn't want a woman. He wouldn't mind that, though it'd be fourth on his list after sleep, food, and more sleep, but yeah, he'd absolutely take a warm, sexy, naked woman under him. Over him.

However she desired . . .

But not this woman, no matter how attractive he found her. Because this woman had a set of eyes that had so much life and emotion in them, he'd drown in her.

The house phone rang, and they both looked at it. "Is that your personal line?" he asked. "Or Marshall's?"

"Well, it started out Teddy's," she said. "But I use it too."

He gestured for her to go ahead and answer it then, since it couldn't be for him. Few if any knew he was here. Certainly not his commander, who was still pissed off that Luke had taken time off in the middle of the media shit-storm.

And not his parents or his sister, Sara.

The only people who might know—his two closest friends, Jack and Ben—were working. Jack, right here in Lucky Harbor as a firefighter, and Ben, off saving the world. Somewhere.

Ben, who'd suffered his own unimaginable losses, would have known to leave Luke alone, but not Jack. Jack would sniff him out sooner rather than later, but Luke wanted to have his head on straight first, because no one saw through him like Jack did.

Ali had answered the phone and was frowning. "You're looking for who?" she asked. "Detective Lieutenant Luke Hanover?" She slid Luke a long look.

People usually had one of two reactions when finding out that he was in law enforcement: They either wanted to see his gun and be shown some self-defense moves, or they ran like hell.

Ali's reaction was somewhere in between, but Luke didn't care. What he cared about was not having anyone know he was here. He shook his head with a "hell no" look. He had no idea how whoever was looking for him had gotten this number but he was *not* here.

"How did you get this number?" she asked whoever was on the phone.

Luke liked the question and wondered at the answer.

"Uh-huh," she said, still looking at Luke. "I see."

Luke pointed to himself and shook his head, his message implicitly evident: He was *not* here.

Ali gave him a sweet smile and then lifted a single finger, indicating that she needed a minute.

Luke gave her his best intimidation stare—which was completely wasted on her because she turned her back to him.

"Yes, of course," she said into the phone. "I understand why you'd want to speak to him."

Okay, they were done here. Luke strode toward her, intending to physically remove the phone from her hand, but then she surprised him again by holding him off with a hand to his chest. "However," she said, "you're mistaken about Detective Lieutenant Hanover being here . . . uh-huh . . ."

She was getting an earful, he could tell. Ignoring the hand still on his chest—which was shockingly difficult to do—he motioned for her to hang the fuck up.

"Uh-huh . . ."

Again he reached for her, and again she pressed on his chest. "Hmm," she said, reminding him he still had no idea what that meant. "Well, as I mentioned, he's not here. Don't call again." She hung up and looked at Luke. "Interesting."

"A reporter," he guessed.

"Yes."

He let out a breath. "Thanks."

"No problem," she said. "I've got lots of

practice dodging callers. I honed the skill with bill collectors and various other annoyances for my mom. Had it down to a science before I knew my multiplication tables."

Luke braced himself for the inevitable questions that most anyone else would have asked, but she surprised him yet again.

"I'll get that phone line shut down for you before I go," she said.

"Thanks. Ali—"

Someone knocked at the door, and he swore.

"I'll get it," she said. She started to head out of the kitchen, but stopped to look at him. "I take it you're still not here?"

"Correct."

She looked at him for a beat, her eyes softening just a little before she vanished. He had no idea what that meant, but a minute later he heard the front door open.

"Mr. Gregory," she said, an obvious smile in her voice. "Everything okay?"

In the kitchen, Luke swore again. Mr. Edward Gregory was the closest neighbor, a disarmingly sweet-looking old man who was actually about as sweet as a rattler.

And once upon a time, for about three minutes, he'd been married to his grandma—which made him Luke's biological grandfather. Not that Ali could possibly know that since he sincerely doubted Edward would have mentioned him.

Luke hadn't exactly done anything to be proud of in his grandfather's eyes, unless one counted getting his sister sent to prison at age eighteen, and then two years later, letting his grandma die alone.

Luke and Edward hadn't spoken in a while, a long while. And for now, he intended to keep it that way.

"Do you need help with the pot I started for you?" he heard Ali ask.

What the hell?

"No, I'm good," Edward said. "I'm heading over to the senior center to take the whole crew to the buffet special."

Luke glanced out the kitchen window. Parked behind Ali's truck was a big, white van with SENIOR CENTER DIAL-A-RIDE across the side. His grandfather was old enough to be in the damn center himself, or at least close to it, but apparently he was driving for them instead.

"I saw an unfamiliar truck in the driveway," Edward said. "Wanted to make sure you were okay."

Luke's truck was two years old. No one here in Lucky Harbor would recognize it except Jack, but Edward Gregory was a wily, old fox. And Ali was clearly kind and caring and all kinds of gullible. She'd probably fall for it hook, line, and sinker and let the old man in.

And wouldn't that just make Luke's day,

having the confrontation that had been brewing for a decade, on top of everything else.

"Oh, aren't you sweet," Ali said. "But I'm just fine, Mr. Gregory. Thank you so much for asking."

Was she actually protecting Luke? It'd been a while since he'd found himself in this position, *needing* help, and he didn't know how to feel. He settled for uncomfortable and off balance.

"You still having problems with that kitchen plumbing?" his grandfather asked.

"Nope, it's behaving now."

Luke looked into the kitchen sink. Yeah. She was definitely protecting him. It was totally clogged. And suddenly, so was his throat. Christ, he was tired. Tired and messed up.

Ali and his grandfather continued to chitchat for what felt like ten years, but in reality was only a few minutes, with Edward continuing to angle for an invite in, turning on the charm full power.

But Ali held her own, laughing and keeping things light, while remaining utterly firm. And in another minute, the front door shut, and she was back.

Luke looked at her. "You deal pot to the geriatric crowd?"

She stared at him and then laughed. She laughed so hard she had to put her hands on her knees and double over. Finally she straightened and swiped at her eyes. "Oh my God, I needed that." She got herself under control with what appeared to be some effort. "No, I don't deal pot. I teach a weekly ceramics class at the senior center." She shook her head at him. "You are such a cop."

Guilty. "A detective."

"So I heard."

The damn reporter.

"A *lucky* cop too," she went on.

His life was such complete shit that he had no idea what she could possibly be talking about. "Lucky?"

"With your neighbors," she said. "Growing up, my neighbors were career arsonists and loan sharks." She shrugged. "The arsonist was nice enough, but if I left my dolls out, he'd set their hair on fire."

"And the loan shark?"

"He wasn't crazy about little kids," she said. "He used to tell me and my sister that he was going to sneak into our place one night and sell us on the white slave market, and then retire off his portion of the profit."

Jesus. "How old were you?"

"I don't know, twelve maybe. He never got the chance. When my mom found out what he'd said, she threw a lamp at his head. That straightened him out pretty quick."

Luke wasn't into civilians taking matters into their own hands, but in this case, the vigilante justice worked for him. "*Good.* And thanks for your help."

She smiled. "I figured you didn't want to socialize."

"No."

"So maybe it's fate that I'm here."

Fate? He'd call it bad luck. "I don't put much stock in fate." He believed in making his own path—even if that way was to fuck up a few times before he got it right. He never blamed something as intangible as fate for his screwups.

He blamed himself.

She stared at him for a moment, her eyes soft, as if maybe she felt sorry for him, of all things. "That's okay," she said. "I believe enough for the both of us."

Well, hell.

He tried to shake it all off, but his eyes were gritty from the exhaustion. "I'm hitting the sack." He walked away and took the stairs down to the basement.

It'd been years since he'd been down here, but not much had changed. The walls were a midnight blue with the galaxy painted on the ceiling. Pluto was still a planet. The door was covered in late '90s radio station stickers, a virtual time capsule to Luke's teenagehood.

Not that there was a lot to the time capsule. His parents, both doctors, had never put much stock in sentiment. They believed in higher education, hard work, and harder, tough love. And the cause, always the cause.

Right now that meant being in Haiti. Back then,

it'd been Doctors Without Borders, which had left Luke and his older sister, Sara, more often in the care of their grandma up here in Lucky Harbor than at home in San Francisco.

Which had worked for Luke.

He'd had a lot of good times in Lucky Harbor, the best times of his life. His first climb. His first ski. His first boat race. His first jump off the pier. His first kiss. And given that Candy Jenson, a senior to his freshman, had also taken his virginity, he'd had just about every possible first here.

Good memories.

At least until several years later, on one particularly stupid night when he'd been with the girl of his dreams. They'd parked up at Pigeon Point to "stargaze," aka have sex, in her daddy's truck. They'd been doing just that when his sister had called him. Twenty years old to his eighteen, Sara hadn't bothered with Luke all that often, but that night she'd been drinking and had needed a ride home.

Luke had still had two condoms left. He'd told his sister to give him a little bit.

But Sara hadn't waited. She'd driven home drunk, blasting through a stop sign and killing an old man crossing the street.

Though Sara had never blamed him for her two years in jail, Luke still hadn't forgiven himself, and their relationship had been strained ever since.

And then his grandma had died two summers

later. Again, he hadn't been the direct cause, but close enough.

He'd not come back to Lucky Harbor since.

The stack of boxes against the wall suggested that at some point this room had gone from housing a teenager to housing extra crap. His grandma Fay had never been able to throw anything of his or Sara's away. She'd been the only sentimental one in the entire family.

Luke took a long look around and nudged the first box with his toe, eyes locking in on a lump of clay—the stupid snowman he'd once made at summer camp. It was missing an eye and a chunk of its head, but his grandma had cherished the thing, which had sat on her desk as a paperweight for as many years as he could remember.

Her desk was still upstairs in the den, but it was empty now, available for whichever tenant wanted to use it.

Luke stared at the snowman, reluctantly acknowledging the damn ache in his chest before shaking his head and heading straight for the bed. Kicking off his clothes and shoes with equal carelessness, he sprawled onto the mattress.

His last conscious thought was the image of Ali standing in his kitchen in nothing but her sexy bra and panties and that smile, the one that told him he was in a whole shitload of trouble, whether he liked it or not.

And for the record, he didn't like it.

Chapter 4

Ali heard the door shut from the depths of the house, and then nothing.

Just silence in Luke's wake.

She cleared up the shards on the floor from the ceramic pot she'd thrown and let out a long breath. Luke Hanover was a force. A big, edgy, enigmatic force. And a cop. A detective lieutenant.

Good Lord.

Her mom loved men, *all* of them, but one thing she'd always imparted to her daughters was a general distrust of men of the law. Ali's growing up years had been like living through a season of *COPS*, and she still tended to twitch when she heard a siren. Though she'd twitched at the sight of Luke for an entirely different reason.

In light of the fact that she was just dumped and therefore temporarily uninterested in anyone with a penis, this was deeply disturbing.

Luke was a good-looking guy, she told herself. Any woman would react. It was the way he carried himself—the sharp gaze that missed nothing and a calm, controlled demeanor even after finding a half-naked woman in his house.

Although, there'd definitely been something in his expression suggesting a tension that had nothing to do with her. The earful she'd gotten from the reporter had confirmed this. Luke had clearly had a week far worse than hers, especially since his had involved dead people.

Clearly Luke dealt with more stress and responsibility on any given day than Ali had ever managed. She felt bad, but at the moment, she had her own problems.

Big problems.

Roof-over-her-head problems. She could stay here tonight, but she had every other night to worry about. Letting out a shaky breath, she lifted her chin. It was what the Winters women did, they faked their bravado. Then they told themselves everything was going to be okay. "It *is* going to be okay," she said out loud to convince herself, because that would make it so. "It's really going to be okay."

But she had no idea how. She didn't charge the senior center when she taught there, and Lucky Harbor Flowers was slower than usual this season. Russell kept talking about his dream, which was to follow his ex-boyfriend Paul to Las Vegas. And that meant closing the shop.

Unless she could suddenly convince him that she could run the shop in his absence, things were going to go bad for her.

Her phone buzzed. It was Leah Sullivan,

pastry chef and Ali's closest friend in town. "Hey," Ali said, going for chipper.

"You okay?" Leah asked.

"Yep," Ali said. "Totally okay."

Leah, a wanderlust soul, was friendly and curious and funny as hell. She seemed to have a knack for recognizing bullshit. "You're lying."

"A little," Ali admitted.

Leah sighed. They hadn't been friends that long, Leah was only in town to run her grandma's bakery while the older woman recovered from knee surgery, but some things didn't take any time at all.

"Men are scum," Leah said. "Even cute Ted Marshall apparently."

"How is this already news?"

"There was a sighting of Ted carrying boxes into a rental duplex. So you're still at the house?"

"Yes," Ali said, not mentioning that she was only staying for one more night. She didn't want to worry or burden Leah, who'd just recently come back to Lucky Harbor after a long stretch away. She worked in the bakery in the same building as Ali, which was how they'd become friends. But Leah was only here to help her grandma, and was staying in her grandma's tiny place. Leah would insist Ali join them, but Ali wouldn't impose.

"I've got fresh éclairs," Leah said. "Excellent breakup food."

"Definitely. I'll come by later," Ali said and clicked off. She could go to her mom's and sister's. White Center wasn't that far, a couple of hours, and Mimi and Harper would welcome her with open arms. But she'd left them and come here for a new start, to make something of herself, dammit.

She had other friends, but no one close enough to barge in on. Pensive over the realization that her life wasn't exactly going in the carefree, fun direction she'd hoped, she finished watering the plants. It was quiet in the house in spite of the big, brooding guy in it. Eerily quiet. She put the watering pitcher back under the kitchen sink and then sagged a little in the silence.

She didn't have to leave right now, but the fact remained that this was *his* home now.

Not hers.

She had no real home. This wasn't exactly a new feeling, but she hated that unsettled spot in her gut, and her fingers itched for a clump of cool, wet clay, which always soothed her. She might have gone out to the garage, where she'd set up a little workstation for herself, but the house phone rang again. She answered to another reporter and gave the same spiel that she'd given the first, but more firmly.

She'd seen something in Luke's eyes, a hollowness that she understood. Clearly he'd escaped to Lucky Harbor for some peace and quiet, and she was willing to fight for it for him. It was the least she could do to earn her keep.

Ali woke up on Sunday morning to a silent house. Luke's truck was still out front, so she assumed he was still sleeping.

She didn't have that luxury. She had a class to teach at the senior center and a life to figure out.

First up: breakfast. If her life was going to hell in a handbasket, well then she was going on a full stomach. In the kitchen, she pulled out the makings for two omelets. She cooked and then inhaled one while standing on the back deck. From here, she could see down the steep stairs to the house's private dock below, which jutted out into the water. She stared at the churning swells, lost in thought.

And worry.

And anxiety.

And lingering temper.

A movement caught her eye. There was a wiry-looking guy trying to get into the bushes along the side of the house. He had a camera in one hand and a cell phone in the other, which he was waving wildly about, trying to shoo something.

Narrowing her eyes, Ali moved closer. "Who are you?" she demanded.

He'd disturbed a few bees, and they were on him. The guy dropped to the ground, losing both his camera and his phone. "You have kamikaze bees!"

Clearly not a local. "Where are you from?" she asked.

He came up to his knees, gingerly looking around. "Are they gone?"

There was still one circling his head. "Yes."

"Whew." He let out a breath of relief and reached for his things. "I'm looking for Detective Lieutenant Luke Hanover. I just want a picture—"

That was all she needed to hear. She grabbed the hose that she'd coiled yesterday after watering the yard and nailed him.

"Hey!" He curled over his phone and camera to protect them. *"Hey!"*

She lowered the hose. "You're trespassing."

He stared at her like she was a loon. "You ruined my things! I'm going to call the cops!"

"Do that," she suggested. "And be sure to tell them you were on private property trying to get a picture to sell to the media when you accidentally ran into the sprinklers."

"I'm not leaving," he said. "Not until I talk to the owner of this house."

Ali lifted the hose again, and he squeaked and then ran off. "That's what I thought," she said, and dropped the hose.

Feeling a little better, she went inside and wrapped up the second omelet and put it in the fridge with a note to her tall, dark, and attitude-ridden landlord:

Luke,

I made you a kick-ass omelet. Thanks for letting me stay the night.

Ali

P.S. I hosed the paparazzi scoping out your back deck so I doubt he'll be back today.

It took her a moment to find her keys, since she'd thrown the key pot at Luke. They were under the table. Grabbing them, she headed out to her class. It was surprisingly hot already, which might have sent anyone else scampering back inside, but Ali was made of sheer, one-hundred-percent resilience.

Or so her mom always said.

Outside, her truck didn't want to start. It was a morning thing, something the two of them had in common. "Come on baby," she coaxed, patting the dash with love. "Do it for me." The sweet talk worked, the truck roared to life, and they were off.

Lucky Harbor tended to roll up its sidewalks at dusk, and they hadn't yet been unrolled. The sleepy town was just coming to life, with little to no traffic on the streets and the shops not yet open for business. The pier was quiet too, the arcade dark, the Ferris wheel still against the morning sky.

On the outskirts of town stood a large, one-story building that had once been a small Army outpost. The barracks had been converted to apartments and then into a senior center.

Inside, Ali was greeted by Lucille. She was somewhere between sixty and one hundred, had a tendency toward velour sweat suits in eye-popping colors, and had a heart of gold. She also had an ear for gossip. She ran the local art gallery and the town's Facebook page with equal enthusiasm. Recently she'd expanded her social media platform to include Pinterest as well. She came out for all of Ali's classes because she had a crush on the men at the senior center, at least the ones who were "still kicking" as she liked to say.

Lucille smiled sympathetically at Ali. "You okay, honey?"

"Sure," Ali said. "Why?"

"I heard about your breakup. It's on Facebook."

Ali stared at her. "Who put it on Facebook?"

"Me." At least she grimaced. "I'm sorry. I heard it from the grapevine, so I wanted to get Ted up on our list of eligible bachelors." She patted Ali's hand. "Don't give him another thought. A man like Ted Marshall isn't ready to be tied down is all. Not your fault."

Ali hadn't wanted to tie him down. She'd wanted . . . well, she didn't know exactly.

Liar, liar, pants on fire. She knew.

She wanted to be loved.

They entered the big rec room for class and

found the usual gang, ex-postmaster and currently a professional hell raiser Mr. Lyon, ex–truck driver and current geriatric playboy Mr. Elroy, and ex–rocket scientist and current ringleader Mr. Wykowski—all of them decades north of their midlife crises. Mr. Gregory was there as well because he'd just driven them back from the breakfast buffet and was helping everyone off the Dial-A-Ride van.

Ali had kept a few of the floral arrangements from the town auction. She unloaded them, setting them around the place so that the seniors could enjoy them. Then she started class. They'd been working on miniature animal statues. It was a thing of Ali's. When she'd been a little girl, she and Harper had sometimes been left alone for long periods of time while Mimi had been at work, and it hadn't always been safe enough to go outside to play. Ali would mix flour, salt, and water together into a homemade clay, passing the time creating palm-sized animals.

The seniors enjoyed it. Leah's grandma Elsie was there, working meticulously on a cat. Mr. Lyons created a lump that he claimed was a grizzly bear. "Top of the food chain," he said. "Like me. Why aren't I on your list of eligible bachelors? I'd kick ass on that list."

Mrs. Burland, a former teacher, smacked him upside the head. "Watch your language."

Mr. Elroy, who'd been watching the exchange

and sliding his dentures around some, grinned at Mrs. B. "I'm making an elephant," he said. "Want to see its trunk?"

Mrs. Burland reached over and flattened Mr. Elroy's elephant with one smack of the palm of her hand.

Mr. Wykowski chuckled. "No worries. His trunk didn't work anyway."

After class, Ali dashed to her truck beneath a sizzling sun. The temp had risen and so had the humidity, and it took forever for her AC to kick in. While she waited, she realized that Teddy still had a presence in her vehicle and that rankled. She ripped down his pic from the dash, yanked out his Coldplay CD, and grabbed his sunglasses from the console. She thought about how beloved Teddy was here in Lucky Harbor—of course no one knew that he was a two-timing jerk—and gave brief thought to tossing his stuff in the trash.

It would be extremely satisfying, but she just couldn't do it. So she let out a breath and headed to Town Hall. Hopefully Gus was around today too, and she could drop everything off in Teddy's office so she wouldn't have to look at it—or him—ever again.

There were cars in the lot, but not Teddy's Lexus. Others cleaning up from the celebration, probably, and maybe some hard-working government employees putting in overtime. Ali shoved

Teddy's things into her purse and took a moment to peek into the rearview mirror. Her hair had soaked up the humidity, frizzing into what now closely resembled a dandelion. Nothing she could do about that, because she'd run out of her drugstore defrizz a week ago. But she could wipe the mascara from beneath her eyes and apply some watermelon gloss, whose label promised to bring forth some serious shine and sexiness. After the past few days she'd had, Ali could have used some fortitude and strength to go with it, but she was pretty sure she wasn't going to get that from a lip gloss. A good stiff drink, maybe . . .

Later, she promised herself. A glass of something strong, a bath, and a serious pity party for one. But for now, she patted down her hair the best she could and grabbed her purse.

Teddy shared an assistant with several other city workers. Aubrey, who was tall, willowy, and beautiful, was standing behind her desk, frowning at her computer while still looking beautiful. And on top of that, *her* shiny blonde hair wasn't the slightest bit frizzy.

"Ali," Aubrey said in surprise, "what are you doing here on a Sunday?"

"I was just going to ask you the same thing."

"Work." Aubrey gestured to her computer, where a Skype screen was open to reveal another woman.

Bree Medina, the mayor's wife.

Bree was in her early forties, though she looked a full decade younger. She was an interior decorator to the rich and famous, and was one cool customer. Ali was glad Bree was not there in person, because in person she had a way of making Ali feel like a bargain-basement special. Plus, Bree's perfume made her sneeze. In fact, just thinking about it made her nose itch.

"Sorry," Ali said. "I didn't mean to interrupt. But I've got some things of Teddy's that I forgot to drop off yesterday." She left out the part about stealing her pencil pot back. No need to present herself as a Level Five Crazy Ex. "Can I leave it all in his office?"

"I can't let you in there," Aubrey said. "It's against the rules. But I can take it for him."

"It's not work related," Ali warned her, leaving out details on purpose. People loved Teddy, she got that. But that's not why she kept quiet about their breakup. She kept quiet because she didn't want to be pitied.

There was an awkward silence.

"What is it?" Bree asked. "The ex-boyfriend box of crap?"

So they did know.

"Facebook," Aubrey said. "Lucille knows all."

"I have to go," Bree said. She looked at Aubrey. "I'll be in the office on Monday with the new office chairs we talked about." And then she clicked off.

Aubrey quit Skype and looked at Ali. "I knew you two lived together, everyone did, but the general consensus was that you two were just friends. At least that's how Teddy always made it sound." She pulled out her keys. "You can leave everything on his desk, but I did *not* let you in there."

"Never saw you."

And so Ali found herself in Teddy's office for the second time in as many days, which was two more times than she'd been here all month. Teddy had been far too busy for far too long. It burned deep that she'd let it happen, that she'd let him put her on the back burner without a thought.

Why had she done that? Why had she accepted less from him than she deserved? Because he was the golden boy? Because she'd gotten herself infatuated with the idea of a relationship?

She sat in his big, leather chair, set his things on his desk, and eyed the blotter scribbled with Teddy's familiar scrawl. *Call CPA. Order cards. Email reports.*

Huh. No *Screw over Ali* anywhere on the list.

She grabbed a new sticky note and let out the beast:

ASS.

She set the note front and center on his desk, next to the things from her truck. She studied her handiwork a minute and decided it wasn't quite enough. She added a few more thoughtful sentences on what she thought of his skills as a boyfriend, and finally feeling marginally better—and grateful that Mrs. Burland wasn't here to smack her upside the head for her language—she exited the office.

Aubrey was no longer at her desk, which was just as well. Ali wasn't sure if she could muster a smile as she exited the building.

Of course it was still hot. Once again Ali made her way to her truck and cranked on the AC, which was making an ominous grinding sound. Today would be a great day for it to break.

She wasn't sure where to go next. She didn't want to crowd Luke in his own home after he'd been so generous by letting her stay an extra night. The flower shop was only a half block away. She could grab her paycheck. Russell would probably be in his office in the back, watching Bravo, yelling at whatever *Real Housewives* show was on. She could spend some time online and see if an available apartment had come up.

With that decision made, she got out of the truck, into the sweltering day, and walked over to the flower shop. The old Victorian building had long ago been divided into three storefronts: the flower shop, Leah's grandmother's bakery, and an old bookstore that had been closed all year.

Most of the other downtown buildings had been renovated in the past decade, but not this one.

It needed a major overhaul, but Ali loved it. The place had quirks and its own charm and character in spades. The flower shop was on the left, painted pastel yellow with white trim. The wood floors creaked and the lights always flickered, but to Ali, those things gave the place personality. It felt like her home away from home.

If she had a home . . .

Russell wasn't here, and as she moved through the front room, she inhaled the familiar scent of flora and tried to relax. She went through the available rentals again, lowering her expectations, trying to find something that would work. There were two, but one was subletting a room in some guy's house, and that felt a little sketchy for a woman. The other was on the outskirts of the county, far more remote and isolated than even the beach house. Not ideal . . .

She looked around Russell's office, which held a tiny desk, two filing cabinets filled to overflowing, and enough room to stand.

Nowhere to sleep.

Knowing she'd stalled as long as she could, she got up to go and opened the top desk drawer to grab her paycheck. But Russell hadn't written it, and one glance at the balance scrawled in his checkbook told her why. He was short again. He'd left her an envelope with half of what he owed her in cash, and a note that he'd get her the rest by the end of the week. Oh boy.

Things were going to be okay.

But she didn't know how. She moved to the office window and looked out. She could see the pier from here. The Ferris wheel was turning. The trees lining the street were swaying. She knew if she opened the window, the breeze would be scented with an intoxicating combo of sea salt, pine trees, and hope.

She craved that. The fact was Lucky Harbor gave off a quiet serenity and strength, and she craved that too. She'd grown up in smoky, noisy, colorful lounges and bars. Mimi Winters had a long work history, from waitress to "dancer," and then back to waitressing when it got too hard on her body. She might not have been all that good with money, but she was good with love. Some would argue too good, as she'd rarely met a man she didn't fall for. But when there'd been trouble—and there *had* been trouble—Mimi had always come through for her girls, and together they'd handled whatever had come up.

Ali had gotten good at handling things, real good. This was just another of those times. Needing to connect to someone who loved her, she pulled out her cell phone and texted both her mom and sister with: *Missing you, how's things?*

Harper replied right away. *Got a hot date with Lenny. Remember Lenny? He's hot as ever and running his dad's plumbing business now.*

Mimi's response was just as fast. *Ali-gator!*

Miss your pretty face! Gotta run, caught some OT to help cover rent. Oh and I'm taking an online business class that's gonna change everything, you'll see.

In Mimi's world, there was always something that was going to change everything. And the thing was, Mimi honestly believed it. Optimism was one of her most endearing qualities, but it also left Ali as the only realistic one in the family. She looked in her envelope again and worked some fancy math before texting her mom back.

Got some extra this month. I'll send.

Mimi's response was immediate: *You're an angel. What would I do without you?*

Exactly what Ali worried about.

Luke woke up with a start, heart thundering in his chest, the vision of a drowned Isabel Reyes crystal clear in his head. Her hair had been floating behind her in a terrible parody of beauty, eyes open in permanent terror, skin so pale as to be translucent.

He'd been there when they'd pulled her body from the water, but he'd seen plenty of dead bodies before. It wasn't the image haunting him now so much as the failure to save her.

It was pitch black in the room, but he didn't need a light to remember where he was. In hell. He sat straight up. It was dark outside. He'd slept all day.

Scrubbing his hands over his face, he let his wits catch up with him. He would've rolled over and closed his eyes to take the rest of the sleep he still needed, but his stomach rumbled in protest. Damn. He reached for his phone and saw he had messages. No big surprise there.

His commander, wanting him to get his ass back to San Francisco in one week, not the three Luke had asked for, because "vacation time was for pussies"—not to mention that it left him dealing with the "media shitstorm" on his own. His mom, reminding him that sometimes things happened for a reason. His dad, telling him to work through it and stay strong. Last was Jack's message, suggesting that Luke not read the news or turn on the TV.

So of course Luke went straight to the browser app on his phone and brought up the news. Yep, the media storm was still raging, with people blaming the DA and the entire SFPD.

And Luke, of course.

That was okay. Luke blamed Luke too.

He was starving. He slid off the bed and staggered up the creaky stairs and into the kitchen. He could drive into town, but he'd have to get dressed, and plus, he had no idea where he'd left his keys. He rarely did. Without turning on the light, he pulled open the refrigerator door.

He had no idea what he was expecting. He hadn't yet stocked any food. He hadn't thought that far ahead. Hadn't thought of anything other than getting away to hear himself think.

Or better yet, not think.

But there was bottled water, milk, eggs, cheese, luncheon meats, apples, oranges, and—hitting the jack-pot—beer. A plate on the middle shelf had a colorful note stuck right on the top of it, from Ali.

He'd nearly forgotten about her.

Curious, he pulled out the plate. An omelet. He'd have preferred pie, but this looked good.

Hell, who was he kidding? *Anything* he didn't have to cook would have looked good to him. He nuked the plate, and then wolfed down the omelet where he stood. He was moving to the sink when he heard a whisper of a sound.

Footsteps.

Luke reached for his gun before remembering he was unarmed and in his boxers. Christ, he needed more sleep.

"Hands where I can see them, dick breath," a female said, and then the overhead light was slapped on.

Turning slowly, Luke came face to face with Ali standing in the kitchen entryway with an umbrella in one hand—aimed in his direction like a sword—and the other hand still on the light switch.

Clearly, she'd been in bed sleeping. Her hair was wild, like an explosion in a mattress factory. Her eyes were huge in her pale face. She wore a thin, white wife-beater tank top and sweatpants that were so big they were slipping off.

She lowered the umbrella and hitched up the sweats. "I thought we had an intruder."

"We do," he said. *"You."* To distract himself from the fact that she was very braless, he eyed her stance. She wasn't new at protecting herself. "Dick breath?"

"Sorry, I was trying to sound tough." She shoved a hand through that crazy hair, looking a little bit wild and a lot off her game, and yet, he thought, there she stood ready to defend his house.

The first person on his side in a good long time.

Firmly ignoring the odd feeling in his gut, he shook his head. "Bad idea, coming up on a pissed-off, hungry, exhausted cop like that."

"I didn't know it was you," she said. "And you're not a cop right now. You're on leave."

He could have told her he was *always* a cop. "What if I'd shot you?"

"Would have ruined my whole day," she said in a tone that told him her day had been shitty. Then her gaze ran over him, and he knew the exact second she registered that all he wore was boxers because her breath caught audibly.

She was aware of him as a man. Ted might have dented her heart but he hadn't broken it.

"Is that a gun in your shorts," she asked softly. "Or are you just happy to see me?"

Chapter 5

Ali worked at not swallowing her tongue, as Luke—after a speculative, edgy look—turned and vanished down the hall without responding to her question.

Good Lord, the man wore nothing but boxers like no one else. She'd known he was good looking, but she hadn't known he had acres of hard sinew that bunched and flexed with his every move.

And she had no idea what she'd been doing baiting him like that. She certainly hadn't expected to feel scorched by heat just from looking at him. The man was drop-dead sexy, that was for sure.

Equally for sure was relief that he hadn't responded to her. It'd been a rhetorical question anyway, one uttered only because her brain had clicked off at the realization that he was half naked. But before she could reboot, he was back, wearing low-slung Levi's, shrugging into a shirt that he didn't bother to button. He had that whole dangerous, brooding air going on, spilling testosterone and bad boy vibes all over the place.

It did something very unwelcome in the pit of

her belly. And lower. She cleared her throat. "I found two possible rentals today."

He didn't speak.

Good to know where she stood. Probably he was so thrilled and overjoyed that he *couldn't* speak.

He went to the fridge.

"One's on the outer edge of the county," she said. "In the Highlands. The other's a room from the guy who owns the hardwood store. Anderson something."

"No," he said.

"No?"

"The Highlands is a bad neighborhood. And you're not renting a room from Anderson. Hell no."

She stared at him, but he was head first in the fridge. "You still hungry?" she asked. "I can make you something." She moved over there just as he turned to her. She tried to nudge him out of her way, her palms settling on his chest, absorbing the heated, hard strength of him.

He didn't budge.

She pushed a little harder and this time he stepped back. "Thanks for the omelet," he said.

"Want another?"

"Sure."

She pulled out the eggs, cheese, broccoli, and a red pepper. Grabbing a pan, she turned on a burner. "Oh, I almost forgot. I have something for you."

His gaze went hooded, and she felt herself

blush. She wasn't sure what he thought she might be offering, but given what she'd said about the gun in his boxers, it was probably far more than she'd meant to offer.

"There," she said, gesturing with her chin to the envelope on the kitchen table. It was the cash equivalent of three nights' worth of rent. Last night, tonight, and hopefully tomorrow night as well.

Optimism. Guess her mom wasn't the only Winters with that particular trait after all. The fact was that she'd hoped to get into a place tomorrow, but he'd just shut down her two current options.

He didn't make a move for the envelope, a fact Ali ignored as she began cutting up the pepper and grating cheese while he just stood there looking rumpled and sleepy and on edge. "Ironic, don't you think?" she asked.

"That you're more at home in my kitchen than I am?"

"The fact that we're complete strangers, and yet we've already seen each other in our underwear."

"Yeah." He stole a piece of cheese and popped it into his mouth. "I noticed that *you* didn't hand me a sweater like I did for you."

She smiled. Her first of the day. Maybe of the week.

He actually smiled back, which had to count for something, especially since he had a pretty great smile. She flipped the omelet and then a moment later transferred it to a plate, placing a few small broccoli spears on top before handing it to him.

He stared down at the broccoli. "I don't like broccoli."

"Why not?"

"Because it's green."

"When was the last time you tried it?" she asked.

"I don't like it," he repeated, as if this answered her question.

"Eat around it."

He stood there eyeing the offending vegetable like it was a bomb, and then his stomach grumbled loudly.

"Eat."

Kicking out a chair, he sat. "Thanks," he said around a mouthful. "I hate to cook."

She smiled. "My mom always said I should know how to feed a man. She says most women assume a guy's most critical body part is considerably lower than his stomach, but they're wrong. She says it's a man's stomach that does his thinking for him, not—" She broke off and felt herself flush. "Anyway, cooking is how she caught all her boyfriends."

"Was your dad one of those boyfriends?"

Ali's dad lived in Tacoma, and last she'd heard, he was a bartender. By all accounts, he was an effortless charmer who meant well, but she knew him as the guy with all the unfulfilled promises.

Long gone were the days where she'd wait by the phone for the call he'd promised, but the memories still made her ache a little bit. "He didn't stick around. The first boyfriend who did was a dentist." She let out an involuntary shudder. "He was a pincher."

"A pincher?" Luke asked.

"Yeah." She opened and closed her first finger and thumb together a few times to demonstrate. "Whenever we annoyed him, he'd pinch. Always where the bruise wouldn't show too. Hurt like hell."

Luke didn't show much in expression or body language, and he had a way of staying very still. But his eyes had gone hard, pissed off on behalf of a young girl he'd never known.

"Your mom let him touch you?" he asked.

"Oh, we didn't tell her," Ali said. "She liked him so much, it would have killed her. But one day we were shopping and she saw a bruise on my sister in the dressing room."

"I hope she kicked his ass," Luke said.

"She took a baseball bat to him." Her smile faded because Mimi had cried for a week when he'd moved out. "She didn't bring another guy home for a long time after that."

"Good." Hooking his bare foot in a chair, he pushed it toward her. "Sit with me."

She put the pan in the sink and sat, shaking her head when he offered her a bite.

"So you learned to cook so you could catch a man?" he asked.

"No. I learned to cook because I like to eat," she said, "not because I want a string of boyfriends. Because I don't." Not until she figured out how to pick them anyway. She watched Luke work his way carefully around the broccoli. "Broccoli has almost as much calcium as milk," she told him, amused. "It gives you strong bones."

His gaze slid to hers, and she felt her face heat again. He had strong bones. And as they both knew, a few minutes ago, he'd had one particularly strong boner to boot. But mercifully he let the comment go.

Setting down his fork, he opened the envelope she'd left on the table, staring in surprise at the cash she'd carefully counted out. "What's this?" he asked.

"What I owe you for a few nights' stay. I prorated what I was paying monthly. I hope that's okay."

He was quiet for a full sixty seconds, and when he spoke, his voice was low. "I got the impression you were hard up for money."

"Not that hard up."

He looked at her for a long moment, then set the envelope back on the table and pushed it toward her with one finger.

She slid it back. "I pay my debts."

"How much does it leave you?" he asked.

She felt a small smile curve her lips. "Worried I won't have enough to find another place?"

"Hell yes."

She laughed softly. "Don't be. I'm not your responsibility." She wasn't anyone's responsibility and hadn't been in a long time.

He went back to eating. When a tiny piece of broccoli found its way on his fork, he gave it a look, but shoved it in his mouth.

She waited, but he just shrugged.

"Don't overwhelm me with praise or anything," she said dryly.

He flashed a quick grin. "It's good," he said. "Really good. You're holding up your end of the bargain." His smile faded. "But I'm not taking your money, Ali."

Bossy alpha. She got up and loaded the few dishes into the dishwasher, trying to pay no attention to the silent man behind her. Hard to do when he rose and put his dish in for her.

A *neat,* bossy alpha.

"You should go back to bed," she said softly. "You look beat."

He gave her a long look, which she decided was best not to decipher, before walking away, leaving her alone with her thoughts.

Ali didn't sleep well and got up before dawn. With several hours before she had to be at the shop, she quietly made her way to the garage.

She pulled on an apron that said Florists Do It with Style. Retrieving fresh clay from her storage bin, she worked it for a few minutes, trying to lose herself.

From the other side of the garage door, she heard a car pull up, but it didn't really register until the doorbell sounded. Startled at the early hour and pissed that another reporter might have found Luke, she wiped her hands on her apron and left the garage, moving quickly through the house to the living room. Prepared to kick some ass, she opened the front door, shocked to find two police officers standing there, flanking Teddy.

"Are you Ali Winters?" one of the cops asked.

"Yes, yes, it's her," Teddy said impatiently.

"Is something wrong?" Her heart dropped. "My mom? My sister, Harper? Are they okay?"

"This isn't about your damn family," Teddy said in disbelief. "It's about the fact that you stole that money to fuck me over. You're *that* pissed at me, that you had to try to ruin me?"

Ali shook her head in confusion. "What?"

"Ma'am," one of the cops said, "we need to bring you down to the station to ask you some questions."

Her heart stuttered to a stop just as someone came up behind her. Luke. She could feel the warm strength of him at her back.

"What's the problem here?" he asked calmly.

"Who the hell are you?" Teddy demanded.

Luke ignored him and waited for the officers to speak.

"We have a situation in regards to a theft that occurred at the town offices over the weekend," the first cop said. "A briefcase of money went missing from Ted Marshall's office."

Ali felt the horror fill her—they thought *she'd* stolen the money?

"It didn't go missing," Teddy said. "She stole it to get back at me for breaking up with her."

"Hey," Ali said, "*I* broke up with *you!*"

The officer went on as if neither of them had spoken. "The missing cash was from Friday night's town auction. According to several eye-witnesses, you were the last one in his office."

"Twice," Teddy said. "You were let into the office first by Gus on Saturday and then again by Aubrey on Sunday. Christ, Ali, how could you do this to me? I thought we were friends, at least."

"Friends don't sneak out in the middle of the night," she said, hating that they had an avid audience soaking up the exchange. "And I didn't steal anything." She recognized one of the cops. He'd been in the shop to buy flowers for his girlfriend. She spoke directly to him. "I've *never* stolen anything. Not once in my whole life."

Well, except she had. She winced. "Okay," she said, "so maybe one time I took a lip gloss from the drugstore, but I was twelve and stupid and my mom made me take it back. I had to work there for free for a whole day to make up for it. I haven't stolen anything since."

The second cop was rubbing his temple. Men did that a lot around her. Apparently she gave good headache.

"You have to believe me," she said. "I didn't take any cash. How much is missing?"

"All of it," Teddy said tightly. He was wearing khakis and an untucked, white button-down shoved to his elbows. He looked like he'd walked right out of a *GQ* ad, but instead of feeling her heart sigh, it hardened. The dreamy quotient of Teddy Marshall had run out.

"So you just showed up here to accuse Ali?" Luke asked him.

Teddy stared at him. "Seriously, who the hell are you?"

"Detective Lieutenant Luke Hanover."

"My landlord?"

"*Ex*-landlord," Luke said.

Ali's stomach was somewhere in the vicinity of her toes, so she couldn't process the exchange of testosterone at the moment. "So what now?" she asked the first cop.

"You come to the station for some questions, ma'am."

"Even though I didn't do it?" she asked.

"Yes, ma'am."

"Ali," she managed. "You keep saying *ma'am,*

and I want to look over my shoulder to see who you're talking to. Why can't you just question me right here?"

"That's not policy, ma'—"

At her glare, he wisely swallowed the "ma'am" part.

"Look, Ali," Teddy said, clearly attempting to soften his voice. Once upon a time that might have charmed her, but not today. "You're pissed at me," he said. "I get that. So just give us the money back, and we'll all go to our separate corners. No harm, no foul."

"I don't have the money; I didn't take it!"

When the two cops just looked at her, she let out a breath. "I didn't."

"Go through her stuff," Teddy said wearily. "There isn't much. It shouldn't take long."

Luke put a hand to Teddy's chest, halting his forward progress. "No one's searching her *or* the premises," he said, still calm but with one-hundred-percent authority. "Not without consent or a warrant."

Ali turned and looked at him for the first time. He was in black board shorts, still damp enough to cling to his body. No shirt. Bare feet. A towel was slung over his shoulder, his hair wet and uncombed.

He'd been in the water, she realized, swimming or maybe on the paddleboard she'd seen leaning against the back deck. She wasn't sure if she was grateful for his intervention or pissed that he clearly thought she needed the protection from a search due to what they might find.

"I didn't do it," she told Luke. "They can search."

"Good." Teddy pushed his way in through the door. "Where's the stuff you took out of Town Hall, Al?"

"I brought the floral arrangements to the senior center yesterday," she said. She pointed to her purse and the box of small ceramics on the foyer bench. "That's all that's left from the auction."

Teddy reached for the box, but the first cop stopped him. "It can't be you, Marshall, sorry," the cop said, and grabbed the box.

Ali heard all her things clink together. "Careful—"

She broke off when he pulled out the pine tree pencil pot.

"What the hell?" Teddy said incredulously. "You gave that to me." He turned to Ali, brows knit together. "You stole it out of my office?"

"Took back," she corrected. "I took it back because you didn't deserve it."

"You *stole* it. Where's the money, Ali?"

"I didn't take the money!"

The first cop pulled something out of the pot.

"Jesus," Teddy said as they all stared at a bank bill wrapper, the kind that was used to hold together a stack of money, exactly like the bill wrappers that'd been used on the auction money.

He whirled on her now, eyes furious. *"Where's the money?"*

"I . . ." At a loss, she shook her head. "I didn't know that was in there."

The cops looked at each other, faces impenetrable, their entire demeanor shifting from fairly relaxed to on guard and far more alert.

"Oh no," Ali told them. "This isn't what you think. That bill wrapper must have been in there when I took the pot."

"So you admit to taking the pot, ma'am?" the first cop asked.

"Well, yes, but . . ." She trailed off at their expressions. Clearly, they thought she was full of shit. She didn't dare turn to look at Luke to see if he felt the same. "I didn't steal the money," she said, suddenly feeling very small and very alone. "I didn't."

Teddy blew out a breath and shoved his fingers through his hair. "What now?" he asked the two cops.

"Do we still have your permission to search the premises?" one of them asked her.

"You don't need her permission," Teddy said. "I shared this place with her. It's half mine. *I* give you permission."

"Wrong," Luke said with that same steely authority in his voice. "You no longer live here or have rights to the property."

Again, Ali didn't know whether to be touched

81

or upset. She went with upset. "Search," she said. "Please. You'll see . . ."

They started with the living room and kitchen. Luke stood by, watchful. Impassive.

Not Ali. Her thoughts raced. Why was Teddy was acting so sure that it'd been her? Had he set her up? And what was the motive for that? Did he think that would keep her quiet about what he'd been doing in his office that night? "Where was the money in the first place?" she asked.

"In my locked bottom desk drawer," Teddy said stiffly. "As you very well know."

"I *don't* know," she said, just as stiffly. But she'd gone through his desk looking for the pencil pot. Had there been a locked drawer? She didn't think so. "You sure you locked it?"

"Yes."

"*Sure* sure?"

"Jesus! Yes!"

But Ali knew that expression and defensive tone. *He wasn't sure.* "You're lying about being sure," she said. "What else are you lying about, Teddy?"

Both officers straightened and gave him a long, appraising look. He raised his hands. "Hey, *I'm* the wronged party here! I put the briefcase in the bottom drawer to keep it locked up until the bank opened so I could deposit it. Hell, it was all just for show to begin with. Most of the money that had been actually collected was in electronic form. But we wanted to display cash that night to make

it look impressive and to encourage more dona-
tions. I had it in my bottom desk drawer. I just . . ."

"What?" asked one of the cops.

Teddy sighed. "Okay, so maybe I can't remember if I locked the drawer. I was in a hurry."

"Doing what?" Ali asked, knowing damn well
what—just not who.

"It's not pertinent," Teddy said.

The cop looked pained, and the look he gave
Teddy said he didn't appreciate being put in the
position of having to push. "It's pertinent. What
did you do directly after putting the money in
your bottom desk drawer?"

Teddy opened his mouth, and then closed it. After
a long pause, he sighed again. "Melissa Mann."

"What?" the cop asked.

Teddy sighed. "I was doing Melissa Mann."

There was a beat of stunned silence.

Melissa Mann was a local manicurist, fun and
sweet and pretty. She worked at the Hair Today
salon a few doors down from the flower shop. Ali
absorbed the hit and stared at Teddy.

Surprisingly, he had the balls to meet her gaze,
an apology there behind his lingering temper.
"I'm sorry, Ali. But we'd been over for a while."

That was not even close to true, but she didn't
dispute it. Because dammit, he meant for him.
It'd been over for him, and she'd not paid close
enough attention to notice. But hell if she'd
admit to being stupid.

"So you had Melissa in your office," the second cop said, "with the money."

"Yes," he said. "Apparently money is an aphrodisiac."

Ali felt the snarl catch in her throat and thought about how satisfying it'd be to wrap her fingers around his neck, but the witnesses were problematic. If she was in trouble for a crime she hadn't committed, she could imagine how much trouble she'd be in for murder.

A hand settled on her shoulder. Luke's. Clearly she'd projected the murderous urge . . .

Teddy took in the touch and narrowed his eyes.

"And afterward?" the first police officer asked him.

Teddy was still eyeing Luke's hand on her shoulder. "I gave Melissa a ride home."

"You gave her a ride home," Ali repeated slowly. "Let me see if I have this right. You stood up your girlfriend, dumped fifty thousand into your desk, maybe forgot to lock the drawer, had sex with Melissa, and then gave her a ride home and left the money there."

Ted grimaced again. "Listen, I realize that makes me look bad."

"Actually," Luke said, "it makes you look like a douche."

Teddy flushed an angry red. "Which still doesn't make me a thief."

The cops moved on to check the rest of the

house, including the bedroom Ali had been using. They went through her drawers, which was embarrassing enough, but then the closet. One of the cops pulled out the *Fun 'N Pleasure* bag that she'd gotten as a gag gift for her birthday from her sister. "No," she said quickly. "Wait—That's not mine—"

Cop number two pulled a Catwoman costume from the bag and then a massive, eye-popping neon-pink vibrator.

Teddy gawked at the sheer size of the thing. "You have a vibrator?"

"It was a gag gift," Ali said, sure she was as pink as the vibrator.

Still standing stoic and steady as ever, Luke eyed the items without a word.

"You have a vibrator," Teddy repeated in disbelief. "Is *that* why we hadn't had sex in two months?"

Once again Luke's hand settled on Ali. Just as well since there were two—no *three*—cops watching. So she didn't go for Teddy's throat, a fact she considered a real feat of restraint.

But it wasn't restraint at all. It was burning humiliation, anger, and something else.

Terror.

And that terror was tripled when the cops finished searching both the house and her truck. Though they didn't find the money, they took her downtown anyway.

Chapter 6

Luke stood in the center of his living room, which looked like it'd been tossed by a couple of thieves.

Hurricane Ali.

He didn't know what to make of the fact that she'd been caught with the bill wrapper. Nor did he know what to make of her being taken to the station for questioning.

But he did know one thing. Marshall—he refused to think of him as *Teddy*—had rubbed him the wrong way.

Still, this wasn't his problem. He didn't know Ali from Adam. What he *did* know was that he didn't want to get involved. He was on break from getting involved. In spite of what his commander wanted, he had nineteen days left on his leave, and he planned on using every single one of them to do jack shit. He was looking forward to it.

But for reasons he couldn't explain, he couldn't dispel the image of Ali at the station, sitting in an interrogation room, in trouble.

He'd always believed in the system. He'd had to. It was what had made his job so important to him. Take down the bad guys and let the courts keep them down—that had been his life, his entire reason for being.

But then that very system had failed him. And he'd failed too. He'd failed the people who believed in the system. And now he was taking a break from people so he couldn't fail again.

Which in no way explained why, instead of putting the house back together, or hell, going back to paddleboarding, he ended up in front of his laptop.

He'd already done that basic search on Ali, but he hadn't gone far. He picked up where he'd left off. Her mother had a record: two arrests for assault and battery, one, apparently, for the baseball bat incident Ali had told him about. Both times the charges had been reduced, and Mimi Winters had been let out on time served. Ali's sister, Harper, had a record as well, for indecent exposure.

Nothing for Ali. Though going back further, he caught a few additional times where she'd been questioned, one for an incident involving her science teacher, who'd allegedly been sexually inappropriate with his students. Christ, he hoped she hadn't been one of them. Leaning back in his chair, Luke stared at his screen. He already knew that she was protective, loyal, and tough as hell. Now he also knew that she'd grown up knee-high in shit, and yet somehow she appeared to come out of it with a sweet kindness that was to-the-bone genuine.

And she *was* innocent in regard to the money. He felt it deep in his gut.

He researched Ted Marshall next. There'd been the basic search done when Marshall had applied for the lease, but Luke went deeper without remorse, because something wasn't right.

The golden boy had certainly sailed through life so far. He'd been raised here in town, was captain of the football team, and had gone on to the University of Washington, graduating with a degree in political science. He'd not gotten into law school, so he'd come back to Lucky Harbor. He paid his bills on time, golfed, and had a fantasy football team that did pretty well. He'd been pulled over three years ago in Kent with a hooker in his car, but the story had later been amended to describe the woman as being an "exotic dancer." Marshall sat on several charitable committees in Lucky Harbor, and as the town clerk, no one had a single negative thing to say about him. He was well known and well liked.

Luke was experiencing bad flashbacks from the whole senator nightmare. Not that Marshall was a secret stalker and murderer. No, Luke suspected he was exactly as he appeared—a guy for whom things either came easy or not at all, because he was just on the wrong side of lazy.

Which also told Luke something else. Marshall wasn't the thief either. He didn't have it in him.

So the question was, did Marshall really believe Ali had taken the money? This was a tough one because there'd been something in the man's eyes, something in his tone, that hadn't rung true to Luke.

He'd been lying.

But about what exactly?

Luke made a call to Sheriff Sawyer Thompson. Sawyer had run wild in his youth, only a few years ahead of Luke. Their paths had crossed professionally on several occasions, most notably when Luke had helped Sawyer track down one of his perps in San Francisco not too long ago.

They bullshitted back and forth for a few minutes, and then Luke asked about Ali.

She was still being questioned. Having the bill wrapper in her possession looked bad, real bad, Sawyer said, but it wasn't enough evidence for an arrest. He said that a toe ring had been found in Marshall's office couch, and it didn't seem to belong to anyone who had business being in Marshall's office.

Or to Melissa Mann.

Luke hung up and chewed on that for a few minutes. *Not your problem,* he told himself. But he was still mulling it all over when his cell rang.

"How's the brooding going?" Sara asked.

He frowned at his sister through the phone. "I'm not brooding."

"Of course you are. You're a professional brooder."

Luke pinched the bridge of his nose. "Did you call for something in particular or just to piss me off?"

"Well, fun as it is to piss you off, I did call for a reason." But then she hesitated.

Shit. "What?" he asked. Sara had come out of prison determined to fix her life. Luke had done whatever he could, paying for rehab—twice—sending her to school—also twice—and finally sitting in the crowd with pride and relief when she'd eventually graduated with her teaching credentials. She now worked with troubled kids in an alternative high school in the Bay Area, and he couldn't be more proud of her.

But she was still a colossal pain in his ass. "You okay?" he asked.

"Yes. I just . . ."

"Whatever you need, Sara. You know that."

She sighed, sounding exasperated. "Okay, stop expecting me to be in trouble every time I call."

He felt a twinge of guilt, but there'd been years when that had been true. Not that he wanted to remind her. "I don't do that."

"Yes, you do," she said. "But this time, *you're* the one in trouble."

"Me? I'm fine."

"Really? Is that why you took off for Lucky Harbor—*Lucky Harbor,* Luke, where you never go

90

anymore? You ran away from the press. What was that?"

"I needed a vacation," he said.

"Is that it? Really?"

"Yes," he said, trying to assuage the worry he heard in her voice. "I told you, I had three weeks of leave that I was going to lose if I didn't use."

There was a beat of silence, as if she was trying to assess the truth from two hundred miles away. "Don't make me come up there," she finally said. "Because I totally will."

"I'm fine," he said, relieved she'd backed down. "I'm just . . . relaxing. Hanging out."

"Good. Then you can also give grandpa a hug for me."

"Sara—"

"He's old, Luke. And getting older. Do it for me."

The doorbell rang. *Saved by the bell.* "Gotta go." Luke clicked off and walked through the house, looking out the window at the white Dial-A-Ride van in his driveway. *Ah, Christ.* He opened the front door and faced the entire gang of Lucky Harbor's biggest troublemakers: Lyle Lyons, Cecil Elroy, Joseph Wykowski.

And their ringleader, Edward Gregory.

Edward and Luke's grandma had divorced in the '70s, when Fay had founded the local historical society to preserve the buildings that made up Commercial Row, and then insisted on running it herself. Back in the day, Edward hadn't gotten the memo about women's rights, not to mention exactly how strong willed and stubborn a Hanover could be. He'd stood firm, and Fay had dumped him.

Edward had moved out, eventually buying the house next door, saying he'd done so to spite Fay. But everyone knew it was because he hadn't gotten over her.

Or her death.

Or Luke, seeing as he'd caused it . . .

Luke leaned against the doorjamb and waited, because whatever this was, it was going to be good.

Or really, really bad.

"Took you long enough to answer the door," Mr. Lyons said, leaning heavily on his cane to peer inside, and then let out a low whistle at the mess. "Holy smokes, boy. You haven't outgrown that party animal stage yet?"

"He didn't do that, you idiot, the cops did," Mr. Wykowski said. "They tossed the joint looking for the dough."

Edward didn't speak. They hadn't been face to face in years, hadn't seen each other since Fay's funeral. "What's up?" Luke asked.

"We called Edward to drive us over here to see you," Mr. Wykowski said. "On account of I lost my license last year and these yahoos are blinder than bats."

"Hey," Mr. Elroy said, glaring at him. "You're the one who tried to drive down the pier and ended up nose first inside the deli. You smelled like pickles for a month."

"I turned at the wrong place. Big deal, we all make mistakes." Mr. Wykowski waved this off as he turned to Luke. "Ali's still at the police station."

"I know."

"Thing is, Ted Marshall's sort of the golden boy around here. Hell, he had the senior center redone last year so we could open up more rooms, and he single-handedly raised the money for the Dial-A-Ride van. He makes sure there's money in the budget for Edward's pay. People love him and trust him. If he says Ali stole the money, everyone believes him. You know what I'm saying?"

"No," Luke said. "Just because someone's a good guy doesn't mean what he says is gold. There's a justice system."

Which he knew better than anyone didn't always work.

"Listen," Mr. Lyons said, "we watch *Law and Order*. We know shit happens. And shit's happening."

"Ali's our ceramics teacher," Mr. Elroy said. "She also gets library books and reads to us. We need to help her. We're all she has."

"And you want me to do what exactly?" Luke asked.

"We figure since she's been staying here, that makes her yours too."

"It's not like that," Luke said.

"What is it like?" Mr. Elroy asked, and every one of them looked at Luke through rheumy, but sharp-as-hell, eyes.

Yeah, Luke, what was it like? She'd come along when he'd wanted to be alone, and she'd gotten his entire house torn up in the search for the fifty large. But the landline hadn't rung in a full twenty-four hours. Ali, whose damn life was circling the drain, had amazingly managed to scare everyone off and give him a chance at his peace and quiet.

In spite of himself, he wanted to help her in return. Not that she wanted his help. The envelope of cash she'd tried to give him was still on the table. Broke as shit, she'd still given it to him, because that was the right thing to do.

It'd been the pride flaring in her eyes that had slain him. She *needed* to pay her way. He was an ass, but not that big an ass to squelch the life that she projected with every single breath. He might be standing in the darkness, wallowing, weighed down by the things he saw on his job, but she wasn't like that. She was light.

And yet she was at the police station right now being questioned.

Alone.

He told himself that she was used to shitty circumstances. Hell, it appeared she was used to shitty men too. Her father, the pincher . . . him. She was used to taking care of herself and others.

And he had no idea why that got to him. But it did. *She* did.

"You still with us, boy?" Mr. Elroy asked. "Now's not the time to go all silent and cranky on us."

Luke hadn't been called "boy" in a damn long time. And few other than Sara dared to call him on the silent and cranky. "Ali's just being questioned," he said.

"What if she needs bailing out?"

"She doesn't."

"But if she does?"

"You could do it," Luke said.

"Yes, and we would," Mr. Wykowski said. "But . . ." He glanced at Edward, who still said nothing, gave away nothing. At seventy-two, he looked as fit and healthy as Sara and Jack had reported and pretty much the same as always— as if he'd just swallowed a lemon.

"We don't have very much," Mr. Lyons said. "We pooled our available cash together from what was left of our social security for the month, but it's not much. We had a poker game a few nights back, see, and normally I'd have taken the pot—"

Mr. Elroy coughed and muttered "bullshit" at the same time.

Mr. Lyons glared at him. "—But I had a little bad luck."

"That's not what happened," Mr. Elroy said.

"Yes, it is," Mr. Lyons said.

"No." Mr. Elroy shook his head. "Eileen Weiselman knew she had a losing hand, so she flashed you her tits to distract you into folding, and you lost. We all lost."

"Okay, look," Luke said, rubbing his temples where he was getting a stress headache. "Ali isn't a thief. I'm sure it's all a misunderstanding that will get worked out."

"But you can't just let her sit in jail while it does," Mr. Wykowski said, horrified.

"She's not in a jail cell. She's being questioned. Big difference. And unless she's charged and arrested—which they won't do without just cause—she won't need bailing out."

"See," Mr. Elroy said, "that's good information. I didn't know that. It's why you need to be in charge of this situation."

"I'm not in charge," Luke said. "Of anything."

"But she's down there with *hardened* criminals," Mr. Lyons said. "You can't let her sit there with them."

Luke sincerely doubted there were any hardened criminals in Lucky Harbor. The daily police reports read like something right out of Mayberry: an elk walking down Main Street, a drunken and disorderly at two a.m., high school punks running over mailboxes. "This isn't up to me," he said. "You know that, right? They're just following procedure."

They all looked deeply disappointed in him.

And then Edward spoke for the first time, uttering only two words. "Get it."

Mr. Lyons nodded and used his cane to navigate back to the van.

Edward just stood there looking at Luke.

Luke ignored them all and thought about Ali. He'd meant what he'd said, she was no thief. She'd probably give a stranger the shirt off her own back. The thought reminded him of what she'd looked like without a shirt in his kitchen, yelling at Marshall's voice mail.

Vibrant. Fierce. *Sexy.*

But she was also sweet and warm. And vulnerable.

And she was sitting in the police station. *Shit.*

His cell vibrated. He looked at the screen. His commander. With a long, slow inhale, he connected. "Hanover."

"Got a death threat this morning." Commander Craig O'Neil's voice was gruff and as commanding as his title. "Aimed at all of us. Just wanted you to know."

"Great," Luke said. "I'll start working my way down my bucket list."

"How about instead you just get your ass back here."

Not a question but a statement. Actually, more like a direct demand. "I'm on vacation," Luke reminded him.

"You're not, you're working a fucking case. Sheriff Thompson called me to make sure I didn't mind sharing you. What the hell?"

Thanks, Sawyer. "What did the threat say?"

"It said 'die pigs.' But he misspelled 'die,' used a Y. *Dye* pigs just doesn't have the same impact. But watch your back just in case."

"Will do."

"How long are you really going to be?"

"Didn't we just do this? Three weeks."

"Goddammit." The commander went quiet for a moment. "How about one?"

"I'll get back to you." Luke disconnected.

"Work problems?" Mr. Wykowski asked.

Luke didn't answer. Mr. Wykowski was a nice guy, but he was close friends with Lucille, which was a lot like being close friends with a PA system. Whatever he told Mr. Wykowski, he had to be willing for the entire county to hear. If he mentioned the threat, it'd be on Facebook in five minutes flat.

Mr. Lyons made his slow way back up the driveway, cane in one hand and in the other . . . an apple pie.

"Homemade," he said, waving it back and forth beneath Luke's nose. "We got it off of Betsy Morango, who made it for her granddaughter. We have to let her in on the next poker game now, but anything for Ali."

"You can't bribe me with pie." Before he'd finished the sentence, his stomach grumbled loudly in a plea for the pie.

The men grinned.

"We all know you're a pie ho," Mr. Elroy said.

Mr. Lyons had two plastic forks tucked neatly into his breast pocket. He took one out and scooped up a bite of the apple pie. "Oh yeah," he murmured, licking the fork. "Good stuff."

Just the thought of it was making Luke's damn mouth water.

Edward was still looking at him steadily. Intensely. Luke had no idea what his grandfather's angle was on this, but one thing he did know: There *was* an angle. "If I agree to step in here, you nosy-bodies have to agree to something too."

"What?" Mr. Lyons asked.

"Ali needs a place to stay until she gets an apartment. You have lady friends." Again he met Edward's gaze. "Surely one of you knows some-one looking for a roommate. She cooks. She does her own dishes. She's . . ." Not quiet. Not easy to ignore. "Cheerful," he finally said, hoping that sounded like a compliment. "She'd be a good roommate for anyone."

Except for him.

"She can stay with me," Mr. Elroy said, and waggled his brow.

Luke wrestled with his conscience and lost. "No." *Christ.* "Never mind. I'll find her a damn place myself." He reached for the pie, but Mr. Lyons held it close.

"Almost forgot, I need another favor," Mr. Lyons said.

Luke gave him a look. "I'm a little busy working on the first one right now."

"This one can wait until you get Ali home safe and sound. Roger Barrett needs to hire you. He's got a problem. He misplaced his '67 GTO."

"He didn't misplace it," Mr. Wykowski said. "He lost it in a poker game to Phillip Schmidt two years ago, remember?"

"Yes," Mr. Lyons said, "with the caveat that when the old geezer died, he had to give it back to Roger. Phillip's been six feet under for six months now, and his grandson Mikey 'The Doper' Schmidt still says he hasn't 'located' the GTO, which is bull-pucky. He's just not done driving the piss out of it."

"You realize that car's no longer PC," Mr. Elroy said, disapprovingly. "It's a gas guzzler."

"Gas guzzler, smuzzler," Mr. Lyons said. "It's a beaut. They don't make cars like that anymore. God rest Pontiac's soul."

Luke shook his head. "And the GTO is my problem why?"

"Because you're the problem-solving guy," Mr. Lyons said.

"Says who?"

"Your grandpa says that's what you do best."

Luke met Edward's gaze. Edward still didn't speak.

"So you're going to help Ali, right?" Mr. Lyons asked.

Luke could smell the brown sugar and baked apples. He needed that pie. *The hell with it.* He snatched it. "Yeah. I'm going to help her." He snagged the other fork out of Mr. Lyons's pocket. He took a big bite and nearly died and went to heaven. "Sawyer said the cops aren't done talking to her yet, not until around two."

Mr. Lyons blinked. "You were already going to help her," he said all accusatorially.

Luke took another big bite. "Yeah."

Mr. Lyons narrowed his eyes. "And Roger? You'll help Roger too?"

"Yeah, but *only* because Phillip Schmidt was the idiot who built that monstrosity on northeast bluffs. It blocks access to the beach from that side of the harbor, so he calls the cops on the kids that have to trespass to get to the water."

Mr. Lyons smiled. "You're a good boy. You're going to be good for Ali. I take her classes, you know, both the ceramics and her floral-design class. They help with my arthritis. She deserves better than to be treated like a common criminal."

Luke turned to Edward. "So what's your interest in this?"

"Oh, he takes Ali's classes too," Mr. Elroy answered for him. "We all do." He smiled. "We love her."

Luke was having some trouble with the image of his tough, stoic, impenetrable grandfather taking ceramics and floral design.

Not to mention—what the hell was floral design?

101

Chapter 7

Ali had a recurring nightmare that changed in details, but at the core it was always the same —she was alone.

Terrifyingly alone.

Sitting on a chair in some chilly room at the police station, her nightmare had gone live.

There'd been lots of questions. *Had she been angry when Teddy had broken up with her? Angry enough to want to frame him?* Because apparently her messages, both the voice mail and the sticky note, indicated a vengeful woman.

Did she know that if she turned the rest of the money in right now that charges would be reduced, possibly dropped? Because apparently she was holding it hostage somewhere.

Did she know that the sticky-note message could also be construed as an actual threat? She didn't know how calling someone an ass who was an actual ass had become threatening, but okay. Fine. Lesson learned.

She'd said maybe she needed an attorney, and one of the cops brought her to a phone. She stared at it in rare indecision. This was new, being on *this* side of the phone call. She'd been on the other side, several times, the first being when her mom had been arrested for property damage after she'd taken that bat to her boyfriend's car. What the cops hadn't known was that Mimi had been aiming for the guy's head.

The second time had been when Mimi had set fire to a different boyfriend's wardrobe. Her mistake had been in using the bonfire to have a party. Mimi had tried to plead temporary insanity on that one, but no one bought it. There was nothing temporary about Mimi's rage whenever she got cheated on.

Both times Ali and Harper had bailed Mimi out using the secret cash stash taped to the bottom of their couch, which was accumulated from her mom's tips. Over the years, that stash had ebbed and flowed, depending on various needs. Christmas. School field trips. Mimi's breast augmentation. And then the second surgery to remove the implants after they'd begun to leak.

Then Harper had taken her turn one year and had gotten arrested for indecent exposure after she'd pulled off to the side of the road to pee in the snow.

Ali still liked to tease Harper about that one.

She could call them, either of them. They'd be here in a blink, their tip stash in tow on the chance that she did indeed get arrested. But Ali wasn't going to call them. She hadn't been arrested—yet—and even if she had, she wasn't

103

going to have them spend their hard-earned money on her.

Besides, neither her mom nor her sister was qualified to offer legal advice, and then there was the embarrassment factor, which on a scale of one to ten, was at an eleven right now.

She *should* call Ted, because oh, did she have things to say to Ted. She stared at the phone some more. Luke. She could call Luke. He'd probably know what she should do. Except she wasn't his problem.

And she needed an attorney, not a detective.

She knew exactly one attorney: Zach Mullen. They'd gone to high school together, and skinny, geeky Zach, the PlayStation master of their neighborhood, had always been the smartest guy she knew, despite his huge crush on Harper. He'd graduated from UNLV law school last year, but it'd been months since she'd talked to him. Had he passed the bar?

She called him and was so grateful to hear his soft, friendly "yo" that she nearly collapsed. "Zach," she said. "Tell me you passed the bar."

"Okay, I passed the bar."

"No, really." She lowered her voice and crossed her fingers. "Did you?"

Zach huffed out a laugh. "Barely, but don't tell anyone that part."

Thank God. "So you're a real lawyer?" she asked, needing to be sure.

"Yep," he said. "A real, bona fide lawyer. I work for a hotel in Seattle in their legal department, though this week I'm in their Los Angeles office. Mostly fact gathering, but they pay bank so—"

"Okay, that's great," she said quickly. "Listen, I have a side job for you. How fast can you get to Lucky Harbor?"

There was a beat of silence. "Lucky Harbor?"

"Yes. I . . . sort of need some legal advice."

Zach might be a sweetheart, and he looked like a good wind could blow him over, but he was also sharp as a tack. "I'm in L.A. until the day after tomorrow," he said. "I've got a late-night flight back into Seattle, and then I'm all yours. What do you need, Ali? Anything."

"I need you."

Ali was eventually released with the caveat that she not leave town. A few minutes later, she was standing on the sidewalk in the bright sun, staring in surprise at the tall, silent Luke, who'd been waiting for her. "Why are you here?" she asked.

"Later. You've got other issues." He pointed at the two women holding up FREE ALI signs in front of the courthouse.

Her mom and sister.

"Ali!" they cried at the sight of her and rushed over. Dropping her sign, Mimi grabbed Ali in close and hugged her tight. "Oh, Aligator! Did they violate any of your rights?

105

Because honey, you have rights, lots of them."

"I'm fine, Mom. All my rights are still intact."

Mimi was wearing white capri leggings and a sparkly gold lamé top. Her gold hoop earrings matched the wide strip of bangle bracelets up one arm and was the same color as her spiked sandals. Her face was creased with worry as she tried to pat down Ali's gone-wild hair.

Ali pulled free and turned to Harper, who was wearing Daisy Dukes and a halter top, her hair and makeup bar-ready. She'd come straight from work and probably raced through the two-hour drive out here.

"Zach called us," Harper said. "Told us you might need moral support until he could get here."

"And moral support means picketing the courthouse?"

"Hey, it works on TV," Mimi said. She smiled up at Luke. "My baby has no manners. I'm Mimi Winters, Ali's mama, and this here's her sister, Harper."

Luke reached out to shake her hand. "Luke Hanover."

Because Mimi was looking at Luke with a speculative are-you-going-to-marry-my-daughter gaze, Ali quickly said, "Luke's helping me out with a place to stay."

"Aw!" Mimi kissed him on the cheek. "Aren't you the sweet one?"

"Mom, I'm paying rent," Ali said.

Mimi cupped Ali's cheek. "Of course you are." She sent a look Luke's way. "She's stubborn, this one, can never accept a helping hand." She looked around. "Where's Teddy? I swear, I don't care how hot he is, I'd like to castrate him. I've got a perfectly good pair of pliers in my purse to do it with too. Should've packed scissors, but the pliers'll be more painful. I'm thinking one slow twist and his doodle will snap right off . . ." She mimed the motion.

"Mom!" Ali quickly looked around. If a sticky note had constituted a threat, she couldn't imagine what packing pliers with the intent to twist off a guy's . . . *doodle* would mean.

"Just sayin'," Mimi murmured.

"Well stop just saying," Ali said. "And castration would mean cutting off his . . . other parts, not his . . ." She gestured vaguely, not daring to glance at Luke. "Doodle."

"Honey, he deserves to be castrated for accusing you of stealing money. You wouldn't steal money. You wouldn't steal anything." Mimi lowered her voice to a whisper and leaned in close. "You don't still steal lip gloss, right?"

"No!" *Good Lord.* "And no castrating. I've got this handled. I'm sorry you made the drive out here, and I appreciate the support, but you should both go back to work. I'm fine."

"We were going to wait until dark and TP

Teddy's new place," Harper said. "Where's he living now?"

"I don't know," Ali said, her second lie of the day. "But no TPing!" She was in enough trouble. "Everything's going to be fine."

"You promise?" Mimi asked. "Do you swear by the tip jar, baby? Because we need you."

"Yes," Ali said, crossing her fingers behind her back. "I swear by the tip jar that everything's going to be fine."

Mimi hugged her again, and she smelled like her favorite body spritz and long-past, sweet memories. "Love you, Ali-gator."

Ali held on for an extra minute and closed her eyes. "Love you too, Mom."

Mimi kissed her cheek and then turned back to Luke. "It was very nice to meet you, Luke."

"You too, Mrs. Winters."

"Oh, please. Call me Mimi. When are you coming home, baby?" she asked Ali.

As she'd been told not to leave town, she was pretty sure it wouldn't be any time soon. "I'll let you know."

"Next weekend? 'Cuz they're filming a new reality show down the street. Something about men and their tools and the women who love them. You could help us get on TV."

"Would love to," Ali said. "But I'm working."

"The weekend after then," Mimi said. "For my surprise birthday party."

"Mom," Harper said, exasperated. "You said you wanted it to be a *surprise*."

"I do. I want to be surprised by both my daughters throwing me a party with friends and flowers and balloons and lots of decorations."

"I don't think you're getting the concept of *surprise*," Harper said.

"And maybe a piñata," Mimi went on, "but with good stuff in it. Too bad men can't fit into piñatas . . ."

"*No men* in piñatas," Harper said. "That's a different kind of party altogether."

"Fine," Mimi said. "But I still want the balloons and flowers. And Ali."

"I'll be there," Ali promised, and watched them get into Harper's car. The engine coughed, emitted a bunch of smoke, and then leaped into gear.

"You crossed your fingers," Luke said.

"What?"

"When you promised her that everything was going to be fine."

Ali turned away. "She needs to think that everything is going to be fine."

Luke pulled her back and looked at her for a long moment. "Cell phone."

"What?"

"I need your cell phone."

She passed it over, watching as he programmed his number into it.

"For the next time you're faced with one phone call," he said. Luke looked into her eyes and let out a long breath. "Look, don't read more into this than it is. If you need me, you call."

"That simple?" she asked.

He shrugged, which she took to mean that he really had no idea, but he'd still do it.

"I wasn't going to call you," she said. "You're on vacation."

"I'm also not getting involved, but neither is working out so well for me."

Her mind had been going one hundred miles per hour since the cops had shown up at the door that morning. The adrenaline was wearing off, leaving her exhausted and far too shaky and emotional to deal with this. Horrifyingly close to the edge, she chewed on her lower lip and ordered herself not to lose it. "Why did you come?" she asked.

"You needed a ride."

Her chest squeezed even tighter. "You're not worried I'm going to steal something from you?"

"Stop," he said, his voice far too gentle for her fragile state of mind. She swallowed the lump in her throat and told herself she was just tired. This was out of control. She was out of control. It was just that for once, she wanted her life to move in a direction that *she* directed. With a sigh, she looked away. Life around her appeared to be maintaining the status quo. There was the usual early evening, low-level traffic. People were just getting off work and heading to the gym, the grocery store, the pier . . . home.

Ali had no idea where that would be for her tonight.

All she wanted was a hot shower and then to go to bed and not wake up again until this whole unbelievable situation had resolved itself. Or until she was old and gray. Whichever came first.

Luke was looking her over. She was still wearing her apron. She had a streak of dried clay across one arm and on one foot. And given the look Luke aimed at her face, she had some there as well. She lifted her chin.

With a small twitch of his lips, he hitched his head in the direction of his truck. He opened the passenger door for her and waited until she pulled her seatbelt across her body before he hit the lock and shut the door. He walked around the front of the vehicle, his stride long-legged and easy. No rush.

When he slid behind the wheel, he put the key in the ignition but didn't start the engine. There was a beat of silence, and then he turned to her, one hand on the back of her head rest, the other on the dash.

She did her best to appear as though she hadn't just been sitting in an interrogation room for hours being questioned about a crime she hadn't committed. But as it turned out, the pretense was far too much for her overloaded emotions, and she closed her eyes, trying to disappear into the seat. If she disappeared, then he couldn't see her fall apart.

"You okay?" he asked.

Her throat tightened further, and she shook her head. Nope. Not okay. Not even close. "Don't," she said.

"Don't what?"

"Don't be nice to me right now. I'll lose it."

With surprising gentleness, he pushed the hair from her face, then clicked open her seatbelt.

It was all the invitation she was going to get, and all the invitation she needed. Turning to him, she burrowed in as steady, strong arms closed around her. He stroked a hand down her back, and she pressed her face into the crook of his neck, soaking in the warm comfort he offered.

It was the safest and most secure she'd felt in far too long, and she wasn't sure she was going to be able to let go.

"Ali."

Afraid he was going to pull away before she was done soaking him in, she squirmed a little closer. "Please, not yet."

A rough sound escaped him, and he tightened his grip. "It's okay. I've got you."

Thank God. For just this one second, someone had her. She didn't have to be strong all on her own. She exhaled a long, shaky breath and concentrated on dragging more air in. After a few beats, she realized he smelled amazing, guy amazing, and that her lips were pressed against his throat. Suddenly it wasn't just comfort she was feeling, but a whole boatload of other things too, with arousal leading the pack. Extremely aware of the big, warm hand moving up and down on her back, she wondered—did he feel it too?

And then she had a bigger problem. Her face was still pressed up against his warm skin, and— look at that—every time she moved, her mouth slid over him.

He hadn't shaved that morning, probably not yesterday either, and his skin was rough with stubble. Deliciously rough. And then there was his scent . . . Yum. She could no more have stopped herself from doing it again as she could have stopped breathing.

In reaction, Luke let out a low, very male sound that called to the most female part of her.

Which answered her question. Yeah, he felt it too.

He said her name again, his hand coming up to cup her jaw, his fingers weaving their way into her hair, tightening as if to draw her away from him.

But he didn't.

Shaken, she inhaled a deep, uneven breath. Her breasts brushed his chest. The first time was accidental. The second time was all her. So was the third, and her entire body got all warm and tightened. What would it be like to have such a man belong to her? To belong to him? To kiss that mouth, feel it open under hers, feel it on her?

The temptation was too much, and her lips slid over his throat yet again. It still wasn't enough. She needed to taste him.

Don't do it . . .

But her day had been complete shit, her brain was full—*too* full—and there was no room in it for logic. None. So she did it. She ran her tongue along the column of his throat, and then because that was so good, she let her teeth sink into him a little bit as well.

A rough groan escaped him. Pulling her back, he searched her gaze for something, though she had no idea what. Probably her sanity.

Too late, she could have told him. She'd lost it.

Whatever he saw, he shook his head.

He was going to pull back. She could feel it in the sudden tautness of his muscles. She gave him her best sex kitten look, but the truth was she wasn't exactly a sex kitten on the best of days, and this was definitely not one of those. But something in his eyes warmed. Still half expecting him to push her back into the seat, she was surprised when he instead pulled her up against him.

"Playing with fire," he murmured. "And one of us is going to get burned."

She managed a nod. Yes, and yes. And for the record, the person getting burned would be her. She was already burning up, from the inside out. A full-blown inferno, and he'd barely touched her. She hadn't even realized until now how badly she wanted him.

Moving slowly, clearly giving her plenty of time to stop him, Luke cupped the nape of her neck, gliding his thumb along the sensitive skin there. Then he slowly leaned in.

She met him halfway, pathetically eager, but she couldn't help herself.

Luke let out a half groan, half low laugh that seemed to be aimed more at himself than her. He shook his head again and brushed his mouth across hers.

When she murmured for more, demanded really, he did it again, and then finally he deepened the connection, parting her lips with his, kissing her deep and hot, banishing every worrisome, unhappy thought from her mind. When they broke for air, he ran his tongue over her bottom lip before gently sinking his teeth into it, just as she'd done to his neck. Heat and desire licked through her like flames, and her fingers curled into his shirt. She wasn't ready to stop, wasn't ready to come back to reality.

He said her name in a silky, rough whisper, covered her mouth with his again, and as before, there was no more thinking.

Hell, there was no more air. There was nothing but this, and she strained to get even closer, thwarted by the console between them. She couldn't help it. Whether merely walking into a room or picking her up from jail, he had a way of commanding her attention. He was steady as a rock, steely. Edgy. Dangerous.

His kiss was all those things too. And he was a master at it, his big hand still gently caressing her neck, liquefying her bones with each delicious stroke of his tongue to hers. His other hand slid down her back, settling low on her spine, holding her still as he plundered.

Completely caught up, she held on tight, working to get closer still. Hell, she'd have crawled inside him if she could. He cupped her ass, and her hips arched to try to meet his in a movement as old as time, but she couldn't get to him. She heard her own soft mewl of frustration, and then he was slowing them down, pausing to rest his forehead against hers. "Damn," he said, stroking the pad of his finger over her wet lower lip. "Did *not* see that coming."

"Didn't see what coming?"

"You."

Chapter 8

Ali had no idea how it'd happened that she'd ended up trying to climb Luke's body, but she blamed his mouth. One hundred percent. "I'm over men," she said out loud so that she might hear it and have it sink in.

Luke didn't say anything to this. He just looked at her with the same intense expression on his face that he'd worn when he'd kissed her, which made her want to beg for another kiss. Instead, she bit her lips to keep them to herself. But as it turned out, she wasn't good at holding her tongue. "It's nothing personal," she said, "but as a whole, men haven't proven themselves all that reliable." She paused. "No offense."

"None taken."

"It wasn't going to be a hardship," she said, "to be over men."

He gave her an almost smile. "Hence the vibrator?"

She felt her face heat. "Okay, that really was a gag gift. And it's not like sex isn't . . . enjoyable or anything. It just tends to lead to bad decisions on my part."

"I can respect that," he said. "But for the record,

sex, when it's done right, is a hell of a lot more than *enjoyable*."

Her body was still tingling from his kisses, so it wasn't much of a stretch to believe that he could make sex far more than *enjoyable*.

"One more thing," he said.

She looked into his deep blue eyes.

"Not all men will disappoint you," he said. "I don't mean me. Because I will absolutely disappoint you. But we're not all assholes, Ali. I can promise you that."

She held his gaze, the man who'd let her stay in his house, the man who'd come for her no questions asked, not even "are you guilty?" Which meant that already he'd done more for her than most of the men in her life. She was still staring at him when her phone rang.

"Ohmigod, Ali," Aubrey said. "They brought you in for questioning? Why? How? *What the hell happened?*"

"Well," Ali said, "apparently after you let me into Teddy's office, I stole the fifty big ones."

"Did you?"

"No!"

Luke reached over and hit END, disconnecting her call.

Ali stared at him. "Why did you do that?"

"You shouldn't discuss the case with anyone," he said. "And especially don't joke about stealing the money."

"But that was Aubrey, Teddy's assistant."

"I don't care if it was the Easter Bunny."

"She's nice. She's the one who let me into his office the second time. She . . ." Ali broke off, her mind suddenly racing.

"She what?"

Ali met his gaze. "She asked me to make sure to never tell anyone that she'd let me in."

Luke's eyes were sharp. "You're friends?"

"Not the go out and share sushi kind, but yeah. It's more the 'your dress is pretty, where did you get it' sort."

Luke shook his head. "Was that in English?"

"We're friends," she clarified.

"You know they found a toe ring in Marshall's couch?"

"Yes," she said. "The cops asked me about it, but it wasn't mine."

"And it's not Melissa's either. So whose is it? And is the owner fifty thousand dollars richer this week?"

She shook her head. "I don't know." She'd been going over and over this in her head until it spun. "I saw the money at the auction like everyone else. The next day, I cleaned up the hall and carried out all the floral arrangements. Then I remembered the pencil pot I'd made Teddy, the one sitting on his desk. For some reason, I couldn't leave it there, so I went in to take it back. But it wasn't on his desk."

"Where was it?"

She paused, remembering how embarrassed she'd been to find it buried. "In his credenza."

Luke blew out a breath. "You went through his things?"

"Yes, but I never saw the money. I grabbed the pot and left. I didn't know the bill wrapper was there until the police found it, and I sure as hell don't know where the money is. I'm thinking Teddy framed me."

"Is there any reason that he'd want to stop the building of that new rec center?"

"I can't imagine why. It's his baby, a feather in his cap. And he likes feathers in his cap." She shook her head. "I've never seen him lose it like he did this morning. He was . . ."

"Scared," Luke said.

She nodded. "Yeah. I think he really believes I stole the money."

"It does have a woman scorned feel to it."

She didn't say anything to that, not wanting to know if he thought her capable of being that scorned woman. "I'm meeting my lawyer tomorrow."

"Who?" Luke asked.

"Zach Mullen." She watched as he pulled out his cell phone. "He's an old high school friend," she told him. "What are you doing?"

"How old is he? He looks twelve." Luke showed her the screen. He'd brought up Zach's

Facebook profile, where indeed his pic revealed a young-faced Zach, clearly fresh from a haircut, since he had a ring of pale skin across his forehead and the tips of his ears. His latest status update—from an hour ago—indicated he was at a sports bar in L.A.

Hooters.

"He's there for business," she murmured. "You're pretty quick with the research. I know you went back to your laptop. What else did you find out about me?"

He just looked at her.

"Come on," she said. "You're an off-duty detective, and I got taken from your house for questioning on the missing fifty thousand. What else did you dig up about me?"

Luke shrugged. "A few things."

"Like what? That I hated elementary school so much I used to hide at the park and my mom had to take off work and come find me?"

"You were a decent student though," he said. "And you took dance."

"I loved dance," she murmured. "But I quit early; I had no coordination."

He slid her a look. "Or you were worried about the cost."

Or that . . .

"You moved around a lot," he said. "There's a few gaps in the known addresses."

She slid down a little farther in the seat. Yeah,

there'd been gaps, which matched her mom's gaps in income, when they'd bunked on friends' couches here and there. "Sometimes my mom would lose jobs if she couldn't keep certain hours. Or . . . whatever."

He nodded, no judgment on his face. And, thankfully, no pity. She hated going back there in her mind, but she hated even more that he knew so much about her. "What else?" she wanted to know.

"You applied to transfer to several different state schools, even getting into a few of them," he said, "but you didn't go. No word why, though I can guess."

She felt a horrifying burning behind her lids. "You're thorough," she managed.

He shrugged.

Ali wasn't sure what that meant, but decided she didn't want to know.

"Tell me about Zach," he said.

"We went to high school together. He's a good lawyer."

"Yeah?" He slid her a look. "How long has he been practicing?"

Ali hesitated.

"How long, Ali?"

"He just passed the bar."

His mouth tightened. "You need someone who knows what they're doing."

"Zach does," she said. She hoped. "And it's not like I've been arrested."

But you could be . . . She knew he was thinking this but thankfully it went unsaid.

"Where to, Ali?"

She knew she should come up with a plan, but suddenly she couldn't speak.

Reaching out, Luke pulled something from her hair.

Dried clay.

He let his fingers linger, then tucked a strand of hair behind her ear. "I've already asked," he said very quietly, very seriously. "But I'm going to ask again. Are you okay?"

She had no idea, but she suspected no. No, she wasn't okay, not even a little bit. She'd been unceremoniously dumped, made homeless, and could be arrested at any moment. It'd been a craptastic week.

But hell if she'd say it. *Couldn't* say it, really, since the lump in her throat had grown to the size of a regulation football. So she nodded instead, acting perfectly okay . . . But she could feel the heat and strength of him, and for one shocking moment, she wanted to crawl into his lap and lay her head down on his shoulder. She wanted to burrow in and feel his arms close around her again. She wanted to feel the brush of his rough jaw as he pressed it to hers and whispered silly little nothings in her ear, like "you're going to be all right."

But he didn't do any of that.

Because he didn't want to be involved. She suspected it was his greatest wish to just be left alone, which, of course, was pretty much the opposite of her wish. "You can drop me at the B and B," she said.

"Stay with me," he said softly. "But you should understand that there are things you don't know about me."

"Are you an ax murderer?"

"No."

"You beat up old ladies?"

"No. Jesus, Ali."

"Do you call your mom every once in a while?" she asked.

Something came and went in his eyes. The very slightest glimmer of amusement. "Yes."

"Then I know enough," she said.

"You don't know that there are death threats being lobbed at me."

This had her taking a beat. "Seriously?"

"I think it's probably just the average, run-of-the-mill nutjob news junkie, but I can't be sure."

"That's okay," she said. "There's something *you* don't know about *me*." She smiled proudly. "I'm a three-time, sharpshooter Lucky Harbor Arcade champion."

"You're an . . . arcade champion."

"*Three* time," she repeated. "Missed that in your research, didn't you? I can shoot all my ducks in a row, ask anyone. Ask Lance, he runs the ice cream shop next to the arcade. I beat him just last week on a break."

Luke laughed softly. "Well in that case . . ."

She smiled, but his faded and he shook his head. "This isn't a joke, Ali."

"As I'm all too well aware," she said quietly. "Look, thanks for the accommodations. I'll pull my weight, I promise."

He looked a little taken aback at the statement. Did he do all the giving in every aspect of his life? If so, it made her ache for him, because she understood. That she'd found this common ground between them felt both unsettling and comforting.

She was going to have to get over that. And him.

Chapter 9

Luke drove up the narrow road toward his grandma's house, the rocky landscape made up of skyscraper-tall granite boulders that had been pushed here twenty thousand years ago, during the last Ice Age.

His passenger stared out her window at the rocks, as still and quiet as the surface of the water in the harbor far below.

This was unusual enough, but there was an element to Ali's silence that worried him. She was giving off a sadness, a sense of loneliness that made him ache for her.

He'd seen her with her family, who maybe rivaled his own family for the crazy quotient. But it was clear that she loved them with everything she had.

He understood that too.

"Thanks," she finally said softly, "for coming for me."

She hadn't called, and that got to him too. She hadn't wanted to be a burden. She'd asked him if he was worried she'd steal from him. The thought had never crossed his mind. She had the face of an angel, but that wasn't why he trusted her.

It was her eyes.

Christ, those eyes.

And bastard he might be, he wasn't usually wrong about people.

"You've done a lot for a perfect stranger you found squatting in your house," Ali murmured. "Or maybe not so perfect when it comes right down to it . . ."

"Perfect is overrated," he said. "And you're welcome, but I didn't do it just for you."

She turned to him. "No?"

"No."

"Then . . . why?"

There were two spots of color on her cheeks, and he wasn't sure if it was pride, temper, or intense curiosity. But any of it was hugely preferable to the brief sheen of tears he'd caught before, which had struck terror in his heart in a way that taking down hardened criminals never had. It was now his sole goal to keep her from crying. To that end, he answered her question more lightly than he would have otherwise. "Because the geriatric gang was going to drive me crazy until I did."

"My seniors?" she asked, shocked. "Why?"

Her seniors. He paused, really not wanting to go there. He thought about omitting, evading, or even out-and-out lying. He had no problem with any of that when it suited him, but for some reason, he had a problem with it now, with her. So he drew a deep breath and concentrated on the road. "Edward Gregory is my grandfather."

She stared at him. "Mr. Gregory, the Dial-A-Ride driver? He's your grandpa?"

"Yeah. He was married to my grandma Fay a million years ago for about ten minutes. When she left him, she changed her name—and my dad's—back to Hanover. My dad's their only kid."

"And he lives next door to you."

"Next door to my *grandma's* house," he corrected.

"Which is now *your* house. So he made you come check on me?"

"He was worried about you."

"And you?" she asked.

Again, he answered lightly. This time for *him*. "I was worried I'd never get any peace if I didn't do as they asked."

There was a long silence from the passenger seat, with Ali studying each passing tree as if it held the secrets to world peace.

He sighed. "Yeah, okay. I was worried too."

She said nothing to this, and he glanced at her. "You okay over there?"

"Just trying to picture you as someone's little grandson."

"Hard to believe, I know. But I wasn't always thirty and jaded as hell. I actually had a childhood, a lot of it spent right here in Lucky Harbor, in fact."

This got her. She turned her head and stared at him. "Are your parents here in town?"

"No, they raised me in San Francisco, mostly. They're doctors, both in Haiti now. When I was younger and they traveled, which was just about all the time, my sister and I came here to my grandma Fay's."

She shook her head. "Still trying to see you as a little boy, having fun, playing in the sandbox."

He smiled. "I was more of a blow-shit-up kind of kid. And believe it or not, I do know how to have fun."

Again she met his gaze, and the air seemed to crackle around them.

"Hmm," she said.

That damn "hmm" left him tempted to pull over and show her *exactly* how much fun he could be. But that would be a mistake.

Showing her anything over and above what they'd already done would be a mistake. Still, he was shockingly tempted, and he let her see that when he looked over at her.

Color bloomed in her cheeks again. "You're a distraction," she said softly. "I don't need a distraction. I need to do some problem solving."

"Are you going to ask me for help?"

"No," she said. "You're not getting involved."

Maybe if they both kept saying it, it would be true. "Right," he said, wanting to drive this point home. "I am definitely on a break from getting involved."

"Because of your last case."

"Among other reasons."

She fell silent, and he was a big enough jerk to be grateful.

"It wasn't your fault," she finally said, quietly. "What happened to that woman . . . Isabel Reyes."

"She might feel differently, if she could say so," he said with a lightness he didn't feel.

The typical late afternoon wind was kicking up as they made the last hairpin turn to the top of the cliffs. The water wasn't quiet now. The sun shimmered on it, lighting up the whitecaps as if they were a million bursts of fire.

Once upon a time, Luke would have been out there on that water with Jack or Ben, stirring up shit in one form or another. Now he was asking for trouble of a different kind altogether by bringing Ali back to the house.

"The news accounts I've read say that the prosecution's evidence got tossed out," she said. "And we both know that once they set the senator free, it was out of your hands."

The knife in his chest twisted a little bit. She was looking at him. He could feel the weight of her gaze.

"Must be a terribly helpless feeling," she said softly. "When something like that happens, and there's nothing you can do to stop it."

"Yeah."

"Why do you do it?"

"The job?" He shrugged. "Someone's got to. And I'm good at it. Usually."

"You didn't fail her, Luke. The senator did. *You* didn't fail anyone."

"You're wrong there," he said. "I've failed plenty." He'd failed his sister. His grandma. And no matter what Ali said, he'd also failed Isabel Reyes. He pulled into the driveway, turned off the engine, and got out of the truck.

He came around for Ali but she was already sliding out, and they headed up the walkway in silence.

Before he could open the door, Ali stopped him with a hand on his arm. He felt the zing of her touch all the way to his soul.

"You manage huge amounts of responsibility," she said quietly. "You face so much, every day. I think you're amazing, Luke. I also think a part of why you want to be alone is because you're feeling vulnerable right now. You're afraid you're going to fail someone else."

And if it was her, if he failed her in any way, it would kill him.

"Luke?"

"No," he said.

She was standing there in her muddy apron and wild hair, looking at him with those big, soft eyes that said she thought he was a hero.

But a hero wouldn't want to push her up against the door and kiss her.

"You haven't failed me," she whispered.

Fuck it, he thought, and giving in to the need swamping him, he backed her up to the door and kissed her. It didn't take more than a single heartbeat for her to wind her arms around his neck and kiss him back.

"*That's* why I need to be alone," he said when they broke apart, breathless. "We have a chemistry problem."

"Yes. I think you're right." She wobbled, and Luke slid an arm around her as he unlocked the front door, noticing he wasn't all that steady either. "Food or shower?"

"Both." She was still looking a little shell-shocked at their combustibility. "Shower first."

He led her inside, blocking the view of the still-trashed living room, standing there until she'd gone straight into the bathroom. Then he turned and faced the destroyed house. Shaking his head, he moved back to shut the front door just as Jack pulled up.

Jack was a firefighter and ran the local fire station. He was still in uniform, complete with the radio at his hip, and he carried a bag of food. They'd been best friends, brothers really, since the summer after sixth grade—which meant there were no formalities.

"You're an asshole," Jack said.

Guy code for *good to see you, man.*

Jack came to San Francisco at least once a

month, almost always staying with Luke. They'd seen each other two weeks ago, when Jack had come down to go sailing on a friend's boat. "Right back atcha," Luke said. "How's your mom?"

Dee Harper was fighting breast cancer and, by all counts, winning the war but it was costing her. And Jack as well.

"She's doing better, much better," Jack said, and started to walk right on in, but Luke shoulder-checked him.

"What?" Jack asked.

Luke took the food. "Thanks for dinner. Add it to my tab." Before he could shut the door, Jack stuck his steel-toe, big-ass boot out, blocking it.

"The size of your tab could feed a third-world country," Jack said.

Actually, the reverse was true, but Jack had a selective memory when it suited him. He also had the whole laid-back ski bum vibe going, but the truth was, beneath the deceptive playfulness, Jack Harper was anything but laid back and easy-going. Maybe he made his way through women like some men went through socks, but he worked every bit as hard as he played.

Luke peeked in the bag. "Orange chicken and spicy beef?"

"And fried rice, just in case the main course doesn't clog our arteries properly." Jack was trying to see past Luke into the house, his sharp eyes missing nothing. "Damn. They really did make a fucking mess."

"What did you know about the missing fifty K?"

"I'm too hungry to talk; I'm wasting away as we stand here. I need to eat. In front of the game."

"The game's not on."

"Yeah, it is."

"It's not on in *here*," Luke said.

"The game's always on at your place."

Down the hall, the shower went on, and Jack's brow went up.

Luke blew out a breath. "Ali Winters."

"She's here?" He grinned. "You were holding out on me." He pushed past Luke and headed into the messy living room. He shoved the cushions back onto the couch and then dropped onto it in a big, lazy sprawl. "Where's the remote? I've only got half an hour before I have to be back at the station."

"You're not staying."

"Aw, come on. It's been forever since I've gotten to see you be an idiot with a woman. Don't ruin my fun."

"I'm not an idiot with women."

"You're a complete idiot with women, and I'll prove it: *Tina Rawlings*."

"Tina Rawlings was when we were *sixteen*," Luke said.

"Yeah, you had sex with her at the lagoon and got caught by her boyfriend. He beat the shit out of you."

"Because he and his entire baseball team jumped me."

"Bowling team," Jack corrected. "It was the *bowling* team, and *I* could've taken them with one arm tied behind my back."

"Hey," Luke said, "some of us didn't get our growth spurt until college."

Jack laughed. "Whatever helps you sleep at night, man. So you and Ali . . . ?"

"No."

"Sure? Because I don't think you have to worry about the bowling team these days. You're not in bad shape."

"I'm not getting involved." How many times was he going to have to say that? He'd come to Lucky Harbor to lose himself for a little while. *Not* to share the place with a woman who made him ache like crazy and had the singular ability to make him want to both howl at the moon and run like hell.

The phone rang, and Luke stared at it like it was a striking cobra.

"You going to get that?" Jack asked.

"Fuck no."

The machine clicked on, and a woman's voice said, "Ali-gator? Just checking in on you—"

"You still have an actual answering machine?" Jack asked. "Man, it might be time to upgrade the place from the 1980s . . ."

Luke strode to the machine and picked up

the phone. "Ali's in the shower, Mrs. Winters."

"Luke!" She sounded pleased to hear his voice. "You were going to call me Mimi, remember?"

He let out a breath. "Right. Mimi . . ."

Jack went brows up again. Luke ignored him. "I'll have her call you," he said to Mimi.

"You're a sweetheart, Luke. Thank you."

"Wow," Jack said when he'd hung up. "Look at you, not getting involved."

Luke flipped him off and snatched the remote from Jack's hand.

"Figured you'd want the 4-1-1," Jack said. "If you kick me out now, you won't get to hear it. But hey, if you're not getting involved . . ."

"Tell me."

Jack grinned. "Lucky for you, I work with a bunch of little girls."

"You work with a bunch of firefighters."

"Who all gossip like girls. The money's still missing, as you know, and actually there's a reward going out on it, but Ali isn't the only one they hauled in. They questioned Ted Marshall further. And also Melissa Mann. You remember her, right? She said—"

"That Marshall was screwing her and he can't remember if he locked the drawer with the money," Luke said.

"Damn, you stole my thunder. Seems Golden Boy's keeping secrets. Melissa said the police searched the office and came up with a woman's toe ring deep in the couch that doesn't belong to her."

"Or Ali," Luke said.

"Okay," Jack said, irritated now. "If you already know everything, why did you ask?"

"Because gossip is usually based in fact," Luke said. "Got anything else? Maybe something on the admin, Aubrey?"

"Nothing on Aubrey. But Melissa did say she believed that Teddy and Ali were just room-mates. Which means Ted had a good thing going. They're going to question everyone who was in the office on the night of the auction, but there's a few problems."

"Like?"

"Teddy isn't talking about any other possible indiscretions. And apparently that whole wing of the building was a revolving door. Several people were back there using the quiet hallway for phone calls, and people were going through on bath-room runs. The janitor had a thing with the caterer in the treasurer's office, one door down from Marshall's office. Reportedly even the mayor's wife was seen slipping out of the hallway storage closet just past the bathroom. Go Mr. Mayor."

Luke stared at him. "Are you telling me that place saw more action than the rest of us saw all year?"

"Speak for yourself." But Jack's grin faded. "The fact is Ali's the one who got caught with evidence. And there's a lot of pressure on Sawyer to make an arrest. She's also the only one with an obvious motive."

"Circumstantial evidence," Luke said. "And people don't need a motive to steal cash."

"She stole a ceramic pot because she'd made it for her boyfriend who'd just dumped her by text," Jack pointed out. "Hello motive."

"She didn't know there was evidence to a crime in it."

"We both know that's weak, Luke."

"I know. And I know something else too, it's not Marshall either. Yeah, he's into politics, but he's a piggy-backer, not a big-plan sort of guy. He doesn't have the stones for this."

"So . . . what? He was framed?"

"I'd bet on it," Luke said. "And somehow Ali got caught in the middle—" He broke off at the sound of bare feet padding down the hall.

Ali appeared. She'd showered and changed faster than any woman Luke had ever known. She was in sweats and makeup-free, wet hair piled up on top of her head, with wavy tendrils framing her face. She headed straight to the kitchen and headed back with a carton of ice cream from Lance's shop.

Luke felt a small smile play around his mouth as she ate right out of the container with a wooden spoon. Ali Winters might be down, but she wasn't out for the count.

She scooped another big bite, and her expression finally relaxed. Until she saw the mess of the house. That wiped the smile right off her face. "Oh no. Oh Luke, I'm so sorry."

"Don't worry about it," he said. "It's seen worse."

"This is true." Jack rose off the couch. "Way worse. We were what you might call wayward teenagers."

Jack had the same height as Luke, but more bulk to his muscle tone. Of the two of them, Jack also possessed the charm, which had gotten him out of more trouble than Luke had ever managed to get into. Jack flashed all one thousand watts of that charm at Ali now.

"Jack Harper. I've seen you around, but we've never been introduced," he said, holding out his hand to Ali, smiling his "reassuring" smile. It was number three in his arsenal, behind his "you can't resist me" and "I want you" smiles. "I'm the best friend, by the way. The better-looking, far more fascinating one, I should add."

"Ali Winters," she said, looking a little dazzled, which made Luke roll his eyes. "Nice to meet you." She glanced at the mess again, but Luke stepped in her way.

"I've heard a lot about you," Jack said.

"I'm sorry," she said, glancing at Luke. "I can't say the same."

"Not surprised," Jack said. "Luke's not exactly a big talker."

139

"No," Ali said faintly, a slight blush coming to her cheeks. "He's not."

There was nothing in Ali's tone to suggest that they'd spent some time in Luke's truck kissing like their lives had depended on it, but Jack knew him better than anyone else on the planet. Proving it, his gaze shifted from Ali to Luke. "Also, he can never find his keys and he snores," Jack said.

"Thanks, man," Luke said.

Jack smiled at Ali. "Hope you're hungry; I brought Chinese. Ben, my cousin and the third musketeer, would've brought a loaded pizza. He's on government assignment right now, and I'm just superstitious enough that I won't eat a pizza until he's home. You need anything else?"

Clearly surprised to be asked, Ali blinked. "No, thank you." Her voice sounded funny and gave Luke a very bad feeling.

Jack didn't miss it either. Jack didn't miss much. "All right, I'll get plates," he said very gently, waiting until he was behind her and out of her peripheral vision to send Luke a steely look.

One thing the two of them had always shared was a hatred of seeing anyone mistreated or taken advantage of. Jack loved Luke, but the message was clear—*don't hurt her more than she's already been hurt.*

When Jack vanished into the kitchen, Ali

moved to the couch, head averted. There might even have been a muffled sniffle.

Oh, Christ. Luke had faced down countless gangbangers, armed felons, and drugged-up perps. He'd faced the worst humanity had to offer, but he'd never gotten the hang of dealing with a woman's tears. Sucking it up, he sat next to her.

She stiffened.

Ignoring that, he reached for her ice cream, thinking to set it down for her, but she surprised him with an elbow to the gut.

"What the hell?"

She hugged the ice cream to her chest. "I told you not to be nice to me right now!"

"I'm not nice. I'm never nice. And Jesus, remind me to never try to separate you from your ice cream again."

Jack reappeared, paper plates and napkins in hand as he took in the scene. "Bad time?"

"Yes," Luke said.

"No," Ali said, and glared at Luke.

Jack nodded in approval. "Keeping him in line. That's good. He needs that."

Luke shot Jack a look, which Jack ignored as he plopped down on the couch right between them. The big oaf actually bounced Ali nearly to the floor and half sat on Luke as he settled in. He took the ice cream from Ali—and didn't get elbowed, Luke couldn't help but notice—and then handed out plates. They divided up the food, with Jack taking the last eggroll.

"Hey," Luke said.

"It'd go straight to your ass," Jack said, and popped the eggroll into his mouth. "No one wants to see that."

Luke ignored this. They were both fit, but extremely competitive. Maybe Jack could kick his ass on a run, but Luke totally had him on the water and the boards.

When Ali finished her food, she pushed her plate away. "Okay, let's hear it."

"Hear what?" Luke asked.

"Whatever information you two have that I don't."

Jack sent Luke a look, and Luke turned to Ali. "Look, at this point it's all really just speculation . . ."

"I'm not some dainty flower, Luke. Spit it out."

Jack grinned at her. "We're going to be great friends, you and I."

"As my friend then, tell me," she said. "Tell me what I'm missing."

"It's about Marshall and his office," Luke said carefully. At the first sign of tears, he'd shut the hell up. "And what else might have occurred there that night."

"I already know what happened," Ali said. "He screwed Melissa on the couch and then screwed me by claiming I stole the money."

"Yes," Luke said. "But the toe ring tells me that in all likelihood, Teddy had more than one woman in his office. And maybe one of those women got greedy. Problem is, the sheriff's department is getting a lot of pressure to make an arrest. Hard to do when the hallway outside his office was Grand Central Station that night." And then he told her about the comings and goings.

Ali stood and paced the room, stepping around the mess of things all over the floor. "So are they checking out Gus, and the caterer, and everyone else, including Mr. and Mrs. Fancy Mayor?" she asked.

Luke nodded. "Yes."

"But I'm the only one who got caught with any sort of evidence," she said quietly.

Luke rose and made his way to her. "We're going to figure this out."

Jack gave him a look at the "we."

"How?" Ali asked.

"We put the evening together like a puzzle," Luke said. "One piece at a time."

"There's a lot of pieces," Ali said, and crouched down to begin picking up.

Luke pulled her upright. "I'll get the mess later," he said. "As for the pieces of the puzzle, we'll figure it out."

Her expression showed her doubt and gave him a pang right in his gut.

Apparently in Jack's too, because he stood as

well. "No one's going to leave you to fry for something you didn't do," he said quite intensely.

Ali managed a small smile. "Thanks. I owe you both."

"No, you don't," Jack said, and kissed her on the cheek. " 'Night."

Luke followed him to the door.

"*Don't* sleep with her," Jack said quietly. "She needs comfort and a friend. And—" he continued before Luke could utter a word, "don't give me any bullshit like you're not her friend because you're not getting involved. You're as involved as I've ever seen you."

Chapter 10

The next morning, the sky was dark and mottled, the clouds tumbling against each other, threatening rain. Instead of putting himself out on the water on a board to be bait for a bolt of lightning, Luke put on his running shoes.

It started to sprinkle as he ran along the rocky beach, but he didn't mind. It kept him cool. The air was salty from the ocean and also scented with pine from the trees. And in spite of the weather, the mountain chickadees were still out singing in force, "cheeseburger, cheeseburger," sounding like The Chipmunks on crack.

It made him hungry.

On the way back, he slowed at the Schmidts' summer beach house, remembering his promise to the Geriatric Gang to locate Roger Barrett's GTO. He walked around the front of the house and took a look through the glass panel across the top of one of the two garage doors.

Yep. There was the '67 GTO.

With a shake of his head, he knocked on the front door.

No answer.

He knocked harder.

Two minutes later, the door was opened by Phillip Schmidt's twenty-two-year-old grandson. Mikey was wearing a bright Hawaiian-print shirt with red and green parrots on it, unbuttoned over a pair of sunshine-yellow boxers. His sun-kissed blond hair hit his shoulders, and he had on small, round, purple-lensed John Lennon sunglasses, a laid-back, surfer-dude smile, and held an unlit joint pinched between his fingers. "Oh shit," he said at the sight of Luke and turned to run.

Luke reached out and grabbed him by the back of his shirt. Mikey, as thin as a pipe cleaner with eyes, ran in the air for a few beats before Luke gave him a little shake and dropped him back to his feet.

"Dude," Mike said, rolling his shoulders, "I have rights."

"Yes, but smoking pot isn't one of them."

"It's called Maritime Law, man. They can't tell you what to do in the ocean."

"You're not in the ocean, and I don't give a shit about your pot. I'm here about the GTO in the garage."

"My grandpa won it in a poker game. Sweet, right?"

"Very. But it's not yours."

"Says who?" Mikey asked.

"Roger Barrett."

"Aw, man, that guy's a hundred and something years old. He can't see past his own nose, and anyway, he's a little cuckoo for Cocoa Puffs." For emphasis, Mikey made the crazy sign, twirling a finger by his ear.

"He's seventy and sharp as a piranha's eye-tooth," Luke said. "Plus he had Lasik surgery. Roger can see better than both of us put together. And he's got one finger on his 'oops I've fallen and can't get up button' to report the GTO as stolen. Get it back to him today."

"Can't. I have, like, plans."

"Cancel them," Luke said.

"No can do. Candy James is coming over today. I'm going to get laid, man. She is one hot piece."

"If you don't return the car, *you're* going to be the hot piece, Mikey. In prison."

Mikey sighed. "Harshing my buzz, dude."

Luke held out his hand. "Keys."

Mikey mopily grabbed a set of keys on the foyer bench and slapped them into Luke's palm. "It's on empty."

Of course it was. Luke started to walk out, then turned back. "You work for that cleaning company that takes care of Town Hall, right? The night shift?"

"Yeah. Why?"

"You ever see anyone there in the offices late at night?"

"Sometimes. People are, like, working hard to keep their jobs, man."

"How about recently?" Luke asked.

"You mean as recently as when your girlfriend

147

stole the money from Ted Marshall's office?"

"Ali isn't my girlfriend, and she didn't steal the money."

"Ted Marshall's a pretty good guy, man. He wouldn't lie."

"Have you seen anything helpful? Anyone else in the office with him, for instance?"

"Maybe I don't feel like telling you."

"You feel like going to jail?"

Mikey let out a dramatic sigh. "The cops already asked me this. I told them I didn't see anything."

Luke crossed his arms over his chest and eyed Mikey over the tops of his sunglasses.

After all of three seconds, Mikey broke eye contact. "If I get fired from another job, my dad's gonna gut me."

"You keep stealing cars, and your dad is the least of your worries. Talk to me, Mikey."

"Okay, so normally when I go in, everyone's gone. Twice this past week, Marshall was working late. Only he wasn't working, you know what I mean?"

"No."

Mikey hesitated. "I don't think I should say, man. He's never snitched on me. I don't want to snitch on him."

"You're not snitching. You're helping me solve a crime so that an innocent woman doesn't get blamed for it."

Mikey sighed. "He was in his office, in his chair, with some hot chick bouncing on him."

"You know her?" Luke asked.

"Hello, she was *naked,* man. Hot as hell. My eyes never got higher than her ass. But maybe she had blonde hair. Maybe. I dunno. She was a real screamer though, if that helps. She kept going 'harder, baby, harder,' which didn't make sense, because she was on top and—"

"Have you seen him working late since?" He was grasping at straws here, and knew it.

"If that was 'working' then I want his job," Mikey said.

When Luke just looked at him, he let out a breath. "No, I haven't seen him"—Mikey used air quotes—"*working late* since."

"Thanks." Luke turned to go.

"If you let me keep the car, maybe I'll remember something else."

"How about this," Luke said. "If you remember something else, you tell me. Fast and quiet. And then—"

"You'll get me the car back?"

"No. But I'll let you live."

Mikey blew out another breath, and Luke left. He filled up the GTO, and because it was dirty and the interior reeked like weed, he also drove it through the car wash and got a pine tree air freshener to dangle from the rearview mirror. Thirty minutes later, he was handing the keys

149

over to Roger Barrett. "Good as new," he said.

Roger couldn't wait to sit in it. Gleeful as a kid in a candy shop, he made Luke join him and cranked up the music.

Neil Sedaka.

They sat there, the windows rattling with "Breaking Up Is Hard to Do," sipping sodas. Just when Luke was thinking he needed a sharp stick with which to poke out one of his eyeballs, Roger turned to him. "About your girlfriend, that cutie patootie from White Center."

Luke didn't bother to sigh. "Ali. And she's not my girlfriend."

"Well, whatever you kids are calling it nowadays then," Roger said. "Friends with benefits?"

Luke choked on his soda.

"You know, Ted Marshall's a good man, right? He takes care of Lucky Harbor, and he gives back. But Ali's good people too. She goes to the senior center. My sister's there. Ali takes the time to sit with her, talk to her, get her involved in the activities. If Ali stole that money . . . Well, I just wanted to say that I know she must have had a real good reason."

"She didn't steal it," Luke said.

"I'm just saying . . ."

A few minutes later, Luke left for home, once again jogging through the morning chill. He took the streets this time, his running shoes hitting the damp ground. He'd meant to steer clear of all Lucky Harbor business. He'd definitely meant to stay clear of Ali.

He'd failed at both.

Ali had had a crappy day. Leah had tried to get her to go out tonight but she wasn't in the mood. Instead, she was in the kitchen licking brownie batter from a wooden spoon like her life depended on it when Luke wandered into the kitchen.

"I smell chocolate," he said, looking hopeful.

He was wearing sexy-as-hell jeans and a white, long-sleeved shirt that was snug across his broad shoulders. He looked even better than the chocolate. "Brownies from a box," she told him. "Comfort food."

"What's wrong?"

She shook her head and reloaded the spoon with more batter.

Taking her wrist, he brought her hand up to lick the spoon in the same spot she'd just licked.

It gave her a hot rush. So did Luke shifting closer.

"Tell me," he said.

She shrugged. "People kept coming into the shop to see the girl who stole the money. And you were right—word is they're getting ready to make an arrest."

"And you're afraid it's going to be you."

"Well, who else at this point?" she sighed.

"Russell's taking two days off and keeping the shop closed. Even he's planning for me to be in jail." She needed to get to the bottom of this now. Determined, she set down the spoon, grabbed her keys and purse, and turned to the door.

"Where are you going?" Luke asked, slapping his pockets, turning in a circle, clearly searching for his keys in the universal bewilderment of men everywhere across the planet. "Ali—"

"Table," she said.

"What?"

"Your keys are on the table."

"Damn, you're good." He scooped them up. "Where we going?"

"To be proactive."

"Yeah? Where's this proactive thing taking place?" Outside, he took her elbow and redirected her to his truck.

"I don't need help, Luke. Not with this."

"Think of me as a wingman," he suggested, and opened the passenger door for her.

Since he was standing there blocking her escape, looking big and bad and absolutely unmovable, she got in. "If you're just the wingman, why are we taking your truck?" she asked.

"Wingmen always drive. Where to?"

"The Love Shack." The local bar and grill was the only nightlife in the entire county.

"I have liquor in the house," Luke said.

"I want to talk to Gus. He told the police he'd holed up with the caterer."

"So?"

"So the caterer was Tara Daniels Walker, and she's *very* married. But Tara's assistant—Callie—dated Gus a few months back and then broke up with him. Loudly."

"What makes you think he's lying?"

"*Someone's* lying," she said. "If it's Gus, why? What's he covering up? Something for Teddy, or himself?"

"Okay, I like the way you think," Luke said, "but this has trouble written all over it. I talked to Mikey Schmidt today."

"The stoner guy?"

"He cleans Town Hall at night. He caught Marshall with a maybe blonde the other night."

She glanced at him. "Melissa?"

"He couldn't say. I need a favor, Ali."

"Sure. Anything."

The look he slid her was pure heat, and she flushed at the thought of doing *anything* for him. *That's not what he'd meant,* she told herself firmly. Get a damn grip.

"When we get there, let me lead." He parked in the parking lot between the pier and The Love Shack, catching her before she could jump out of the truck. "Wait," he said. His phone was ringing. Holding onto her purse—clearly a man who knew how to slow down a woman—he punched SPEAKER on his phone, which was still lying on the console. "Hanover," he said shortly.

"Oooh, so official," a woman said. "Odd, for a man on vacay."

"I'm . . ." He glanced at Ali. "Busy. You okay?"

"You mean, do I need you to save me?" the woman asked. "Never fear, little brother, I do not. *I'm* trying to save *you*."

Luke's sister, Ali thought with way more relief than she should have felt.

Luke's brow knit in annoyance. "I'm fine, Sara. Just—"

"Busy," Sara said. "Yeah, yeah, I get it. I heard about you and the cute florist."

Luke stared at the phone, and Sara snorted into the silence. "You were seen kissing her in your truck on Main Street in Lucky Harbor, Luke. What did you expect? Anyway, you've got some reporters here who want—"

"Tell them no," he said with steel. "Tell them to stay away from you or I'll get restraining orders. Tell them—"

"Got it, Ace. I can handle this. What are you doing?"

Luke tightened his grip on Ali's purse when she tried to break free. "Working."

"Liar," Sara said. "You never answer the phone when you're working. It's the cute florist, right? Tell me about her."

Luke pinched the bridge of his nose. "I'm hanging up now."

Sara laughed at him. "I'll start. Her name's Ali. Jack says she's pretty. Maybe I should get a few days off work and come up to get a look at her myself."

Ali felt a warm fuzzy flow through her, which was rudely chased away by a blast of reality by Luke himself.

"It's work," he repeated.

Work . . .

"Uh-huh," Sara said, sounding amused. "Love you."

Luke punched END and looked at Ali. "Ready?"

Oh, yes. She was ready. She was ready to leave his truck. *Alone.* "I'll handle this," she said.

"Never hurts to have backup, Ali."

"I won't be more work to you."

He gave what might have been a very small sigh. "You don't know my sister," he said. "If I'd told her anything else, she'd drive up here and butt in."

She unhooked her seatbelt.

Behind her, Luke did the same. "Let me do the talking."

Over her dead body.

"Listen," Luke said, going for reasonable. His mistake, because it'd been a while, but he should have remembered that angry women were never reasonable. "You're looking pretty riled up. You need to—"

Ali slid out of the truck and headed to the bar with purpose.

"Go in low profile," he finished. *"Shit,"* he muttered behind her when she didn't slow down. He followed her inside and watched as she walked right up to the bar where Gus was sitting with a few other guys over beers.

Luke nodded to the guy behind the bar—Ford Walker, co-owner of the place, ex–world sailing champion and all-around good guy.

"Can I have a minute?" Ali asked the janitor.

The big guy smiled down at her. "Hey, Ali. Luke. Heard you two were a thing now."

"Remember the other night?" Ali asked him.

"When I let you into Marshall's office? Yeah." His smile faded. "I'm sorry you got caught."

"I didn't steal the money," she said, looking like steam might start coming out of her ears. Or her hair. The hair was pretty wild today, but he liked it.

He liked *her*. Way too much.

"Right." Gus nodded adamantly at her. "You didn't steal the money."

"Can you tell me who else you saw in the hallway that night?" Ali asked.

"Well," he said, scratching his beard, "just as I told the police, it was hard to keep track. That hall was busy as hell."

"Could you give it a shot?"

"Sure. Mrs. Medina wanted to see the Lost and

Found, which was in the storage closet. Then, while I was waiting on her, Ella came in to make a phone call in private. Only she ended up yelling at her sister, so it really wasn't so private at all."

"Ella?"

"From the post office. And then Aubrey came in to see why people were in the office to begin with, and she got all up in arms about it. And then there was Ted himself . . ." Gus blushed a bit at that. "But I suppose you've already heard . . ."

"That he had Melissa in there?" Ali asked politely.

Gus downed his drink. "Yeah. I didn't know, Ali. I swear it."

Gus's mountain-sized friend snorted.

Luke agreed. As the janitor, nothing happened in that building that Gus didn't know about.

"And you," Ali said to Gus, "you were there with Callie, right?"

Gus went very still, only his eyes sliding to the giant next to him. "Uh, who told you that?"

"It's what you told the police," Ali said calmly. Except she wasn't calm at all. Her eyes gave her away. Was Luke the only one who could see it?

Gus's friend set down his beer and glared hard at Gus. "You were with Callie?" he asked. Actually, it was more of a shout.

"Now, now, Buddy," Gus said quickly, raising his hands. "In all fairness, you did say you two were just friends, so—"

Buddy punched Gus in the mouth. "In all fairness," he said.

Luke grabbed Ali and hauled her back just as the two men tumbled to the ground, Gus's long legs taking out the two men on the other side of him.

"Hey!" one of them yelled. "You spilled my drink!" And then he jumped into the fray too.

His friend dove in as well, and pretty soon beers and fists were flying in a full-out bar brawl. Ford hopped over the bar to break it up, and Luke helped him separate the idiots from the idiots.

Afterward, Ali was staring at him. "Wow," she said.

"What?"

"You just waded into the flying fists and yanked them apart like it was no big deal, like you didn't even notice the danger."

He could have told her that it was no big deal. He'd been in a lot worse danger than a damn bar fight, but she was looking at him all impressed, and it was kind of nice. He led her outside, where they ran into a woman going in.

Aubrey.

In a navy blue suit, looking elegant and chic, hair perfect, she looked startled to see them. "We got cut off on the phone," she said to Ali.

"Yeah." Ali slid Luke a glance. "Sorry about that. Listen, careful in there. It's crazy tonight."

Aubrey took a look at the bar's entrance. "What's going on?"

"A little fight," Ali said.

"Seriously?" Aubrey pulled out her phone. "Did you call the police?" She turned to Luke. "Aren't *you* the police?"

"It's handled now," Luke said. "How often do you work late?"

"A lot." Aubrey gave him a wary look. "Why?"

"Just wondering if you've ever seen anyone else late in Marshall's office."

Aubrey was quiet for a beat. "You're on vacation, which means you're not a cop right *now*, right?"

"Right," he said. *Cop rule numero uno: be able to lie your ass off right to anyone's face.*

"So this isn't official or anything."

"Absolutely *not*," Luke said without hesitation.

Aubrey nodded, then glanced apologetically at Ali. "I think it's possible that Teddy's been seeing someone else."

"Besides Melissa and me?" Ali asked.

"Yes."

"Who?"

"I don't know," Aubrey said. "I'd have told you before, but until you came into the office the other day, I really thought you and Ted were just roommates."

Aubrey entered the bar, and Ali, looking a little deflated, fell silent. Luke took her hand. "Come on."

159

That she let him lead told him it was time for more ice cream. So he took her to the pier and bought her a triple cone from Lance at the ice cream shop. Then he took her hand again. At this time of night, the pier was quiet, and once they walked past the arcade and Ferris wheel, they had the night to themselves. They walked in silence to the very end and stood there looking out at the ocean, lit by a streak of light from the moon. Water slapped rhythmically against the pylons. The sound always calmed Luke, and next to him, Ali let out a soft sigh.

"That got me nowhere," she finally said, leaning against the railing, licking her cone like she meant business.

He tried not to stare and failed. Christ, he wanted her to lick him like that. "We knocked on some doors," he said. "We shook things up."

She turned to face him. "And now what?"

He stroked a finger along her temple, tucking a strand of hair behind her ear for the sheer pleasure of touching her. Then he leaned in for a kiss. She tasted like chocolate and trouble. Big trouble. "We wait for the dust to settle."

"We?"

"Yeah. We." He let his hand fall from her. "But—"

"Yeah, I know." She pushed away from the railing and started walking back to his truck. "It's a short-term 'we.'"

Chapter 11

It was two in the morning before Ali got Luke's kitchen back together. She was heading to do the den next when she got her usual daily check-in text from Harper: *Made good tips tonight! Next time you come home, dinner's on me.*

Ali managed a smile. Exhausted, dusty, and a little sweaty, she swiped her forehead and texted Harper back. *Sounds good. How's Mom?*

The money you put in her account made her day. You okay? You don't sound okay.

You got not okay from sounds good?

It's in the tone . . .

Ali rolled her eyes. *I'm fine . . . 'night. Sweet dreams.*

Don't let the bed bugs bite!

It was an old mantra, and it made Ali smile again as she went back to cleaning up. Two hours later, she'd worked her way to the living room, and it was a disaster. Besides Luke's things, her own pottery was still unwrapped and scattered on the floor.

After the bar brawl, Luke had once again told her to ignore the mess, that he'd get to it in the morning. "Get some sleep," he'd said, and had vanished into the basement to presumably follow his own advice.

But Ali couldn't sleep, and she couldn't ignore the house anymore. When she'd first seen it, she'd felt sick to the bone. The place was a mess, mirroring her own life. But it was *her* life and not Luke's. *She'd* brought this disaster to his home. And since she had, it was important that she clean it up.

She'd already straightened the bedroom she'd been using and had packed up her stuff while she was at it. She'd tortured Luke enough with her presence. When she was done here, she would go to the Lucky Harbor B&B, and then to the first apartment that was ready, and hope to God her Visa could handle the weight.

It would be okay.

She'd always been spectacularly good at denial, at not looking back, at keeping one foot in front of the other. Nothing about that had changed. She'd landed on her feet before, and she would do it again. Knowing it, she took her first real deep breath since . . .

Since too long to remember.

At a whisper of sound behind her, she whirled around to find a heavy-lidded, tousled-looking Luke in the doorway, hands braced over his head on the jamb.

"What, no umbrella this time?" he asked.

She relaxed her hold on a ceramic pot. "You nearly got this upside your head."

A ghost of a smile crossed his face. He'd clearly come straight from his bed. He was wearing only a pair of black basketball shorts, disturbingly low on his hips, putting all his hard muscles directly in her line of sight. If she touched his abs, she'd find them rock hard. She knew this because during their kiss in his truck, she'd copped a feel.

And there. That. *That* was what her mind had kept going back to all these past hours while she straightened up. Their kiss. How he'd tasted. How his mouth had slanted over her own, his tongue gliding along hers . . . She didn't have to think about the heat they'd generated; she was sweating just remembering it. "Sorry if I woke you," she said, surrounded by the disaster she'd brought to his door. Averting her face, she concentrated on righting the books.

He didn't say anything, so she turned back and found him still looking at her, his own gaze hooded. Sleepy. And something else, something that made her throat burn.

Dammit.

"Thought I told you I'd get to this in the morning," he said.

"It *is* morning."

Padding barefoot into the living room, he headed to the coffee table. Its big drawer had been dumped onto the floor. Crouching, he began tossing the things back inside.

"Luke, stop."

He didn't stop.

"This was my doing." She caught his arm. "I've got this."

His eyes held hers, not at all sleepy anymore, his muscles beneath her fingers corded. Warm. Then he went back to work. He finished the drawer and looked around, frowning when he saw the box of her pottery still scattered. He reached for the first piece, a miniature lion that she'd created last year, when she'd first come to Lucky Harbor. It represented courage. *Her* courage.

Luke stared down at the lion for a long moment, then very gently ran the pad of his finger over the mane. "It's amazing. It looks so real."

"Thanks."

"You sculpted this?"

She nodded.

"Then painted it?"

She nodded again.

He looked at her collection of animals sprawled out carelessly, toppled over like carnage. "These must have taken you a long time."

"Years." She shrugged at his questioning gaze. "My mom used to work a lot of nights. After my sister would go to bed, sometimes I'd stay up." Waiting for Mimi to come home. "It was something to do."

"Each piece means something to you," he said.

"Yes."

"What does this lion mean?"

164

"I made him when I first moved to Lucky Harbor." She paused. "He's my . . . roar."

A small smile crossed his lips. "You already have courage in spades, Ali." He grabbed a piece of the packing paper, then very carefully rolled up the lion as if it was the most precious thing in the world.

Ali opened her mouth, but then, unable to speak, closed it again.

Without another word or glance her way, as if he knew how painful this was for her, Luke reached for another piece of her pottery. An owl. He held it up to her.

"To remind me to try to be wise," she said softly. "No stupid decisions."

"Like sex."

Okay, that hadn't been exactly what she'd meant, but it didn't matter. Her body was reacting to the way he'd said "sex," and a shocking heat of arousal washed through her. She swallowed hard, but nodded.

Another smile. He rolled up the owl and set it carefully in the box with the lion. Over and over again with each piece, the whole time showing a respect for her things in a way the police hadn't.

Ali never really expected much from the men in her life. That way it wasn't a surprise when they didn't come through. But Luke kept surprising her, and it was unexpected to say the least.

He was unexpected.

An hour later, dawn broke. Shortly after that, the sun slanted in the huge picture windows, casting them in gold. "Done," Luke declared, tossing aside the broom in his hands.

They'd been quiet so long that she jumped. "The garage—"

"Was already a mess," he said. "Leave it. Go to bed, Ali. Get some rest."

She looked at the boxes and bags lined up in the hall. Her things.

His gaze followed hers. "You packed," he said flatly.

"Yes."

"Where are you going?"

"The B and B," she said. "Just until something pans out."

He stepped closer. "Why?" he asked.

She took in the high angle of his cheekbones, his strong jaw, the column of his throat. His broad shoulders were stiff with tension. He was holding back, and it was costing him.

"Ali, why?"

"Because . . ." His hands went to her hips. God, he was beautifully made, all tough, sinewy lines and smooth skin, which she knew would be heated to the touch. And oh, how she suddenly needed to touch. She lifted her hands to his chest. "Because . . ."

His eyes pinned her, his sheer force of personality making her go weak in the knees. And that wasn't all. He wanted her. There was no question; the proof of it was pressing into her belly.

And at that realization, she got weak in a lot more places than just her knees. But she didn't go weak for a man anymore, no matter how much she wanted to learn her way around his body and satisfy them both. Indulging herself—just for a minute—she let her hands roam.

Oh yeah, warm to the touch. *Hot* to the touch, really, his muscles smooth and hard. She could feel his heart beating beneath her hand, steady as a rock, flowing through her fingertips to mingle with her own pulse. He held himself very still, his big body just barely brushing hers. He didn't want to take advantage, she knew that. Sweet.

Except he wasn't sweet. And she wasn't feeling so sweet either. She was feeling dangerous as she kissed one corner of his delicious mouth. And then the other. Just a taste, she promised herself. "I'm going," she said, "because of this." And then she kissed him again, not just a taste.

Beneath her fingers, his muscles jerked, but he didn't make a move. That's okay, she had her own moves. She skimmed her hands up, around his neck, into his silky hair, and then fisted it, pulling his head closer to hers.

With a rough groan, his hands tightened on her, thumbs splaying across her stomach, rubbing her own heated skin. Pulling back a fraction of an inch, he looked down at her, his gaze dark and full of desire. It was irresistible and so was the way he watched her, his body seeming to shudder when she pressed more closely against him.

And then he kissed *her,* his tongue tracing the curve of her lips until she allowed him entry. He hooked his fingers in the hem of her tank top, slowly drawing it up, exposing her inch by inch.

Dipping his head, he looked his fill. Drawing a long, serrated breath, he slowly traced the lines of her ribs with his fingertips before cupping the curves of her breasts.

She loved the way he seemed to tremble when he touched her. Or maybe that was *her* doing the trembling from the feel of his palms searing her skin. He had a way of driving every thought from her head. Everything, except for need.

And right then, in that moment, the only thing she needed was him. "Luke."

Lowering his head, he put his mouth on her breast, taking the peak between his teeth, flicking it with his tongue before tugging gently.

He tightened his grip on her hair, and she cried out before she could stop herself.

"Stop me, Ali."

Was he kidding? Her nails raked across his back for more, making him inhale sharply.

"You're not ready for this," he said against her skin. "For me."

If she were any more ready, she'd be in flames. "Not your call, Luke."

With another groan, he pressed his forehead to her shoulder. "Then I'm not ready for you," he said. "I can't give you what you want, Ali."

"I don't want anything." But the magic spell was broken, and she stepped back, pulling her tank down, entangling her hands together to ensure she kept them off of him. "I'm going to go."

He blew out a breath, and then shook his head. "The B and B is in high season. They're charging tourist prices."

She knew one of the owners; Maddie, the middle sister, came into the shop weekly to buy flowers for the inn. Ali thought she would give her a good deal, but he was right—it was still going to be out of her price range. "Fine," she said, "I'll go stay with my mom and commute from there."

"Have you seen gas prices?" he asked. "That's a stupid idea. And you're not stupid."

"Stop it, Luke."

"Stop what?"

"I'm not staying here just because you suddenly feel sorry for me."

"Okay, then stay so we can have wild, up-against-the-wall sex," he said.

Her breath caught. She wasn't even sure what wild-up-against-the-wall sex would feel like, but she had a feeling she'd like it. A lot. And yet she knew that he was merely trying to rile her up so she wouldn't do something awful, like cry. "I'm not a pity case."

"I don't have the capacity for pity," he said. "Hell, Ali, stay here because . . . I need you."

Stunned, she stared up into his face, which was cast in granite. Apparently she'd met her match in stubbornness. "You *need* me," she repeated doubtfully.

As if on cue, the phone rang, shattering the early morning quiet. He pointed to the phone and then to her. *See? Need you.* And then he vanished down the hall without another word.

The phone rang again.

Ali looked at it, weighing the price of the B&B along with the danger to her bank account against the price of staying here and endangering something even more fragile—her heart.

No contest on which decision would cost her the most. And yet she headed to the phone and used her apparently pent-up frustration getting rid of yet another reporter looking for Luke.

Chapter 12

Zach showed up that afternoon in a suit that emphasized his beanpole body, a messenger bag strapped across his chest, and thick black-rimmed glasses on his nose. His jet-black hair was in spikes. His eyebrow piercing glittered as he scooped Ali in for a big hug.

Zach's familiar ease faded when she introduced him to Luke. Oh, his warm chocolate eyes were friendly enough, but reserved, as the two men sized each other up.

Luke was his usual steely intense self as they shook hands, and Zach reverted to geeky awkwardness, though he maintained eye contact. Ali gave him credit for not peeing his pants.

"So you're licensed in the state of Washington?" Luke asked him.

Ali gave him a long look. "Luke . . ."

"Yes," Zach said, and pushed his glasses higher on his nose. "I'm licensed in Washington."

"How many trial cases do you have under your belt?"

Ali grimaced. *"Luke."*

"If Ali gets arrested, and if the case goes to trial," Zach said, "this would be my first solo. But we both know even if it gets that far, as a first-time offender she might end up with restitution over time served. The record would be the worst part."

"Might isn't good enough," Luke said. "And how about the fact that she's innocent?"

"Of course she's innocent," Zach said simply. "It's Ali."

Ali smiled at him, sent Luke a hard look, and brought Zach to the kitchen table, where they discussed the case at length. Zach asked questions that might have had her head spinning, except he had a way about him. Sweet. Calm. It allowed her to concentrate on the task at hand, telling him all they'd learned about the comings and goings the night of the auction.

Zach looked over his notes. "So you took your pencil pot back without looking inside it."

"Yes, except it wasn't exactly mine. It was his, a little bit."

"How little?"

"One hundred percent."

Zach looked up from the iPad, expression wry. "You mean you stole it."

"Well, if you want to get technical, yeah. I stole it. I guess I shouldn't admit that to my attorney, right?"

Zach smiled gently at her. "You can tell me anything, Al. I'm not a cop." He slid a silent Luke a long look. "And the only cop in the room is off duty."

So Zach had done his own background search.

Whatever Luke thought about being baited by Zach, he kept it to himself. He was good at that.

It was a lesson Ali would be well served to learn herself.

The next morning, Luke was woken just before dawn by a text from his commander.

Need you back for internal review on Reyes case. There's prep work the size of the California debt. Stop with the small town PI shit and get your ass back here.

Luke thumbed his way to the browser and searched for the latest reports. It wasn't pretty. The first article he pulled up called the SFPD a complete failure. Luke tossed the phone aside and tried to tell himself he didn't give a damn. But he did. Only a week ago, his job had been everything to him, his entire being wrapped up in the reputation and ego of it. That had been who he was.

Now, far from San Francisco, he didn't feel like that same guy.

He'd lived the fast-paced, adrenaline-rushed job for years, and he'd thrived on it. But he wasn't thriving anymore. It wasn't the danger he faced on the force, or the darkness of the things he saw, or the slogging knee-deep through shit on a daily basis.

He missed life here.

He'd left Lucky Harbor, exiled himself really, and not looked back. And in doing so, he'd cut himself off from the happiest times of his life. In coming back, he underestimated the pull that the wild, hauntingly beautiful, resilient Pacific Northwest had always had on him.

Now there was something else pulling at him as well—the equally wild, hauntingly beautiful, resilient Ali Winters.

Rolling out of bed, he pulled on swim trunks. Out back, he balanced his board on his head and took the steep stairs down to the water.

The harbor was quiet. By the time he'd set the board in the water, the sky had lightened from black to purple. The water was icy cold and would clear his head.

Or kill him.

He pushed off and began paddling. And then there was nothing but the sound of his board skimming through the water, the occasional splash of a zealous fish, and the chirping birds that were waking with the dawn.

Alone.

Quiet.

It was the closest to heaven that he could imagine. He paddled out past the pier and harbor and into the open water. He pushed himself hard, until his heart pounded and he couldn't catch his breath. It felt good. Here, in the zone, he couldn't think, couldn't obsess, couldn't regret.

An hour later, muscles quivering, he stopped, panting as the sun beat down on him. He cooled down by making his way back slowly, enjoying the early morning. As he entered the harbor again, he passed the pier and the Ferris wheel, and saw a female jogging along the water's edge. She was built like a Victoria's Secret model, and her long blonde hair flowed behind her.

Melissa Mann.

Shading her eyes with her hand, she took him in, a wide smile crossing her lips. "Well, look who the tide dragged in," she purred as he slid up on the beach and got off his board. "Heard you were back," she said, "and looking for trouble." She waggled a brow and gestured to herself. "Meet trouble with a capital T."

He had to laugh. She was right. She *was* trouble with a capital T. The very best kind of trouble. "How's the salon going?" he asked.

"Running it now," she said proudly. "Come by sometime. I'll give you a buff and shine." She smiled. "On the house."

He smiled too, knowing that they both understood he wouldn't. "Heard you were at the auction the other night."

"I was. Everyone was." She cocked her head and studied him a moment. "You've got quite a cop face on, Luke. Why don't you just ask me what you want to know?"

"You're sleeping with Ted Marshall."

Melissa laughed. "Somehow, I don't think that's jealousy I hear." She was still smiling. "You've been gone a long time. There's a new dog in town. He's a thoroughbred, but a dog is still a dog."

"And by dog you mean . . ."

"Just what you think. Ted's single and enjoying the life. Maybe our . . . enjoyment was mutual a few times."

"He had a girlfriend."

"Ali Winters? He always said that they were just roommates."

"That doesn't bother you?"

"What, that he's really only exclusive with his own dick?" She smiled again and shrugged. "He's actually pretty careful. He's got political ambitions. He likes it that everyone likes him. Plus, it's not like I'm looking for a relationship. He's a good guy, not to mention hot. And he always springs for dinner first."

"On the night of the auction, did you see anyone else with him?"

Melissa gave him another smile. "I don't kiss and tell, Luke. You know that."

He ignored the reference to the one and only night the two of them had shared, back when they'd been nineteen and drunk as skunks on the pier behind the Ferris wheel. "Did you even see the money?" he asked.

"Nope. He did put a big briefcase in the bottom drawer of his desk though. I saw that."

"He lock it?"

"The police asked the same thing. I don't remember either way."

"After," he said. "What happened after?"

"Aubrey came in, and she got *all* pissed off, asking Ted what he'd have done if someone had seen us." She rolled her eyes. "Like he's running for president or something."

"Then what happened?"

"We left separately. He insisted on that. He really does like to keep his private life private."

Which was tough shit, because "Teddy's" life, private or otherwise, was about to be blown wide open. "Thanks, Mel."

She smiled. "Was I helpful?"

"Yes."

She looked him over for a long beat, taking in his wet gear. "If you need anything else, Luke, you look me up."

He smiled at her, but he wasn't going there. He had a different woman on his mind.

Back at home, he got out of the water, carried the paddleboard up the stairs, and leaned it against the deck. He looked up at the house. Today was day two of Ali's enforced leave, thanks to Russell's taking off to Vegas, and Luke had no idea what she might be doing. Not that it mattered, of course. It didn't. Not in the slightest.

Shit. It mattered. It mattered a whole hell of a lot.

He grabbed the towel he'd left for himself on the deck. He was rubbing it over his wet head when he realized he could hear voices coming through the kitchen window. Glancing in, he saw Ali at the island cooking something that smelled amazing and had his mouth instantly watering. On the other side of the island, cozied up on one of Luke's barstools, sat Zach. Ali was listing off characteristics of Leah Sullivan, and why Zach should ask her out.

"She's funny," Ali said, "and has a great personality—"

Zach groaned. "Great personality? That's the kiss of death right there."

Ali's eyes narrowed. "What does that mean?" she asked in a tone that would have had Luke changing course pronto.

But Zach apparently wasn't versed in the *Don't Go There Department.* "You know," he said. "When you say someone has a great personality, it means that they're . . . *not* hot."

"Wow." Ali shook her head. "And here I thought you were better than the rest of your gender." She shrugged. "Your loss, because Leah's *totally* hot."

"Yeah? How hot?"

"Forget it, you've ruined it."

"Aw, man." Zach wasn't in a suit today. Instead he wore skinny-cut, black jeans, an equally tight-to-his-scrawny-chest black button down, and a bright pink tie that matched a few pink streaks in his dark, spiked hair. He still looked twelve. He eyed the omelet Ali was cooking, licking his lips like he was starving.

Ali flipped it onto a plate, pushed it to Zach, and then turned to the door as Luke let himself in.

"Hey," she said. "Yours is next."

Zach stuffed a big bite into his mouth as he eyed Luke. "You don't knock, you just walk in?"

Luke looked at Ali, letting her field this one.

Ali sighed, and she flipped the next omelet. "Luke's living here too, Zach."

"Your mom didn't mention that. She just said he'd given you a place to stay."

"It's not what you think," Ali said.

"No?" Zach asked. "Because what I think is that you're too kind for your own good, and *someone*"—he glanced at Luke so as to leave no doubt who the "someone" was—"could take advantage of you."

"First of all, I'm not all that kind," Ali corrected. "And second, *Luke* is the kind one, letting me stay."

Not feeling particularly kind, Luke strode across the kitchen. He'd intended to shower. Instead, he parked himself on a barstool, sprawling his long legs out, making himself at home in his own place.

Ali gave him a look that he wasn't quite sure how to interpret. Annoyance, definitely. Maybe even some affection too.

179

He could match her on both. But he found himself oddly out-of-sorts at the vibe between her and Zach—which made no fucking sense. They were obviously very fond of each other. And just as obviously, they were old friends with the same level of comfort that he and Jack and Ben had. He didn't read any sexual tension between them.

Not that it mattered. Because it didn't.

What *did* matter was Zach's ability to defend Ali, if it came to that. And Luke wasn't at all sure the kid—who, granted, seemed sharp and eager to get this right—could handle the case.

Zach was scrolling through the notes he'd made on his iPad the day before. "So is there anything else you can think of that I need to know?"

"Yes," Ali said. "I talked to Edward this morning. He gets up early because once a week he enjoys driving the seniors to the early morning buffet at a casino in Tacoma."

More like he enjoyed the early morning Texas hold 'em table, Luke thought.

"The ground-breaking ceremony for the new rec center is scheduled for next weekend," she said. "The mayor himself donated fifty grand to make up for the missing funds."

"Wow," Zach said with a low whistle, "I'd like to run the mayor's financials to see where that money came from."

"It came out of his retirement account and is supposedly legit," Ali said. "Edward had some other interesting news too. He said that Mr. Wykowski was also in Teddy's office the night of the auction. Mr. Wykowski didn't say anything, because he was hiding from Lucille and her posse, who were chasing him. Mr. Wykowski says that it's rough being eighty-two and single, because the women that go to the center outnumber the men two to one."

Zach snorted orange juice out his nose. *"Dammit."*

"And Mr. Lyons was in the hallway too, using that bathroom," Ali said. "Because the main bathroom . . . um, smelled like something died in there." She flipped Luke's omelet. "And then later, Mrs. Burland ended up in the office too. Says she got lost trying to find the coat room. She needs cataract surgery, but hasn't saved up the eight grand yet, which takes her off the suspect list because she can't see past her own nose. Plus she threw out her back last week trying to keep up with Lucille and can't even carry a purse. So it's unlikely she stole anything, except possibly someone's coat that she mistook for hers."

"None of that came out in the police report," Luke said.

Ali shrugged. "Probably no one thought to ask your grandpa."

"I spent summers here," Luke said with a shake of his head. "And I'm still blown away at how he knows everyone else's business."

"Oh, he knows yours too," Ali said.

This gave him pause. "What did he say about me?"

"That I shouldn't trust the man who once blew up all the Town Hall toilets."

"Hey, I was just a kid," Luke said, in his defense, over Zach's choked laugh. "And anyway, that was all Jack and Ben's doing. Mostly Ben's to be honest. He was good at blowing shit up."

Ali smiled. "He said you'd say that."

Luke shook his head. "What else?" he asked, as she transferred the omelet from pan to plate and handed it to him. He dug in, and flavor exploded in his mouth in a harmony of deliciousness. He hadn't realized how starved he was, and he closed his eyes to enjoy it. When he opened them again, Ali was looking at him.

"You know something else?" she asked.

"No." He stuffed another big bite in his mouth rather than tell her that, yes, he knew something else—her ex was a serious dick.

"If you know something that will help," Zach said, "you need to tell us."

Luke set down his fork and gave Zach a look that had the lawyer pulling back just a little bit. Brave but not stupid. Good to know. "The only thing I've got is what we all already know—there are more women in Marshall's life. I think whoever else was in his office the night of the auction is the key to this whole thing."

"We'll find her," Zach said, sounding far more sure of himself than Luke would have thought possible, considering the guy looked like he'd walked off an '80s punk rock poster. "Ali, did you see anything interesting in his office the next day?"

"No. I was only there for a minute both times. The first visit, I just grabbed the pencil pot. The second time, I . . ." She broke off and nibbled on her lower lip.

"What?" Zach pressed.

"I guess I was still pissed about what I'd heard the night before and—"

"Tell me again," Zach said, "what you heard."

She shuddered. "Teddy in the throes."

Zach grimaced. "Other than that."

Luke took in Ali's expression. She wasn't sad, she was pissed, and he was glad. Marshall didn't deserve a piece of her heart.

Neither do you . . .

"Anyway," Ali said. "I set his things on his desk."

"I read the police report, Ali, that's not all you did," Zach said.

She winced. "So I left him a sticky note telling him what he could do with his text breakup, where to stick it, how to stick it . . . that sort of thing. Big deal."

Luke already knew this, but he felt the pride fill his chest again. "Nicely done, by the way."

She shifted, looking embarrassed. "I threatened him. The police frown on that."

"You could plead temporary insanity," Luke said, wanting to lighten the mood.

Ali rolled her eyes, but looked far less vulnerable, and Luke nearly smiled because damn, she didn't need her ceramic lion or the owl. She had guts and brains in spades.

It'd been a long time since he'd ached to be with a woman for more than what they could give each other in bed. This was the problem with Ali, she made him ache. There was just something about her that drew him in, leaving him defenseless against her.

Not good.

"How bad is that note?" Ali asked Zach. "Bad? Or *bad* bad?"

"Bad isn't the right word," Zach said. "Let's go with . . . a little difficult."

She just looked at him. "You don't want me to freak out about writing that I was going to do something to him, and then something happened."

"I don't want you to worry," Zach said, and once again Luke felt his reluctant respect for the guy increase.

Zach glanced at the time and rose. "Gotta get to work." He turned to Luke. "If you learn anything else . . ." He pushed his business card toward him. "I'm all ears." He gave Ali a kiss on the cheek and sent Luke a long, unmistakable look that said *I'm watching you* as he moved to the door. "Stay in touch, Al."

Luke walked him outside.

At the end of the driveway, Zach faced him, eyes

cool, smile gone. "Not that I have to defend myself to you, but I can handle whatever happens here."

"You sure?" Luke asked. "Because you need to be fucking *sure*. She trusts you."

"She *should* trust me. I've known her since grade school. And you've known her for what, five minutes?"

Luke had to give the puppy props. He had sharp teeth.

"Are you sleeping with her?" Zach asked.

"None of your business."

"She's my friend and my client. She's very much my business. And she's watching us right now, so try to look like you don't necessarily plan on kicking my ass."

Luke turned and glanced at the window, indeed finding Ali watching them. He lifted a hand in greeting.

She narrowed her eyes.

Zach smiled and waved at her, then turned his back to the house to slide Luke a measuring look. "Don't even think about climbing into her bed," he said. "She's way too vulnerable for the likes of you right now."

Having been told the same thing by Jack, Edward, and his own conscience, Luke felt himself getting pissed off. "I'll worry about me. You worry about the case."

"Fine. But I'll be watching you," Zach said.

"Yeah? Right back at ya."

Chapter 13

Luke waited until Zach drove off before turning to the house.

Ali was gone from the window.

The place stood as it always had, a little bit quirky, a lot worn, but steady as his grandma had been.

His home away from home for just about all his life.

His grandma had worked hard for many years, but in that last year, she'd finally retired. Her hobby had been painting, and she'd used the garage as a studio. Luke had loved it there, the scents of the oil paint and his grandma's candles, the huge beanbag chair that had been his to crawl into and watch her work. The cookies she'd always had out . . .

Shaking his head at the memories, he punched in the code for the garage door and watched it open, blinking in surprise.

Because there was Ali, paintbrush in hand.

Clearly seeing something in his expression, she put down the brush. There was a table between them, a work table. She made no move to go around it, leaving him to assume she needed the barrier.

He got that. He needed a barrier from her too. He just didn't know what the hell kind of barrier could possibly stand between her and his damn heart, since she was making dust of the walls he'd had in place by just breathing. It was her sweet courage, and the capacity she had for caring about everyone and everything. It was the way she kissed him, as if she was desperately clinging to the fleeting pleasure before it vanished. It was the fierceness with which she protected his privacy. It was her smile.

It was everything about her.

"It's going to be okay, you know," she said.

"Your life, you mean?" he asked.

"And yours."

For months, he'd been operating deep in negativity and bad shit. There'd been no light at the end of the tunnel. His glass was half empty. No silver lining . . .

Not Ali. Her world had fallen apart too, and yet she looked at things completely differently. It wasn't that she wore rose-colored glasses. No one who'd grown up as tough and fast as she had *could* wear rose-colored glasses. She simply chose *not* to live in the dark.

He admired and respected the hell out of that. He looked at the table and saw that she'd been painting a small ceramic bowl shaped like a canoe.

"I hope you don't mind," she said, gesturing to the table and her work. "We need a new key

187

bowl." Since she'd chucked the other one at his head . . . He smiled at the memory.

"My grandma painted in here too." He looked to the other side of the garage, where Fay's shelves still stood. He could almost see her, standing in front of her easel, the sun slanting in the window, casting her in a glow as she created magic out of a blank canvas. "I used to sit at her feet and watch." He pointed to the sheet-covered beanbag chair. "I even gave it a shot myself when she bugged me about it."

"Were you any good?"

"Not even a little bit." He lifted a shoulder, surprised to feel warm at the memories, not regretful.

She came around the table. "So you lived here with her?"

"During the summers," he said. "All my life, until she died."

Her smile faded. "I'm sorry."

"Yeah, me too." He stared at the garage wall. "She shouldn't have died like she did."

She touched his arm. "What happened?"

He blew out a breath and ran a hand over the back of his neck. "Mornings weren't her thing. We all knew it. Sara used to joke that in order to wake her up, we ought to just stand in the doorway and throw a two-by-four at her and then run like hell."

She smiled. "My mom's like that."

"I learned young to leave her alone until she'd had her caffeine. Then the summer of my sophomore year in college, I was here working for a lumber company, and one day I got her up too early. Jesus, she lit into me and we got into a big, old fight." He felt that familiar clutch of guilt. "I knew she needed me to move some boxes and furniture around for her, but I was a total dick about it. I left early for work and didn't come home for my lunch break like we'd planned. After work, I went out on the water, and after that, hit a bar with the guys. I didn't come back here until late." He paused. "I found her on the bathroom floor. Stroke."

"Oh, no," Ali said softly, voice thick with pain for him. "Oh, Luke, how awful."

He'd never forget the horror and gut-wrenching fear that had taken over his body at the sight of her. He'd dropped to his knees and tried to find a pulse, but she'd been cold and long gone. "It'd happened hours before. She probably lay there wondering where the hell I was and why I didn't help her."

She touched him, ran a hand down his back, saying nothing for a long moment. "How long until you were able to come back to the house?" she asked.

"Ten years."

She went still, clearly doing the math. "This is your first time back?"

"Yeah." He wished like hell that he could see his grandma standing there painting, smiling, full of life, just one more time. She'd always been so forgiving. So willing to love him, no matter what. And there'd been plenty to forgive, most notably the incident two years prior to her death, when he'd screwed up in a different way.

By failing Sara.

He'd failed them both, and Luke would give just about anything to be able to tell his grandma how sorry he was, that he never should have left her like he had. That he'd regretted it every single day since. That she was the reason he tried so damn hard these days to make sure he had nothing else to regret. "It was a long time ago," he said.

"You and I both know that doesn't matter," she said quietly.

He stared down into her face, which was creased into an expression of honest concern. In the here and now, she had plenty to be worried about. Instead, she was worried about him and something he'd gone through ten years ago. "Yeah. I'm okay."

"You're probably ready to get back to San Francisco by now," she said softly.

"Actually," he said, "I love it here. I always have. But I need to get back. My commander's been calling."

She nodded, accepting, which wasn't the same thing as being indifferent to his imminent departure, because she was the least indifferent person he'd ever met. She felt things to the bone. In fact, she had a capacity to feel things that he'd never had.

Or maybe it'd been so long he'd just forgotten how.

She could change that. At the thought, his chest tightened and burned with a need that wasn't just physical, though there was that too. He wanted to let her warmth wash over him, wanted to feel things like she did.

Just for a moment, a single moment.

Or maybe two . . .

Hitting the touch pad on the wall to shut the garage door, he stepped close to her, sliding his hands up her bare arms to cup her face.

She met him halfway, winding her arms around his neck, her sweet kiss stealing the very air from his lungs. When her tongue touched his, it sent a bolt of hunger through him so strong he wasn't sure he'd survive it. Pulling her up against him-self, he enjoyed the feel of her, including the way her heart pounded hard into his.

When they broke apart, she stared up at him, breathing unsteadily. He touched her jaw, and she took his hand, wordlessly turning, tugging him with her. Into the house. Through the kitchen. Into her bedroom.

The walls were sky blue with sheer white

drapes blowing gently in the breeze, beyond which lay a view of the water.

Home . . .

But by far, the more heart-stopping view was right in front of him. "Ali," he said, his voice low and gruff. He wanted this. Christ, he wanted this. But . . .

She shut the bedroom door, leaning back against it to smile at him. "You look like you're facing some sort of forbidden fruit."

Truer than she could have imagined. He knew damn well that being with a man meant something to her. Lots of things meant something to her. He admired that about her—greatly—especially since he wasn't feeling much for anyone or anything these days.

She could change that, a small voice inside him said, *if you let her.* He opened his mouth with no idea what he was going to say, but she pushed off the door and came close, pressing a finger against his lips. "Shh a minute," she whispered. "I just want to see something . . ."

And then she went up on tiptoes and kissed him again.

He heard himself groan, and then his arms tightened around her as he opened his mouth wider on hers, willing to let her lead, to let her take this wherever she wanted to go.

She kissed him back, deeper, and his heart started to pound because he knew *exactly* where she wanted this to go.

Same place he did. Still, he shouldn't let it happen. He shouldn't . . .

And yet he couldn't bring himself to pull away. Just one more taste, he thought. One more touch. His hands skimmed up her back, bared by her halter dress, and she arched into him seeking more.

God. God, she was so sweet, her lips clinging to his, her fingers digging into his arms like he was her anchor. And when she moaned and rubbed up against him, he knew.

He was in trouble. Deep trouble.

He'd been fantasizing about her, just like this, melting in his arms, taking everything he gave her and wanting more still. The reality of it was even better than the fantasy. She was warm and soft and eager. *His.* A ridiculous thought that didn't stop him from taking, from slanting his mouth over hers more fully and cupping her breasts, sliding his thumbs over her pebbled nipples. He wanted her in his mouth, every part of her, and was tugging on the tie at the back of her neck toward that very goal when someone rang the doorbell.

They broke apart and stared at each other.

"Wait here," he said, and gently nudged her aside to open the bedroom door.

He took his time walking through the house so as to not open the door with a full-blown hard-on. But looking through the peephole took care of that.

Ted Marshall stood on his doorstep.

Chapter 14

Ali followed Luke through the house and then went still when he opened the front door.

Teddy stood there in a business suit that, unlike Zach's, fit him perfectly.

"What are you still doing here?" he asked her, looking just as shocked as Ali.

What was *she* doing here? "Oh no. *You* first," she said, going for polite, but not quite making it.

"I'm looking for my backup cell phone," Teddy said. "I was going to ask the new tenant if he'd found it."

"You sure you don't want to accuse me of stealing it?" Ali asked, not even in the realm of polite now.

"Did you?"

Luke slid a hand to the nape of her neck.

Right. She had no idea if Zach could defend premeditated murder. "You might want to close your eyes," she said to Luke, "so that you don't have to testify against me."

He smiled.

"Oh for crissake," Teddy grumbled. "For the last time, *you* were the only one in my office who had a motive." He pulled off his expensive reflector aviator sunglasses, the ones she'd used to think made him look so hot, and stared at her. "So what's going on here anyway? And what's wrong with you? You're all . . . flushed."

Extremely aware of her kiss-swollen lips and just-made-out hair, Ali stormed off to the kitchen, opened the junk drawer, and—shock—found Teddy's spare phone. Grabbing it, she slammed the drawer and brought it to the front door. "I didn't steal it, and for the millionth time, I didn't steal that money either."

"Then who did?"

"I don't know!" She tried to take a calming breath. It didn't help. "And I don't even know why you thought it would have been me."

He sighed. "You need the money. You always need money."

Low blow. It took her a minute to catch her breath. "There are more important things than money," she said. "And have you thought that maybe one of your other girlfriends might have done it?"

Guilt flashed for a single beat on his face. "Look," he said, "whatever Melissa and Aubrey have told you is—"

"Aubrey?" Ali stared at him. "You had both Melissa and Aubrey on the side? Seriously?"

Ted's face had closed up. "All I'm saying is that you've been misinformed—"

"Stop," she said, lifting a hand. "You're just reinforcing your ass-ness."

"Fine. I don't have to explain myself to you anyway." His gaze flicked to Luke. "And what's going on between you two? You found a way to stay here, huh?"

This time Luke tensed, and Ali grabbed *his* hand. "Don't bother," she murmured.

Luke didn't take his eyes off Teddy, but he kept his thoughts to himself, looking *extremely* dangerous to Teddy's well-being. "You've got your phone," he said quietly. "Leave now."

"I'm going, but I want to talk to you first," he said to Ali. "Alone."

He was very brave, or very oblivious. Either way, Luke didn't budge, and Ali was choking on all the testosterone. "Oh for God's sake." She turned to Luke. "It's okay."

When he still didn't budge, she stepped outside and shut the front door. "You have two seconds," she said to Teddy.

Teddy eyed the front door warily. "My attorney advised me to stay away," he said. "But you really embarrassed me, Ali. At work. In town. I thought we were okay, that we had a good run and then it was over, no hard feelings. So I have to know—why did you do it? You had to know you wouldn't get away with it."

"I *didn't* do it—"

"I'm trying to work my way up to council and then to mayor," he said, "and you made everyone doubt and mistrust my judgment."

"*Me?* You were sleeping with half the town! You made yourself look bad."

"Ali, you broke into my office and stole back a stupid ceramic pot that you'd given me. That's just ridiculously stupid. Stupid and childish."

"I didn't break in." But she flushed because he was right, on all accounts, and she hated that. "Yes, okay, it was stupid and childish. But I was hurt. You'd walked away without so much as a look back. You didn't deserve the pencil pot."

"Forget the fucking pot!" he yelled, and then made a visible effort to relax. He even poured on a little Teddy charm. "Look, I was just trying to be nice, okay? You were cute and fun, and when you had to get out of your apartment, I wanted to help you out. So I offered to share a place."

This stunned her. "I thought we were a thing."

"Okay, yes, we had a thing. But you weren't *my* thing."

She stared at him. "You could have told me," she finally managed.

"You're right, I should have told you. I should have said that I'd made a mistake. That you weren't my type."

"And what is *that* supposed to mean?"

He sighed. "Forget it."

"Tell me."

"Fine," he said. "We're . . . different."

"You mean you're a cheating bastard and I'm not?"

197

He sighed again, the put-upon ex-boyfriend, suffering through the breakup talk. "That's not what I meant."

No, actually, she knew what he meant, she knew exactly. He'd come from money and she'd come from nothing.

"I want that money back, Ali. I mean it." And with that, he strode off the steps like he owned the world.

She'd have given just about anything to be holding the new key pot she was making so she could wing it at the back of his thick skull. In fact, she whirled around looking for something, anything, to bean him with.

"Later," Luke said, joining her on the porch after clearly having listened to the whole exchange. "I'll hold him down for you."

"When?" she demanded.

"When you don't have witnesses."

She followed his gaze to Mrs. Gibson, who lived on the other side of Luke's grandfather's house. Fifty-something, she was a local teacher, soaking up the spectacle from her doorstep.

Luke waved at her.

Mrs. Gibson returned the wave and went inside.

"We'll make Facebook before the hour's up," he muttered.

Luke could feel Ali vibrating with emotions.

"I really want to hit him," she said.

"Bloodthirsty," he murmured, taking her hand, running his thumb over the pulse racing at her wrist. "I like it."

She didn't look at him, and he realized she was shaking. "Hey," he said softly, pulling her inside, turning her to face him.

She looked down, so he bent his knees to put them nose to nose. "What are you doing, letting him get in your head like that?" he asked.

"I—" She pushed him. "I don't know."

But he knew that she did know. She hated that someone believed she might have stolen that money, hated knowing that anyone thought she was a thief, even if that someone was the cheating bastard Ted Marshall.

"Forget him, Ali."

She covered her face. When she shuddered, his heart stopped.

"I'm not crying," she said through her fingers.

"Thank Christ." But his relief was cut off by the solo tear that tracked down her cheek. Drawing in a deep breath, he pulled her in close. "Ali," he murmured helplessly.

"Don't," she said, muffled against his chest.

"Forget it. I'm going to be nice to you for at least a second. You'll have to just stand there and bear it."

"No, I mean I'm all sweaty now. I think it's the fury."

Her body was overheated, her skin damp. He

didn't care. He lifted her chin and looked her over.

"I'm a wreck," she said, trying to turn away. "A complete wreck. And a fraud."

"Why, did you take the money?"

"No!" She took in the teasing in his expression and squeezed her eyes shut. "I wanted to be someone different here," she said, and broke his heart. "Not an invisible nobody florist's assistant from White Center."

"Do not listen to him," he said, maybe a little harshly, but he wanted her to hear him. Really hear him. "You're not a nobody. And you *are* a florist, a great one. You also teach ceramics. Hell, Ali, half of your students are in love with you. You care enough to be nice to nosy, old men. You helped a stranger avoid the rest of the world, even when he was a total ass. You'd give that stranger the last of your paycheck simply because you thought it was the right thing to do."

"It *was* the right thing to do," she said. "And you weren't a *total* ass."

"You'd probably give away your heart and soul if it was needed," he said. "But that would be a shame, because you're one-hundred-percent heart and soul. You're the real deal, Ali, the way the rest of us have forgotten how to be."

"I have . . . faults."

"Yeah," he agreed, "but they're not the ones Marshall said." He ticked them off on his fingers. "You wear your emotions on your sleeve, and you care. Hell, most people would say those are *good* things."

She snorted, and he smiled, relieved. "But one thing you're not, Ali, is invisible. You're standing right here, strong and beautiful—"

"No—"

"Beautiful," he repeated fiercely, stunned to find that he meant it from a very personal standpoint. He stared at her, impacted on a visceral, physical, and mental level by her. "So beautiful," he whispered, and then he kissed her.

Ali didn't think anyone had ever told her she was beautiful before. It should've felt like a cheesy line, but it didn't. Mostly because though she knew he meant it, she also knew he didn't *want* to find her beautiful.

In some twisted way, it was that reluctance that made her feel better. She didn't want to feel anything for him either. She didn't want to feel anything for anyone ever again, and yet she wasn't hardwired that way. "I'm all sweaty," she said again, even as her hands fisted in his hair.

"That's okay," he said silkily, his mouth brushing her temple. "We're going to get even more so."

The words made her shiver. So did the way he pressed her up against the wall right there in the foyer.

"I thought we were a bad idea," she said.

"We are." Her halter top slid down, revealing her bare breasts. He'd been so smooth she'd not felt him undo it. Then his fingers caught in the hem of the sundress, and he slid it up to her waist.

He sure was quick when properly motivated. "So this is what?" she asked breathlessly, already so excited she was rubbing her thighs together. "A pity fuck?"

His smile was heated and wicked as he kissed her. "That's a two-part question," he said. "Yes to the pity part, but it's not for you, it's for Marshall."

If she'd had enough air in her lungs, she would have laughed.

"Now," he said, pressing closer so there was no mistaking his intent—as if she could mistake anything about his pinning her to the wall with his hard body. "As for the fuck part . . ." He kissed her again, until she nearly forgot herself.

"Are you sure?" she managed to ask, staring up into his gorgeous blues. "Because you weren't sure a few minutes ago."

He rocked into her, and she felt exactly how sure he was. It tugged a moan from her, and she let her head fall back. This gave him better access and he took it. Lowering his head, he kissed her throat, her jaw. The corner of her mouth.

"What changed?" she managed to ask.

He licked her pulse point. "Watching you turn all violent when you got pissed off."

Oh, God, his tongue. "That was sexy?"

"Yeah. Big time." A big, warm, callused hand slid into the back of her panties and palmed her bare bottom. "Everything you do is sexy."

His mouth and the placement of his talented hand were driving her crazy. *He* was driving her crazy, and she struggled to get closer to his big, tough body. "Luke?"

He didn't answer, presumably because his lips were busy moving along the curve of her jaw, her throat, her breast, teasing her nipple, which had long ago tightened for him. But they had to talk first, or at least *she* had to talk. *"Luke?"*

"Hmm."

"I haven't been intimate with Teddy in weeks. You know that, right? You heard him mention it when they were searching the house."

He lifted his head and met her gaze.

"I just wanted to make sure you really knew," she said softly. "Once we moved in together, things got . . . weird. After only a few weeks, he started working late, and then he got allergies and snored. He slept in a different room than me, and . . ." *For the love of God, Ali, zip it and let him do you.*

Pushing her hair back from her eyes, he traced a line along her jaw. "It's been a long time for me too," he said quietly. "So long I can't remember the last time." He kissed her shoulder. "I have a condom." He gestured with his chin to his wallet, which lay on the small foyer table at her hip.

She started to reach for it, but he dipped his knees and ran his tongue around her nipple and then sucked the tight bud into his hot mouth.

She moaned, and her head fell back against the wall. She arched, trying to get him to take more, and felt him smile against her damp skin as he made his way to her other breast. His fingers trailed down her quivering stomach and then slipped between her thighs. "Mmm," he said. "Hot *and* wet."

And then he dropped to his knees.

"Luke . . ."

Not bothering to answer, he stroked the pad of his thumb over her panties, but apparently that wasn't nearly good enough, because then he caught his fingers in the sides. "Pretty," he said, "but they have to go." Slowly dragging them down, he kissed her just beneath her belly button. And then lower, letting his teeth graze over her, his rough jaw scraping her soft skin. His lips applied pressure, and his tongue brought to mind all the wicked things he might do to her. Her knees wobbled.

"I've got you," he murmured, a big, callused hand gliding up the inside of her legs. He kissed first one inner thigh, and then the other, and then . . . in between.

Her hips jerked.

"Easy," he murmured, and gripped her hips

tightly, holding her to the wall while he gently, but thoroughly, began to take her apart with his tongue and teeth. It was the sweetest, most exquisite torture. Dying to have him inside her, she begged, "Please," her pulse racing, her heart pounding.

But he still teased.

"Luke . . ."

"I like the way you say my name," he said, his mouth against her wet flesh.

She had her fingers in his hair, holding on as he drove her out of her mind with slow, hot laving of his tongue, leaving her trembling and beside herself. And still he took his time, until finally, God finally, he took her to the edge and nudged her over.

When she finally caught her breath and her eyes fluttered open, Luke surged to his feet, one arm around her lower back, the other just underneath her butt as he hoisted her up.

"Wrap your legs around me," he said, voice low and rough with need.

She did, wrapping her arms around him too, drawing him tightly to her.

"The condom," he said, eyes as intense and heated as his voice.

With shaky fingers, she opened his wallet and dug out the condom. "Here?" she breathed. "Now?"

"Here. Now."

His words should have felt presumptuous, pushy.

205

Aggressive. Instead, she was more aroused than she'd ever been, making needy little whimpers as she tore at his clothes to get skin to skin.

With calm, steady ease, he took over. He undressed them both, and then, pressing her into the wall to free up his hands, rolled on the condom.

She quivered just watching him. Then his hands were back on her, sliding along the underside of her thighs, angling her hips. And then, hot, fierce, eyes on hers, he slowly thrust into her in one sure stroke, pushing to the hilt and holding there, giving her nowhere to hide.

She didn't want to hide.

For once, just for this once, she wanted to let go and revel in the delicious sensations of being wanted, cherished, needed, and not worry about what came next. Rocking into him, she tried to match his rhythm, but she was pinned and unable to move. He could move though—and did—pulling out only to push back in, his body taking hers along for the ride.

She cried out, the sound of her pleasure echoing through the house. Her last thought before her mind shut down completely was for the neighbors—specifically, Luke's grandfather.

Please, she thought, *please let Edward's windows be closed.*

Funny, Ali thought hazily some time later from flat on her back on the foyer floor, the moments that marked the most important things in a woman's life. For her, it'd been graduating high school, moving out of White Center, learning that she was strong no matter what happened, and . . .

Getting busy with Luke Hanover up against the wall.

Her body was still quivering, little aftershocks of sheer pleasure, and she was pretty sure she couldn't have moved to save her life.

Beside her, Luke stirred, then came up on an elbow and looked down at her, his eyes still dark with heat. "You good?"

"I moved beyond good a few minutes ago."

He was thinking about smiling, she could tell. "How far beyond?" he asked.

"The stratosphere."

She thought maybe that would tug a smile from him, but it didn't. In fact, he looked a little stern as he helped her up, holding her steady until she found her sea legs.

He moved away, presumably to deal with the condom, but he didn't come back. She found him a few minutes later standing at the kitchen sink, hands braced on the countertop, staring out the window at the ocean.

She took a moment to soak him in, because he could still steal her breath. Wearing only his board shorts and nothing else, he was all tanned, smooth skin and lean sinew.

Paddleboarding did a body good.

Though he didn't move as she walked into the room, the muscles of his back and shoulders were tense.

"Hey," she said, "having an orgasm is supposed to relax and rejuvenate you. You don't seem relaxed or re—"

"I'm leaving. You know that right? I'm going back to my job in San Francisco. I don't know when exactly, but soon. I have to."

She drew in a deep breath. She knew all too well, which was a bitch of a problem, considering she'd promised herself not to do this again, not to follow the same patterns as her mom and sister and fall for a guy who would leave her. "I know."

"I want you to get a restraining order against Marshall so he can't come back here and bug you again."

"I don't think he will," she said. "And besides, we both know he hasn't done anything to warrant an order. Plus I'll be getting an apartment. The search has been slowed down a little by the fact that no one wants to rent to a thief, so—"

"Stay here."

"What?"

He turned to face her, gaze unfathomable. "Keep the house. You can get a roommate if you want. I don't care. I just want you to stay here."

"Luke—"

"The house suits you. My grandma would like knowing there was someone here who loved it as she did."

How was it that she wanted to both comfort him and jump him again at the same time? "Luke." She moved to him, slipping her arms around his waist, laying her cheek against his chest. "It's okay that it was just sex. I knew that going in. You don't have to feel guilty."

"It's not guilt." His arms came around her, and he pressed his cheek to the top of her head. "I just . . . Christ." He squeezed her. "That wasn't just sex."

Her heart squeezed, but then he took one look at her face and blew out a breath. "I don't know what the fuck to do with this, Ali. I'm leaving."

"I know."

"This can't happen again."

"I know that too." She stared up at him, a little blown away by the intensity of his words and the fierceness of his expression. Not possessive, exactly, but definitely protective. Something inside her cracked open just a little bit and let him in, which was terrifying her because he was bound to disappoint her.

They always did.

Chapter 15

Ali was up at dawn the next morning and was off and running for work, not allowing herself to let her mind wander. She couldn't *afford* to let her mind wander, or she'd get mired down in the fact that the money still hadn't been found. That she was still the only viable suspect at this point.

That she'd slept with Luke.

Okay, so there hadn't been *any* sleeping involved. Which meant that every single minute of it was imprinted on her brain—the best collection of minutes in her entire life.

She hit the flower market in Seattle for her weekly supply run. While she was there, she took an extra few minutes to drop off a bag of donuts and coffee for her mom and sister, which given the decibel of happy squeals they let out, made their day. Then she hightailed it back to Lucky Harbor to unload the week's supplies for Russell's shop.

There was a low wind howling through the quiet rooms, echoing the unsettled feeling in her gut. It was still early when she opened for business and got to work on the preordered arrangements that were due that day. Russell didn't show up to help. She knew he wouldn't show up until well after noon. And when he did, he'd be out of sorts and unhappy, as he had been from the day Paul had moved to Vegas without him.

Ever since their breakup, Russell kept talking about the shop's lack of profit, and how he wanted to close up. But Ali still believed the place had something to offer Lucky Harbor. If Russell would only give her some of the reins that she'd been begging for, she'd show him how much.

But he'd taken the business over from his sister. It wasn't a life's passion for him, and he'd not put much, if anything, into developing the business. He had a base of fairly steady customers, but hadn't shown any particular interest in catering to them. Nor had he put any effort into attracting *new* customers or cultivating more business.

Ali had all sorts of ideas, but no power. She wanted to create a website where people could order online, from the convenience of their own home or work. But Russell wasn't interested. He didn't want to be bothered with computer work, no matter that Ali had offered to do all of it.

Stymied there, she'd toyed with some changes, incorporating live plants, ceramics, and other local artists' work too, but Russell had been frustratingly resistant. Determined to show him, she spent some time now clearing space to make some displays. She worked hard at it and was proud and breathless when Russell showed up.

But he went straight to his office without a word, not even noticing that Ali had rearranged the shop.

"Hey," she said, following him back, "you okay?"

"I talked to Paul last night," he said, turning to her with a light in his eyes that she hadn't seen in a while: excitement. "He said he was sorry for being such a crazy, possessive bitch, can you believe it? A man who can admit he was wrong."

"That's sweet," she said.

"I know. And he thinks we should make up." He plugged his cell phone into the wall. "My battery died, and I'd left my charger here. I want to see if he called or texted."

"I hope he did," Ali said. "Um, about the shop . . . I rearranged some of the front. I wanted to show you—"

"Be a doll and get me some coffee?" Russell asked, eyes on his phone.

"Sure."

"And see if Leah has any pastries? Get a dozen assorted shipped to Paul, but make sure there are palmiers. Paul loves palmiers."

"Okay," Ali said. "And speaking of Leah, I was thinking it might be cool to offer a same-day delivery special. Flowers and pastries. We could do themed baskets, like birthdays and—"

"O-M-*G!*" Russell squealed.

"You like it?" Ali asked, relieved. "I'm so glad because—"

"No, Paul texted! He bought me a ticket to Vegas for next weekend!"

"But . . ." Ali's mind whirled for a reason to not close the shop again. "You'll miss the big groundbreaking ceremony for the new rec center."

"Let's see . . ." Russell held out both hands, miming weighing something between them. "Getting laid . . . watching a bunch of pretentious town council members slap themselves on the back and pretend to shovel some dirt around . . ." He grinned and rose to his feet and swept Ali off hers and kissed her soundly. "Long weekend alert ahead, Doll! *Woot!*"

Woot.

Later that afternoon, after a long day on her feet, Ali was sitting on the back-office work counter. Leah had come over with the leftover custard puffs for the day, and the two of them were inhaling them like they were going out of style. A daily tradition.

"Can't believe how busy we were today," Ali said. Their afternoon had been wonderfully successful for a change.

"It's you," Leah said, also on the counter, mouth full.

"Yeah?" she asked. "You think it's the way I

rearranged the shop floor and displayed ceramics as well?"

"No. Well, yes. But you know the police are getting really close to an arrest, so I also think people are coming in to appease their curiosity. They want to see if you're looking guilty. Or wearing twenty-dollar bills."

Ali blew out a breath and eyed the last puff. After what Leah had said, reminding her how close she was to jail, she suddenly needed that last puff more than air.

"Go ahead, have it," Leah said. "Probably you need the strength to keep boinking Luke."

Ali, who'd just taken an unfortunately big sip of tea, choked.

Leah had to hop off the counter and pat her on the back. "You don't blink at the idea of wearing twenty-dollar bills," she said, "but you nearly asphyxiate yourself on the thought of boinking Luke?"

"Stop saying that!"

"Which part?" Leah asked innocently. "The wearing twenty-dollar bills, or the boinking Luke?"

"You know what part!"

Leah smiled. "The boinking then. Probably I should have mentioned that my custard puffs are aphrodisiacs. So really, it's not your fault."

Ali grimaced. "That's not what we did. *Boinking.*" She paused. "Not exactly."

Leah's auburn hair was piled on top of her head,

tendrils slipping free to frame her face and her startling green eyes. She looked at Ali for a long moment before her smile slowly faded. "Uh-oh."

"No." Ali shook her head. "No uh-oh."

"Oh there's definitely an uh-oh," Leah said. "If you can't joke around about the boinking, then there's a *huge* uh-oh."

"And why is that?"

"Because that means it's not just boinking."

"Okay, you have *got* to stop using that word," Ali said.

"I mean who could blame you," Leah mused. "Luke's hot as hell. But . . ."

When Leah trailed off, Ali looked at her. "But what?"

"He's . . ."

Ali's stomach tightened uncomfortably. Most likely that was not panic, but the four custard puffs she'd just consumed. "Too good for me?"

"What? No." Leah leaned in and gripped her hand hard. "*Hell,* no. If anything *you're* too good for every man on the planet. It's just that Luke's not exactly diamonds and heartstrings, you know? And you are."

"No, I'm not." Diamonds and heartstrings implied being a keeper, and she wasn't sure she was cut out for that. But Leah gave her a long look, and Ali sighed. "Okay, so I dream of that *eventually,* but—"

"No buts," Leah said firmly. "Look, Luke is

tough and hard and badass, and everything else that makes up the fantasy, you know? But you need the reality, Ali. You deserve the reality."

On Monday, Ali was behind the counter putting together a happy birthday bouquet of roses for a customer when Aubrey walked into the flower shop wearing a perfect dress, perfect high-heeled sandals, and perfect, smooth, straight blonde hair.

Ali hadn't seen her since Teddy had dropped his little I'm-also-doing-Aubrey bomb, and frankly, she could have gone a lot longer without seeing her. Like, say, forever. Instead she tightened her grip on the roses and accidentally stuck herself with a thorn. "Ouch!" She put pressure on the wound with a napkin and glared at Aubrey.

"Don't look at me like that," Aubrey said. She held out a brown bag. "Here."

"What's that?"

Aubrey sighed. "Teddy told me he told you. So I guess it's an *I'm sorry* present."

Ali came around the counter and peered into the bag. It was a tube of hair anti-frizz.

"It's the stuff I use." Aubrey ran a hand over her hair. "It costs nearly a million dollars, but I figured I owed you."

"Since you slept with Teddy, you mean."

Aubrey winced. "Okay, yes. Yes, I slept with him. But in all fairness, he really did tell me that

216

you and he weren't a thing. I'd never have slept with him otherwise. I can promise you that."

"No?"

"Hell, no," Aubrey said, looking pissed off. "I actually thought I had a shot with him. With his heart, I mean." Disgusted, she leaned on the counter. "He was always so sweet and kind and warm and funny. And charming! I mean, I really thought . . ." She sighed and shook her head. "Look, for what it's worth, I asked about you. He said he was moving out. But then after the auction, everything came out about you, about Melissa, and I felt so stupid. I really thought I'd been his one and only. But I wasn't even his number *two* and only," she said tightly.

Ali set down the napkin and studied Aubrey more carefully. "So you didn't know about Melissa either?"

"No. When I found out, I dumped him. I even threw his phone at him. Broke it too." She winced. "Apparently I have a temper."

"Enough to steal the money?" Ali asked hopefully and already knowing the answer. Aubrey might be too pretty, but she wasn't a thief.

"No. I didn't steal the money." Aubrey's eyes narrowed. "*Hell* no."

"Just checking."

"And for what it's worth," Aubrey said, "I don't think you did either. Or Melissa."

"So who does that leave?"

Aubrey shrugged. "Half the town?"

Yeah. Great.

"So we're still . . . friends?" Aubrey asked.

"We weren't ever really friends," Ali admitted. "I'm too jealous of your hair."

Aubrey pointed to the anti-frizz. "No longer a problem."

After Aubrey left, Ali went into the bathroom and flipped on the light. *Eek.* She read the directions and squeezed out a dime-sized dollop, and like magic, the frizz vanished. It didn't end up quite as smooth and shiny as Aubrey's, but Ali stared, entranced by her own hair. *Nice.* "Best breakup ever," she announced to her reflection. "Lost a man. Gained a maybe friend." And the best hair product she'd ever had.

She locked up the shop and called Zach, filling him in about Aubrey.

"I just talked to Luke," he said. "He ran a financial search on everyone involved."

"Can he do that?"

"No," Zach said. "But you tell him that, because he's one bound and determined man to save your cute hide. Anyway, no one's made any suspicious deposits, including Aubrey."

"Wait." Ali shook her head. "You and Luke are working together?"

"Only for you, babe."

Ali drove to the beach house on autopilot.

Hungry, she headed into the kitchen and went straight to the refrigerator.

"Stop," Luke said. "Seriously, you've got to stop."

At the low, authoritative voice, Ali automatically went still before realizing he not only wasn't in the kitchen, he also wasn't talking to her. She went to the window and found him on the deck with Edward.

"You can't bribe me with food," Luke said to his grandfather.

"Everyone can be bribed with food." Edward lifted the foil on the plate he held.

"Pastries," Luke said reverently.

Ali found herself wanting to smile. Luke had been busy, either holed up on his computer or working outside replacing the wood siding that had rotted out over the past few years. During these small renovation projects, Ali had found that she could stare at him in a tool belt for just about as long as she could stare at him in his swim trunks. She'd wondered if he was avoiding her to be alone or because he didn't want to be tempted by her.

She already missed him. Not that it mattered.

"Not just *any* pastries," Edward said, wafting the plate beneath Luke's nose. "*Leah's* cream puffs."

Luke inhaled deeply. "There's brushed sugar on top of the whipped-cream puffs."

"Uh-huh, and they're loaded with butter too. They'll corrode your arteries, but you'll die happy."

"Living's overrated," Luke said, and took one. "You know you haven't spoken directly to me in years."

"*You* haven't spoken to *me* in years."

"Two-way street," Luke said, mouth full, but still managing to sound unimpressed. "We going to talk about it?"

Edward popped a pastry into his mouth.

Luke nodded. "So we're going to keep ignoring it then. Sticking with something we're good at."

Ali thought about what it'd be like to go years without speaking to her mom or Harper and felt her chest tighten. It would hurt, badly. She imagined that's what she heard barely masked in Luke's voice now.

Hurt.

Wanting to help, she moved to the back door, if for no other reason than to alert them of her presence, but then Edward spoke again.

"Sara says you're doing good," Edward said.

Ali hesitated because they were almost actually talking, and if she butted in now, they'd stop.

"You didn't bring these pastries over here to tell me that you know I'm good," Luke said.

"Okay, fine. I brought them so that you'd think about continuing to help Ali."

Luke stared at him. "Let me give you some

advice," he finally said, "stick to what you do best, which is butting out of the stuff that matters."

Ali sucked in a breath. *Walk away, Ali. Just leave them to this.* But she couldn't. She ached for them and wanted to somehow fix it. Again she reached for the door, but Luke sighed, his voice softer when he spoke again. "And I'm going to keep helping Ali. Jesus. You think I wouldn't? But I'm leaving soon, you know that."

"When?"

"If my commander had his way, I'd already be gone."

"Then you need to hurry up," Edward said. "Figure this shit out now. You getting anywhere?"

"Yes, but too slowly," Luke said, sounding frustrated. "This town, for all the rumors, likes its secrets."

"Positive thinking, boy-o," Edward said. "It's all about positive thinking."

"Yeah? Since when?"

"Things change," Edward said, so quietly that Ali almost missed it. "People change. It's never too late to get to the bottom of all the secrets."

"You sound like a fortune cookie," Luke said.

"This isn't a game, Luke. This is every bit as important as any of your big, fancy city cases."

"Hell, I know that. How could you think I don't know that?"

"Because you're taking your sweet-ass time getting to the bottom of it. You're the hotshot.

Make it look like Mr. Fancy Town Clerk *gave* her that money."

There was a stunned beat of silence.

"She didn't steal the money," Luke finally said.

Ali didn't know which shocked her more, the fact that Edward thought she'd stolen the money ... or that Edward would suggest that Luke frame Teddy.

"Okay," Edward said, "of course not." He paused. "But seriously, if you go with the angle that Marshall *gave* it to her—"

"How about the angle that she's *innocent*," Luke said.

"Well, sure, but that's going to be a challenge, isn't it? I mean she was caught red-handed with that money band in the pot."

"She was framed."

Ali couldn't breathe. She simply couldn't drag air into her chest. She brought her hand up and pressed it against her rib cage but it didn't help.

"You think she was framed," Edward said.

"Yes," Luke said.

"You think she's innocent."

"Yes."

Edward's voice filled with relief. "Good. Then you'll help her. Even after you leave, you won't be able to stop yourself. It's what you do."

"You haven't read the papers lately, I take it," Luke said dryly.

"It's what you do," Edward repeated firmly.

"Stop reading your own press. And also, Eddie Kitzsky needs your help. He thinks his guys are stealing from the till at the bowling alley."

"So why doesn't he fire them?"

"Because they're his nephews, and his wife'll kick his ass. He wants you to catch them at it and then kick their asses for him so he can stay married."

Luke bit into yet another pastry and let out a heartfelt moan—a sound that did something unspeakable to Ali's good parts.

"So good," Luke said, licking sugar off his lower lip. "Pastries should always be for dinner."

"Might want to slow down a little," Edward said. "That's your fifth or sixth one."

"So?"

"I used to be able to eat like that," Edward said wistfully. "The night of the auction I ate a ton, and then sat on the pot whole next day because of it."

Luke went still. "You were at the auction?"

"Everyone was at the auction. I drove the seniors, who were like a bunch of drunken sailors on a four-day leave. I'm telling you, you get old and suddenly you can't hold your liquor any-more. Or your bladder."

"You were at the auction," Luke repeated.

"Just said so, didn't I?"

"There's been some problem with the surveil-lance cameras on the building," Luke said.

223

"Apparently they've been down for several weeks, but it's not in the budget to fix until next quarter. You see anyone come out with a big bag?"

"Like a purse?" Edward asked. "Only every woman in the place."

"No, this would've been bigger than a regular evening bag," Luke said. "Something the size of a large briefcase or duffle bag."

"I see where you're going with this," Edward said, "but I wasn't looking. I was playing Angry Birds on my cell phone while the crowd dispersed. What about the gas station across the street from Town Hall? Maybe their cameras caught some action."

"I'll check with Sawyer. Thanks."

"I gotta go take my pill." Edward started to walk away and then stopped. "As for you, get to it already. And by get to it, I don't mean *get to it*. Not with Ali. She's too sweet for you."

Luke frowned. "Why do people keep telling me that?"

"Because it's true." Edward walked away, around the side of the house and out of sight.

Ali had to hustle to look busy. Ears burning, she began making breakfast for dinner.

Don't get to it . . .

Too late, she could have told Edward. And anyway, sleeping with Luke—again—was the *last* thing on her mind.

Except it wasn't. Not even close. Right now, it

was the *only* thing on her mind. He might have honed his instincts by being a detective on the hard, tough streets, but he knew how to apply them to making love. He could read her body and know what she needed before *she* knew. He loved to touch. He loved to kiss, loved to taste.

He was magic.

But that was beside the point. The point was her life was out of control.

And Luke's life? Also out of control.

Around her, the house was quiet. Too quiet. Had Luke left too? Gone out on the water on his paddle-board? Begun another renovation project? Gone around the front to come in and then gone to bed? If she'd eaten an entire plate of pastries for dinner, she'd need to go to sleep too.

She turned back to the stove. When the phone rang a minute later, she jumped, and then answered breathlessly.

"I'm looking for Luke Hanover," a cool female voice said.

Another reporter. *"How are you people getting this number?"*

"This is Angelina Montclair from the *Chronicle*. Tell him I'll give him a fair interview, facts only. Tell him—"

Ali hung up.

The phone immediately rang again, and she snatched it up, getting angry. "Stop calling here or I'll—"

"He *needs* to give this interview," the reporter said, tone firm. "If he doesn't, his career's going to be in the toilet. If he wants to save it, he needs to—"

Ali hung up again, and then on second thought, pulled the phone from the wall. And even though she'd been expecting Luke to walk in any minute, she still nearly leapt out of her skin when he came up behind her. He crowded her so that she could feel the heat of him at her back. Her eyes drifted shut to better savor the experience.

"Protecting my honor?" he asked, voice low enough that she couldn't gauge his mood.

"Yes," she said breathlessly. "And it's turning into a full-time job."

"Except for when you're eavesdropping," he said.

Well, crap. She turned to face him and winced. "Okay, yes, I was eavesdropping. Some people turn to alcohol or chocolate. I eavesdrop." Her face was heated. "It used to be the only way I could learn stuff from my mom, not that *that's* an excuse. I'm sorry."

"Don't be," he said quietly, something in his voice making her chest tighten. "You don't have to eavesdrop with me, Ali. I'll tell you whatever you want to know—always."

She searched his gaze for a clue to his thoughts, but got nothing. "I wanted to tell you I was there, but you two were talking, and I didn't want to interrupt. Are you going to help Mr. Kitzsky?"

"Yeah. His nephews are idiots, but not completely moronic. They know where their bread's buttered. I'll clunk their heads together, and that'll be it." He looked over her shoulder into the pan. "Smells great."

What smelled great was him. It was all she could do not to turn her head and bury her face in the crook of his neck and inhale him.

"I'm guessing that omelets are your specialty," he said, sounding a little amused. She hoped.

"Yep." She flipped the omelet, but then had to admit the truth. "Actually . . . omelets are the *only* thing I can cook."

He tipped back his head and laughed, and the sight was so innately sexy that he took her breath. "Do you really think the gas station might have footage of the thief walking out of Town Hall with the money?" she asked.

He stole a slice of cheese and popped it in his mouth. "So you did hear everything."

"Including the part where your grandpa thought I stole the money? Yeah." She tried to sound neutral, but was pretty sure she failed.

Luke let out a breath and reached around her to turn off the burners. "If you were listening, then you heard exactly how much he cares about you."

She didn't say anything to that. She couldn't. There'd been a lot of people in her life who'd claimed to care about her. It didn't always mean much. "He tried to bribe you with pastries to help me."

"I can't be bribed." He met her gaze. "You know I never do anything I don't want to do."

Her heart gave a little treacherous leap. He was in board shorts again, as sky blue as his eyes, with a drawstring that was loose. One little tug, she thought. His muscles were taut, his skin damp. He'd been paddle-boarding.

She had no idea why the sight of him, a little wet and a lot hot, made her both of those things as well. "I don't either . . ." she whispered, "do things I don't want to do."

"Liar." He stroked a finger along her cheekbone and then tucked a wayward strand of hair behind her ear, lingering at the sensitive skin there.

She shivered, and his eyes heated. "You're a pleaser," he said.

"Was," she corrected. "*Was* a people pleaser. No more. I've turned over a new leaf. I only please myself now."

A very small smile curved his mouth, and he lowered his head so that they shared their next breath. "There's an image," he murmured. "You pleasing yourself."

She let out a low, nervous laugh, and he bent to nip her lower lip.

"I'd want to watch," he said.

Oh, Lord. "I think we're getting off the subject here," she managed.

Eyes on hers, he slowly ran his hands up her arms and then back to grip her hips. Okay, the hell with getting off subject, she thought, as his mouth brushed hers with just the lightest pressure. She heard a moan, *hers,* and at the sound, Luke got more serious about the kiss, taking it deep and hot until she swayed toward him.

A long, delicious moment later, he pulled back a fraction and looked down at her. She realized her fingers were curled into his biceps and that she was actually trying to tug him closer. But he wrapped his fingers around her wrists and pulled her hands away, taking them down to her sides. "We said we weren't going to do this," he said.

Aroused from head to toe, she nodded. "Right." And then shook her head. "Why is that again? Is it because the first time was so awful, or because people keep telling you not to sleep with me?"

"If I can't be bribed, I sure as hell don't give a shit what people think." His voice was low and incredibly sexy, and he tightened his grip on her wrists, still restraining her from touching him.

Which was suddenly all she wanted to do.

"As for it being awful," he said, "we both know it was the polar opposite of awful."

"So . . . ?"

"So we said we weren't going there," he

229

repeated, and she wasn't sure if it was disappointment or relief when he let her go and turned away.

"Actually," she said to his back. His bare back. Tanned. Sleek. Ripped with strength. "*You* said that we weren't going to go there. Because even though you're leaving and it was so awful, I still want to. Go there, that is."

With a half laugh, half groan, he faced her again. "Ali. We can't."

"I know." His board shorts were low, revealing gorgeous abs, cut obliques, and a most impressive erection. At the direction of her gaze, he let out another tortured-sounding laugh and then walked out of the kitchen, vanishing into the depths of the house.

A few seconds later, she heard a shower go on.

It was several minutes before she could breathe or swallow. Still shaky, she divided the omelet, leaving half on a plate for him.

She ate, listening to the water run, noting that he stayed in there a *long* time, during which she did her best not to imagine what he was doing.

Or how she'd rather be doing it for him.

Chapter 16

The next day on her lunch break at the flower shop, Ali called her mom to check in.

"I just set up your sister with a guy from the security office at the casino," Mimi said. "He wears a gun and everything."

Harper and a guy with a gun—seemed like a nightmare waiting to happen. "Mom, maybe she wants to meet her own guys."

"Honey, we all need a little help here and there. You still seeing that very good-looking Luke?"

"We're not seeing each other, not like that," Ali said.

"Well why not?"

Yeah, Ali, why not? "Because I don't need a boyfriend," Ali said.

"Well of course you do, Ali-gator. Every woman needs a man to make her smile, to make her feel pretty, to buy her clothes . . . Don't you like him?"

Ali sighed. "To tell you the truth, it's a little confusing just how much I do."

"Aw, love's not really all that confusing, not when you get right down to it," Mimi said. "You either feel it or you don't."

Said the woman who'd felt it more than most.

But Ali thought about that as she arranged and delivered flowers all afternoon. Did she feel it for Luke? *Could* she feel it for Luke? And given that love had never done a damn thing for her, why would she want to?

Lucille came in to buy some flowers for Mr. Wykowski. "He's under the weather with hemorrhoids," she said. "I wanted to cheer him up with my stripper-pole jazzercise moves, but I threw out my lower back in class last week, so dancing's out."

Ali did her best not to picture Lucille in a stripper-pole class.

"Looking for new Intel," Lucille said. "You didn't confess, did you?"

"No."

"Good. Make 'em sweat."

"I didn't steal the money," Ali said, beginning to feel like a broken record and getting a little pissed about it too.

"Of course you didn't, honey. You're far too sweet. Don't pay attention to anyone who says otherwise. Keep your chin up." Lucille patted her hand, paid her for the flowers, and left.

Just before closing, Zach called to check in. "How are you doing?" he asked.

"Holding my breath," Ali said. "I think I'm about to be arrested any second. I'm not crazy about wearing stripes, Zach."

"Actually," he said, "the jumpsuits are orange in your county."

Ali laughed and then covered her mouth. "It's not funny. Oh my God, Zach. This is so not funny."

"You won't get arrested," he said.

"Because there's not enough evidence?"

"No, because your sister said if I got you out of this mess without an arrest, she'd consider sleeping with me."

Ali choked out another laugh, this one with more real amusement, and hung up. She was closing up when Russell poked his head out of his office. "Hey, cookie, thinking about cutting out Thursday for Vegas."

Ali did her best not to show her dismay. *More* days off wasn't in the plan; she needed the money. "But Thursdays are good business days."

"I know, but Paul's making the big bucks doing the stars' makeup and hair. He bought us tickets to Celine."

"I don't think Celine's still playing."

"She's a drag queen. Great reviews."

Russell was absolutely glowing—though that might have been his spray-on tan, hard to tell. Ali didn't have the heart to tell him how badly she couldn't afford this. "How about I run the shop for you while you're gone?" she asked.

His smile froze a little; it was the expression of a man who didn't know how to tell his beloved little floral designer that though he was fond of her, he didn't trust her to run his shop.

"I can do it, Russell," she said earnestly. "I want to do it so badly, to stay here in Lucky Harbor and make something of this place. Let me show you."

He inhaled dramatically, then blew it out. "I don't know. You have an awful lot going on."

"Which is why I need this." She paused. "Unless . . . you don't trust me with your money—"

"It's not that," he said quickly. *Too* quickly. "It's just that I'm a control freak. You know that. I can't let anyone else run the show. It's all me."

"I understand." But she didn't, not really. Nursing the invisible wounds that only a pastry of some kind could cure, she headed next door to the bakery. The closed sign was up, but the door hadn't been locked yet. The bakery was empty except for the big guy leaning negligently against the glass display counter dressed head to toe in his firefighter gear.

Jack.

"Hey," she said, surprised to see him, "where's Leah?"

"Boxing up some goodies for the fire station."

Leah came out of the back holding a pink box, looking flushed and irritated. "Next time," she said to Jack, smacking the box up against his broad chest, "don't show up at the last minute. Not everyone is moved by your pretty face and the way that uniform somehow manages to show off your ass."

Jack grinned. "And that's not even my best part."

Leah rolled her eyes.

Jack leaned on the counter, all tough, male grace as he worked at charming Leah. "I'll be sure to tell all the fires to put themselves out so that we don't piss off the best pastry chef this side of the Continental Divide."

Leah blew a stray strand of hair from her face and narrowed her eyes. "Only on *this* side of the Continental Divide?"

"In all the land," he corrected.

"Hmmm," Leah said.

Jack studied her face. "You're still mad about the other day."

"You think?"

He laughed. "Hey, you're the one who left your computer signed into your Pinterest account. I merely pinned a pic of you from last Halloween wearing an eighties leotard and leg warmers."

"Yes, with the tagline that read ' "Keep On Loving You" by REO Speedwagon is the theme of my life!' " she said.

Ali snorted, but swallowed it when Leah sent her a look.

"On second thought, give me those pastries back," Leah said to Jack. "You don't deserve them."

He held the box above her head and pulled out

his wallet, presumably to pay, but Leah sighed, shook her head, and pushed him out the door. "Go. Get out before I do something regrettable to you with those pastries."

"Promises, promises," Jack said, playfully tugging on a strand of her hair as he left the shop.

Ali was grinning. Leah pointed at her. "Stop that. I don't want to talk about it. He thinks he's funny."

He was. Very funny. "It was nice of you," Ali said, "not charging him."

Leah sighed. "All the firefighters have been fighting that bush fire out in Desolation Flats, and he's coming off three long, hard, hot days. They need a pick-me-up."

"Or like you said, *pretty face in a hot uniform.*"

"We're just friends, have been forever. We went to high school together."

The door opened, and the bell jingled again. Both women turned to watch Luke walk in. He was in long cargo shorts, a surf shop T-shirt, and an opened button down, the very picture of a guy on vacay—except for his watchful, alert gaze. He smiled at Leah and then gave Ali the "come here" gesture.

Ali moved toward him, brushing against him as he held the door open for her. Outside, she blinked at the bright sun. "What are you doing here?"

"Looking for you."

She wanted to ask if this was a social or business visit, but his face gave her the answer even before he spoke.

"Talked to Sawyer," he said. "He's still working on getting the surveillance video from the gas station. Apparently the owner's been on vacation, and the son—who was supposed to run the place in his absence—closed the place down and went fishing for a few days."

Ali wasn't surprised. This was, after all, Lucky Harbor. Lucky Harbor had its own sense of time, and it rarely ticked along with the real world. "In the meantime," Luke said, "I've got something else." He pulled out his cell phone and brought up a photo. "You recognize this?"

It was a close-up of the Silver Pine pencil pot she'd taken from Ted's office. It'd been confiscated as evidence when the police had come to the house. "Yes," she said, "of course."

"Do you have a signature for your pottery, something that identifies it as yours?"

"I carve my initials into each piece."

"And then you add a star to the glaze?"

"A star? No," she said, confused. "Why? What's going on?"

"Sawyer let me take a look at the evidence. Professional courtesy." He zoomed in on the little pot. "See that?" he asked. "You've got a crack on the inside."

"Well, I made that pot months ago. It's been manhandled and—"

"I'm not questioning the quality of the pot, Ali. Look closer." He zoomed in even further. "See it?"

"Yeah, there's something in the crack . . ." She squinted. It was a sliver of something blue with a tiny white star on it. "Huh."

"Odd, right?"

"Yeah," she said. "Very. What's a nail tip doing stuck in the crack of my ceramic pot?"

Luke stared at her. "Nail tip?"

"Looks like the tip of an acrylic fingernail to me. But I don't have fake nails, and I never use fingernail polish because it chips so easily with the work I do."

Luke shook his head, and then shocked the hell out of her by leaning in and giving her a quick, hard kiss on the mouth. "Hot *and* smart."

She felt the glow from her toes to the roots of her hair, and in some very interesting spots in between. "You think whoever this nail tip belongs to was the one who put the bill wrapper in the jar?"

"I think it's possible."

"I don't know anyone with blue fingernails with white stars," she said.

"How many people live in this town?"

She shrugged. "We've grown to five thousand-ish, I think."

"And half of them are female . . ."

"There's only one beauty salon in town," Ali said. "And it's just two buildings down." She went still. "Melissa runs it."

He nodded. "But her nails are green-and-white stripes right now."

She didn't want to know how he knew that. Okay, so she did. She totally wanted to know. In fact, her immediate reaction was nearly to blurt out, "How do you know this?" but her brain reminded her that they weren't "involved." Which meant she had no business in his business, even though he had just kissed her in public outside the bakery. And given that she'd thought she and Teddy had been a thing when they obviously hadn't been, she clearly wasn't all that up on the rules of Defining Relationships 101. "Can you text me this pic?" she finally asked. "I want to send it to Zach."

"I'll send it to him."

"Okay, but I still want it." She wanted to go see Melissa herself.

Evening was coming. Dusk at the base of the Olympic Mountains was fickle as hell. Though the day had been warm, with the drop of the sun came a drop in temperature, and Ali wrapped her arms around herself.

Luke pulled off his outer shirt and held it out for her. She gratefully slid her arms into the soft cotton and hugged it close to hold in his lingering body heat.

"I'll send you the pic," Luke said quietly, "but I don't want you showing it around." He met her gaze, his own very serious. "I want you to trust me to do it."

"But—"

"Look, I know that this is *your* life, and you like to handle things yourself. I get that. I respect that," he said. "But say that you're sleeping with a bunch of women who don't know about each other. And then one of those women discovers that you're also sticking it to half the town. What do you do?"

Ali stared at him. "Sneak into his office and take back a gift?" she joked weakly. But her humor faded fast. "Or . . . steal the cash in his possession to make him look really bad." She sighed shakily. "Damn. I really walked right into this."

"You got in the middle of someone's plan," Luke agreed. "And that someone has fifty big ones under their mattress and is feeling pretty damn safe right now—at least until you start stirring shit up, shifting the blame from you to them." He met her gaze, his own very serious. "I'm going to let Sawyer know that the star isn't your signature and the fingernail should be run through forensics with the other evidence. And you . . ."

"You want me to be careful," she said softly.

He leaned in and gave her a kiss, right there on the sidewalk. "*Very* careful."

She nodded and then smiled because she could see the fierce determination in his eyes. To get to the bottom of this mess. To protect her. And seeing it, she felt her own fierce determination too. Along with something new.

Hope.

Chapter 17

Normally, Luke's favorite time of day was the opposite of what his grandma's had been—dawn's first light. But not on the days after he stayed up until two in the morning to catch the two knuckleheads closing up their uncle's bowling alley and skimming from the top of the day's take.

Luke didn't have to knock their heads together. As it turned out, they ratted on each other, and Luke was confident he scared the shit out of them and that their skimming days were over.

He finally fell gratefully into bed, but was woken only a few hours later at the ass crack of dawn by the buzz on his phone as an email came in from his commander.

Time's up, Hanover. Be here by this weekend to prepare for Monday's review.

Well, hell. Today was Wednesday, and his gut clenched at the thought of leaving now. He hadn't finished painting the house. Or repairing the beach stairs. Okay, so he hadn't even started the stairs, but he'd planned on it. And he wanted to see Ben. Luke had hoped he'd be back by now.

He didn't want to leave without seeing him. Nor did he want to go before Ali's case was resolved.

Hell, he didn't want to leave. Period.

Pushing out of bed, he slipped into swim trunks and got on the water before the sun came up. He'd get to that painting, and also fix the cranky plumbing so there'd be no problems after he left, but first this. He paddleboarded through the silent water, watching the sky burst into light. The wind was at his back, and beneath him the water was so clear and deep that he could see schools of fish speed through the current, racing him.

It was the closest thing to a religion he'd ever had. The church of the wind and surf.

He paddled until his arms were quaking with exhaustion and then headed back. At the dock, he pulled his board out of the water and came to a stop.

His grandfather was sitting on the dock, feet dangling as he smoked a cigar, watching Luke through a ring of smoke.

Luke leaned the paddleboard against the dock, glanced at the stairs up to the still-dark house. "Early for you, isn't it?"

Edward shrugged.

Fine. Not up to bashing his head up against the blank wall of his grandfather's stubbornness—hell, he still had a concussion from the last time—Luke started to pick up his board and go. But he stopped, blew out a breath, and turned

back. "Thanks for making me think about the surveillance tapes."

"Guess you're not an island all unto yourself
then, huh?"

Luke thought of the nice, hot shower he'd
intended to take and the omelet he'd been hoping
to talk his pretty tenant into fixing him. Instead
he voiced what had been bothering him for ten
years. "You still blame me?"

Edward took a long drag on the cigar and
contemplated the orange glow of ash on the tip.
"That was never the question."

"No?" Luke thought of his grandma Fay's
funeral and the family gathering afterward, right
here on the beach in fact. Fay had been widely
beloved. Everyone had come, milling around,
crying, telling stories, laughing . . . just wanting
to be together to commiserate about the loss of a
woman they'd all cared about.

Luke would never forget how Edward had
stood on this very dock, his back to the crowd,
staring out at the water.

Silent.

Luke could remember the heaviness in his gut
looking at his grandfather's proud, stiff shoulders
and the tightening in his own chest when he'd
walked up to him, until they were standing side
by side.

All of Luke's life, Edward had been a rock. A
hard-ass, tough, rugged rock, with little to no

softness. Even so, Luke had never so much as seen the man lose his temper. Not once. He'd certainly never seen him brought to his knees by grief. But that's what had happened, and on that day when Luke had lifted his own head, there'd been tears streaming down Edward's face.

The sorrow had nearly choked Luke, sorrow and regret and guilt, but he'd somehow managed to speak. "It was my fault." He could remember saying those four words clearly, quickly, like ripping off a Band-Aid. Just as he could remember Edward's response.

Or lack of.

Because Edward had said nothing at all, not a single word. He'd simply given one sharp shake of his head and walked off.

Away from the house.

Away from Luke.

He'd vanished for a few days, which wasn't unusual for Edward. He went off on trips all the time. Back then, he'd still been working as a fish and game warden, so his disappearance had been considered normal. Everyone knew he and Fay had been separated for decades. Just as everyone knew that it hadn't mattered. He'd still been head over heels in love with her, and clearly devastated by her death.

A week later, Edward had resurfaced, but by then Luke had gone back to San Francisco. Sara had still been in jail, and when Luke had gone for his weekly visit with her, he'd told her everything.

Sara, always the mediator, had tried to soothe Luke by telling him to stop with the guilt. In no way did anyone, *especially* their grandpa—a man who'd hurt Fay himself—blame Luke for Fay's death. Just like no one blamed him for Sara being in prison.

But Luke knew she was wrong. Because *he* blamed himself for both of those things.

Water continued to slap up against the pylons of the dock and the shore. The air was scented with pine, wet sand, and cigar and filled with the roar of the high tide hitting the rocky shore.

Edward took another long drag on his cigar.

"You know those things'll kill you," Luke said.

"They haven't yet."

Luke waited but Edward didn't say anything else, just sat there taking in the view. And yet Luke knew damn well he wasn't here for the view. He waited some more and got nothing, so he stretched out on the dock, leaned back on his elbows, and let the morning rays dry and warm him.

"You're finally claiming the house," Edward eventually said.

Ah. *There* it was. Luke threw an arm over his eyes to block the bright sun. "You're still pissed off she left me this place," he said.

"I was never pissed off that she left you this place."

"No?"

"No. Christ," Edward grumbled, "how can someone so smart be so stupid?"

Luke assumed that was a rhetorical question and kept his silence.

"I was pissed that you let her memory go to waste," Edward said. "That you left here without looking back. That you stayed away. That you don't give a shit about anything or anyone." He paused. "That you forgot about her. Us."

Luke sat back up, fury and grief fighting for space in his throat. "No. Hell no. You don't get to say that to me."

"Just did, boy-o."

"I've forgotten exactly *nothing*," Luke said. "I live in San Francisco. My job's there."

"And what, that job's kept you busy twenty-four seven for ten years? Is that what I'm supposed to believe?"

"Yeah, actually. The job's pretty demanding, which you damn-well know."

Edward nodded. He'd worked in law enforcement. He did know. "So you're here now because why? The going got rough?"

Luke stared at him. "You think that's what I do? I just walk away when the going gets rough?"

Edward shrugged. "If the shoe fits . . ."

Luke pressed the heels of his hands to his eyes, but nope, nothing was going to take care of the new headache brutally kicking in behind his lids. "Fuck it," he muttered, and pushed to his feet.

"Fuck this." He grabbed the T-shirt he'd left on the railing, shoved it over his head, and was striding away when he heard his grandfather mutter, "Walking away again."

Luke whipped back, his emotions far too close to the surface now. But he'd started this, he'd damn well finish it. "I didn't walk away from her. She *died.*"

Edward got to his feet, a slow painful movement that had Luke feeling yet a new stab of guilt. When had his grandfather gotten old?

"You walked away from *me,*" Edward said. "From the town that loved you. You closed yourself off and never looked back. *That's* walking away. *That's* what you do."

"I'm here now, aren't I?"

"For how long? Until something bad happens?"

"No, until I have to go back to my life."

Edward just shrugged and turned away, dismissing him. Luke did the same, striding up the stairs to the deck and shoving the back door open. Ali, standing at the stove, gave a startled squeak and whirled around, wielding a wooden spoon like a weapon. When she saw him, she sagged, a hand to her heart. "Jesus, Luke."

He headed straight through the kitchen, intending to put a lot of space between the two of them so that he didn't scare her into next week with his bad attitude.

"Made you an omelet," she said.

He shook his head. "I'm good."

"I left out anything green."

Well, shit. The scent of her cooking was making his mouth water, and right on cue, his stomach rumbled. He turned back to face her and found her eating up the sight of him.

His body, already revved up on adrenaline, reacted predictably, but he didn't move toward her. Refused to touch her when he felt so out of control. "I can't do this right now, Ali."

"Do what?"

"Be civil."

"How about eating. Can you eat?" She pointed to a kitchen chair, and Luke had no idea why, but he sat.

Face creased into an expression of adorable concentration, she flipped the big, fluffy omelet onto a plate and pushed it his way. She poured him an orange juice and then repeated the whole thing for herself. As if realizing he needed some space, she hoisted herself up on the far side of the counter, her legs folded beneath her, eating with him in companionable silence.

"Thanks," he said when he'd finished.

She nodded, hopped off the counter, and went to pass by him. With no idea what he was doing, he snagged her wrist.

She turned to him, a question in her eyes. Then with a soft smile, she stepped between his legs and cupped his jaw. "Maybe I can help make you feel a little better," she said quietly, and bent and gave a gentle kiss to one corner of his mouth.

He closed his eyes against the assault of emotions that battered him. "Ali."

She simply kissed the other corner of his mouth.

So sweet, he thought. So warm. "Ali, I can't—"

"Be civil. I know." She straddled him. "So don't. Be you, Luke. And let me be whatever you need."

He was staggered. "I won't use you."

"I wouldn't let you," she said simply, and pulled off her tank top, leaving her in a pink bra and gauzy skirt. She unhooked her bra and let it fall away.

He closed his eyes and took a deep breath, but it didn't matter. His body didn't need to see her, she was already imprinted on his brain. "I'm leaving in a couple of days," he said. "I have to be back in San Francisco this weekend."

"Okay."

Beautiful, satiny, smooth skin, sweet curves . . . His hands came up and cupped her breasts, his thumbs brushing over the tips.

She sighed in pleasure, and he figured it was a good thing he was sitting down, because she knocked the wind from him, every time he was with her. "Be sure, Ali."

Pulling back, she smiled into his gaze, eyes calm and direct. No sign of the nerves that suddenly lived in his gut.

"Don't worry." Her lips were close enough to brush over his with every word. "I know what this is."

Oh, thank Christ she knew. Because he sure as hell didn't.

Very gently, she pulled his shirt up and off, humming her approval as her hands slid over his chest. Her hips rocked, the core of her pressing down on his erection. He groaned and leaned in, pressing his face to her heart.

"I also know what this isn't," she murmured, her hands sliding into his hair to hold him at her breast.

When the words sank in, he started to pull back, but she tightened her grip. "I'm going to rock your world, Detective Lieutenant Luke Hanover, and you're going to rock mine."

He didn't know how she did it. She took him outside himself and made him feel nothing but in the moment, with her. Turning his head, he ran his tongue over her nipple, loving the way she sighed in pleasure, melting against him.

"And then," she said huskily, breathing heavy, "we're going to go back to being just friends."

They *were* friends, he realized with some surprise, though he had no real clue as to how or when that had actually happened. But it had, so her words disturbed him because they weren't *just* friends.

Not even close.

If they did this again, now that they'd become even more emotionally invested in each other, it'd be far more mind blowing than just rocking each other's world. He already knew that.

Did she?

She looked into his eyes, her own warm and full of emotion, so much emotion that his throat tightened. Yeah, she knew.

And yet she was once again putting him first, ahead of her own problems.

It was going to be hell to walk away from her while wanting more and knowing he couldn't have it.

Wouldn't have it.

But he didn't have the strength to go yet. He wanted this. For right now, he wanted nothing else. They could have this, he told himself, and they could keep it just what it was. Light. Easy.

But even he recognized the lie.

She kissed his jaw. "Looking pretty serious for a man who's got a sure thing in his lap, half naked," she murmured.

She was right. He slid his hands up her slim back, urging her to lean into him so that they were chest to chest. He kissed her shoulder and then nipped the spot.

Teasing.

She was already panting a little, rocking her hips, stroking his ego—among other things. He nipped her again, a little harder, and then made a move for her nipple again, sucking her into his mouth. The hungry sound she made egged him on, and so did the way she tightened her fingers in his hair with every little tug of his mouth.

"Luke. *Please, Luke.*"

Oh yeah, he was going to please. He pushed the hem of her skirt up to her waist. "Hold this."

She reached for it reflexively, freeing up his hands. Running the pad of his finger over her tiny, sky blue cotton panties, he caught the material and scraped them aside, giving him a view that made him groan out her name. She was wet and glistening. For him.

She rocked against him again, and he tore open his board shorts, giving himself some desperately needed room.

"Oh," she whispered, all breathy, staring down at him with flattering raptness.

He reached for her, then stilled, letting out a long string of oaths. "No condom," he managed.

"I'm on the pill."

Her trust meant more to him than he could have possibly imagined. But how the hell was he supposed to keep this light when everything about it felt more like . . . everything?

She was still holding her skirt up like he'd asked, and it was the sexiest thing he'd ever seen. Pulling her in, he wrapped his arms around her, kissing her deeply, wondering why he even bothered to keep his distance. There was no distance with her. None.

She returned his kisses with wild abandon. "It's crazy . . ." she whispered against his mouth, "what you do to me."

"Tell me," he said. "Tell me what I do to you."

"You look at me like I'm the best thing you've seen all day. You make me feel . . . I don't know. Pretty. Sexy. And important to you. You make me *feel,* Luke."

She was all those things to him. And she made him feel too. She made him feel so fucking much that his heart was going to burst through his ribs. "Ali," he breathed, and then slanted his mouth across hers. He'd meant to just make a quick connection, but she moved with him, taking the kiss hotter, deeper, pressing her body to his.

It turned him inside out and upside down and sideways. She was all he'd thought about, dreamed about since he'd returned home, her hot, curvy bod, warm, soft skin, her wild hair flowing over his shoulders and arms. She murmured his name like he was the best thing that had happened to her all day, and he gave himself up to her, sucking on her lower lip, sliding his tongue to hers, ravishing her until they were both trembling. "Raise up," he said, voice hoarse.

She eagerly scrambled up, giving him the room he needed to slide into her. The sensation of filling her rocked his world. Hers too, if her wild breathing meant anything. Holding still, giving her a moment to adjust, was the hardest thing he'd ever done.

"I love that too," she whispered.

He kissed the frantically beating pulse at the base of her neck. "What?"

"The feel of you." She arched against him wordlessly, demanding more. "Your mouth on me."

He made his way along her jaw to just beneath her ear. "What else?"

With a shiver, she tightened her grip on his hair. He didn't care if she made him bald, as long as she didn't let go. "That you know my sweet spots."

"You're one big, sweet spot."

She bit his lower lip, and when he sucked in a breath, she laughed at him softly.

He laughed too. Laughed, while so close to her that he could feel her heart beating. It was the most amazing thing he'd ever experienced. Cupping her sweet ass in his palms, he thrust into her.

She stopped laughing and moaned his name again as her own movements brought her closer to the edge.

"God, Ali," he said, voice low and thick. He couldn't help it, watching her take her pleasure on him was turning him on so much he could hardly draw a breath. "You're so beautiful. Every time I see you, I just want to drag you down and have my way with you." Her hips were driving him insane, and he tightened his grip, trying to slow her down so he didn't lose it in a spectacularly embarrassing fashion.

But she obviously thought his control was of the superhuman variety, because she cupped his face and leaned in, letting her breasts lightly brush his chest again. She smiled at him, the hot little minx.

He smiled back.

And then they were kissing, devouring each other, lost in the moment. He knew she was close, straining for it. Wanting to watch her, wanting to push her over the edge, he stroked a thumb over the sweetest of all her sweet spots.

She tore her mouth free to pant for air, gripping his wrist to hold him there.

Stroking her both inside and out, he watched as she began to tremble.

"Luke."

"I know."

"Don't stop."

"I won't."

She came, flying over the edge with his name on her lips. He tried to hold on, tried to hold back, but it was too late. He was lost. Lost, and yet somehow found. It was as simple and terrifying as that.

Chapter 18

Luke concentrated on dragging air back into his lungs. He was still in the kitchen chair, with Ali's dead weight on his chest. Maybe one day they'd actually make it to his bed.

Except they weren't going to have a "one day."

Ali hadn't moved at all. Luke stroked a hand down her back, relieved to feel her breathing. "I didn't kill you then."

"Death by orgasm," she murmured, still not moving. "Not a bad way to go." But after another long moment, she sighed, rose, and began to put herself back together, covering up that amazing body.

A damn shame.

Luke managed to find his legs and took their plates to the sink. When he turned back, he caught her staring at his ass.

She blushed. "You have some dirt on it, that's all."

"I was sitting on the dock."

"Talking to your grandfather."

"Eavesdropping again?" he asked.

"No, since I couldn't hear the words." She

paused. "But the body language said plenty. Are you close to him? It's hard to tell."

"Used to be." He paused. "I thought he blamed me for my grandma's death."

"Oh Luke," she murmured. "No."

He shrugged. The truth was the truth.

"And now?" she asked.

"He says he was mad at me for leaving Lucky Harbor."

She came close, invading his space, running her hands up his chest to cup his face. He wasn't buried deep inside her body, but the gesture was just as powerful. "Her death wasn't your fault," she said.

"And the leaving?"

"Were you supposed to stay here just to make him happy?" she asked.

"There was no making him happy."

Ali's fingers massaged his skull, melting his bones. He'd just had her, and he wanted her again.

"You seem pretty fond of blaming yourself for everyone and everything," Ali said. "Wonder why that is? You don't want to be happy?"

"Happy?" Unsure how they'd gone from post-orgasmic glow to this, he shook his head. "There's not much to be happy about, and I'd have thought that you'd know that better than anyone."

Ali cocked her head and studied him with what he was certain was more than a dash of pity. "You think I should be unhappy?" she asked.

Even as he sensed a trap, he opened his big, fat, stupid mouth. "Aren't you?"

She went still a beat and then pulled back. "Why? Because someone I thought I could trust walked out on me with nothing more than a text? Because I think my boss is going to close the flower shop and I'll lose my job? Because I've been falsely accused of a crime that people in town actually believe I committed?" She gave him a little push that actually wasn't so little. "I'm not defined by someone I thought I was dating, Luke, or what I do for a living. I'm not defined by what people think of me. My happiness comes from within, and I—"

Oh shit. Her voice broke.

She shook her head and pointed at him. "And here's the thing."

Oh, good. Thank God. There was a thing. He listened, desperate to get past this without her tears.

"I know I might *look* like a ball of fluff," she said, "but I'm not. Not even close. And the fact that I get up each morning and put a damn smile on my face is the same as . . . Batman putting on his cape."

"I—"

"I'm not done. It's . . . protection. It's my shield. It's me waving my middle finger to the world, because I *choose* to be happy. The bottom line, Luke, is that I know what matters and what doesn't." She gave him a look that would have wilted the plant on the kitchen island if she hadn't been taking such good care of it. "And I'd think that *you* would know that better than anyone."

With his own words thrown back at him, mocking him, she turned and headed for the door.

He sighed. "Ali . . ."

But she was gone.

Luke was woken the next morning by a call from Sawyer. "The video is in," he said. "We found nothing, but it's all yours if you want it."

Luke *did* want it. He rolled out of bed, and twenty minutes later he was on his way. He made a pit stop at the beauty salon. A brunette in her early twenties was opening the shop. "Melissa's first appointment isn't until noon," she said when he asked. "I don't expect her for a few hours."

"I'll come back," Luke said. "But out of curiosity, have any of you done a blue manicure with white stars lately?"

"Actually," she said. "Melissa—"

"Is right here . . ."

Luke turned to find Melissa standing there.

"You're looking for a manicure," Melissa said with a broad smile. "A blue one at that. Wow. I so did not see that one coming. I mean I've heard San Francisco can turn a man, but you, Lieutenant

Sexy? You've got so much testosterone that you *ooze* pheromones. Please come back to the straight team. We need you."

He blinked. "What? No." *Jesus.* "The manicure isn't for me."

"Well, that's a relief."

"So?" Luke asked both women. "A blue manicure?"

"Didn't you have a blue manicure last month?" the brunette asked. "We were experimenting with the new spray brush, remember?"

"Didn't keep them blue for more than a few minutes," Melissa said casually, and sipped from the coffee in her hands. "Now if you'll excuse me, I've got a last-minute emergency appointment." She started to walk into the studio, then turned back to Luke. "I'm the only game in town, but it's not far to other salons," she said. "In fact, there's one not too far down the road in Ocean Shores, and they specialize in original nail designs. You might check with them. But just out of curiosity, why are you asking?"

"Nothing important," he said.

"Uh-huh." She gave him a long, speculative look, then vanished inside.

Thoughtful, Luke walked back to his truck and found Jack in the passenger seat, slurping coffee like his life depended on it. There was a look on Jack's face that had Luke's gut clenching. "Ben?"

Jack's expression immediately lightened. "No, man. He's fine, as far as I know. I haven't heard from him, but last time he emailed, he was pretty sure he'd be home soon." He jutted his chin toward the salon. "You get yourself a nice cut and color?"

"Yeah, real nice. What are you doing here?"

"Leah's dating some new guy. I ran him," Jack said, "and he's got a record."

"You ran him? Since when does a firefighter run people?"

"Hey, I have friends in high places, okay? And it was for the common good."

Luke shook his head. "What's his record?"

"He's got a library debt."

Luke stared at him. "Well, hell, Jack. We should string him up for that."

"Hey, if he can't keep a library book safe, he sure as hell can't take care of one little pastry chef."

"So you're waiting here to tell her that?"

"No, I'm going to tell *him* that. I'm waiting for him to get out of there. He's currently sucking up to Leah, looking for date number two."

Luke laughed. Jack and Leah had been friends since their school days. The kind of friends who moved each other's parked cars to different streets, or set them up on bad blind dates for the sheer entertainment value. But this curiosity about who Leah was dating was new. Very new.

Jack wasn't a possessive guy about anything. He'd lost his dad early in a tragic fire. Since then Jack hadn't taken much of anything too seriously—except his job. "You're crazy."

"Says the guy who just came out of a beauty salon," Jack said.

Luke stared at Jack, trying to figure out the odd tone in his voice. "I thought you and Leah were just friends."

"Yeah, and friends don't let friends date potential felons," Jack said. "And aren't you supposed to be back in San Francisco?"

"Aren't you supposed to be putting out fires?"

"I'm just coming off four twenty-fours and going straight to bed."

"Not yet you're not." Luke turned over his engine and pulled out into the street.

"Hey," Jack said.

"I need your help," Luke said.

At the sheriff's station, they were directed to Sawyer's office. He took them to the one and only spare room—the interrogation room. There they had a computer and the gas station's surveillance tapes from the night of the auction.

"We've been over them," Sawyer said, "there's nothing."

"Well, if there's nothing . . ." Jack said on a yawn.

"So where does that leave you?" Luke asked Sawyer.

Sawyer shook his head. "We've run Ted's and

Ali's financials. Nothing sticks out. We've gotten forensics back on the office prints. Everyone and their mother was in that office. The only real evidence we have is the bill band found in Ali's possession."

"And the toe ring and the blue acrylic nail tip."

"With nothing to connect either of them to the crime," Sawyer said.

"Melissa says there's a salon in Ocean Shores that specializes in original nail designs. Whatever that means."

Sawyer shoved a hand through his hair. "Okay, that definitely did not come out when I talked to her. I'll check on that."

"And how about Melissa's financials? She might be feeling spurned . . ."

"We're still looking at her, yes. But . . ."

"But what?"

"Ali stole the damn ceramic pot," Sawyer said. "That looks bad. None of the other players had anything, including motive."

Luke's gut churned. "An arrest on circumstantial evidence? *Weak.*"

Sawyer sighed. "Small town mentality here, man. Give me a break."

"She's innocent. If you didn't find anything on the video, that tells us either the money wasn't taken out that night at all, or the thief didn't leave by the front door because they had access to the back door."

"Like an employee," Sawyer said. "I know. Working on that. Also, we've put out word that there's a reward. Five grand. That might help."

Luke hit a key on the computer so that it booted up.

Jack groaned. "Let me guess. We're going to watch all of the video."

Luke turned up the volume. Jack sighed and took a seat. "Yeah. We're going to watch all of the video."

Two hours later, they'd watched people come and go from the building and it'd yielded nothing but a gut ache from all the soda and chips they'd consumed from the vending machine down the hall.

"Can I go to sleep now?" Jack asked, yawning wide.

Luke's phone rang. His commander. *Shit.*

Jack looked at him. "Problem?"

Luke answered. "Hanover."

"Tell me you're here in San Francisco," the commander's voice boomed, loud enough for Jack to wince.

"Not yet," Luke said.

The commander's response was a string of oaths. "What the hell are you doing there?"

"I'm still on vacay," Luke said. "Resting."

"If only," Jack muttered.

"Resting," his commander repeated.

"I'll be back in town for the internal review on Monday," Luke said.

"See that you are or don't bother coming back at all."

Luke opened his mouth, but the line was dead. He thought about what would happen if he left town now. He'd get to keep his job—a job that, until recently, had defined him. *Still* defined him, even if he felt he'd let everyone in San Francisco down.

But if he left now, Ali was possibly going to be arrested for a crime she didn't commit.

"If you get yourself fired," Jack said, "you could—"

"No," Luke said.

"You don't even know what I was going to say."

"I don't care. I'm not going to get fired."

Jack sipped his soda and thumbed one-handed through his phone for a minute.

From inside Luke's pocket, his own phone vibrated. He pulled it out, saw the incoming text from Jack, and slid him a look. "Really? You texted me?"

Jack opened a package of peanut M&M's. He tossed one up in the air and caught it in his mouth.

Luke shook his head and read the text out loud. "Take a job here in Lucky Harbor." He looked at Jack. *"What?"*

Jack shrugged. "You know you want to stay close to Ali."

"I can't."

"Why?"

Luke sighed and scrubbed a hand over his face. "I'm not right for her."

Jack coughed and said "bullshit" at the same time.

"Look," Luke said, "I'm on a roll right now with screwing things up. I'll disappoint her. In fact, I already have. She deserves better."

"She deserves to be allowed to make up her own mind," Jack said. Then he shrugged again. "Or you can just keep things all fucked up, retire, and then paddleboard for the rest of your life. You know, if real life is too hard for you."

After her ceramic class at the junior college, Ali drove through town toward the beach house. It was a dark night, a jet-black sky littered with stars that twinkled like diamonds. She headed up the hill, getting more and more tense until she pulled into Luke's driveway. At the sight of his truck there, she let out the breath she hadn't realized that she'd been holding.

He was still here.

Not for long, she reminded herself, and got out. She waved at Edward, who was getting out of the Dial-A-Ride van.

"You hanging in there?" Edward asked.

"Always."

He smiled at her clearly standard response, but his surprisingly sharp eyes said he wasn't

266

fooled. "You're a sweet girl," he said, "sticking around to watch out for him."

She let out a low, mirthless laugh. "You have that backward, don't you? You know that Luke watches out for himself."

Edward nodded. "He does. He also watches out for everyone else, always."

She knew this to be true. She'd managed to hold onto some good resentment when it came to Luke thanks to their last conversation, but she found herself softening now.

"But I'm really talking about his heart," Edward said. "You're watching out for his heart. No one does that. He doesn't usually allow it. But he's allowed it with you. Either you pushed him into it, as his grandmother always did with her nosiness, or he cares about you. A lot."

Ali slowly shook her head. "I think you've misunderstood—"

"You care for him, too."

"Well, of course," she said. *Way too much.* "But—"

"No use backtracking now. It's all over your face."

She sighed. "Anyone ever tell you that you're a little nosy too?"

He smiled. "You'll do, Ali. You'll do. Here's some advice—he thinks he's so big and bad, thinks that nothing can get to him. But we both know otherwise. He's been hurt and disappointed by people who've claimed to care about him. You won't do that. You love him. You're good for him."

She stared at him. "I don't—" She closed her mouth, her heart picking up speed. She couldn't find her words. "We're not . . ." She shook her head and spoke the one truth she knew for a fact. "He's leaving."

"You're good for him," Edward repeated with utter steel. "We all see it."

She was almost afraid to ask. "Who's all?"

"I take it you don't go to Facebook very much." He smiled again. "Probably for the best."

Shaken, Ali went inside. The house was empty, but Luke had painted the living room. She walked through the kitchen, where her attention was caught by a movement outside the window. She grabbed a flashlight and headed out to the dock, finding Luke sitting there in the dark, feet dangling in the water, head tipped up, staring at the stars as if they held the secrets of the universe.

There was a bottle of Scotch at his side. "What are you doing?" she asked.

"Drinking."

Hmmm. She sat next to him and eyed the bottle. One-third gone. She eyed Luke. Probably also one-third gone. He'd been on the water, she guessed, given that he was in his board shorts, which were so low tonight as to be almost indecent. His long-sleeved T-shirt was thin and fit to his leanly muscled torso, his mouth turned up in a trouble-filled smile as he studied her right back.

He looked like sex walking, and at just the thought, her body quivered. "I'm mad at you."

"You might have to get in line," he said. He hesitated. "I'm sorry I was a dick."

She sighed. "You weren't. I care about you, Luke."

Tilting his head up, he met her gaze, his own fathomless. "Ali—"

"I care," she repeated. "But I'm not going to let what I feel for you—no matter how it turns out—define my happiness. No one but me can do that."

He looked at her for a long moment, then the corners of his mouth quirked. "You're the strongest person I know, did you know that?"

She stared at him, stunned. "No."

"You are." He tipped the bottle back and took a long swallow. When he was done, she held out her hand for the bottle.

With an amused glint in his eye, he handed it over.

It took less than a second for the liquor to burn a hole clear to her belly, and she coughed.

He patted her on the back and took the bottle back, and also another shot. She looked at his profile, barely outlined by the night sky, and felt her heart clench. Either she was having a heart attack or everyone else was right—she really was falling for him hard and fast. "Do you believe in love?" she asked.

It was his turn to choke, and he lowered the bottle, swiping his mouth with his arm as he stared at her.

"I'm just asking," she said quickly. "Not declaring or anything."

"Okay, but *why* are you asking?"

Fair enough question, but she'd sort of hoped he'd let it go. "People keep suggesting that maybe I'm falling for you."

He stared at her. "I don't think I'm authorized to have this conversation."

"Hey, I'm not saying it's true or anything," she said defensively. *Sheesh.* "But I guess now I know how you feel about it."

He caught her when she would have made her escape, moving faster than a man with a third of a bottle of Scotch in him should be able to move. He held her next to him on the dock in the dark, with the crickets singing and the water slapping up against the pylons below them.

So peaceful. So devastatingly peaceful.

"I enjoy your company," he finally said.

She turned her head and gave him a glare— wasted on him because he was staring out at the water as if transfixed.

"I even crave it," he said, sounding insultingly surprised. "More than I'd thought possible."

"Well gee," she said, "thanks."

He looked at her then. "But much as I do, you know that this isn't leading to a walk down the aisle, a tricycle in the yard, or us getting old and sharing dentures."

"Do people actually do that? Share dentures?" The alcohol had made its way through her system now so that she felt nice and . . . buzzed. "Because that's kind of ick . . ."

"Ali."

"Yeah." She blew out a breath and nodded. "I guess I knew all that already, since we're supposedly not going to have more sex, even though we already blew that." She paused. "But tell me again why we're supposedly not going to have more sex?"

He paused, like he was having trouble remembering himself. "Because someone's going to get hurt."

"Ah." She nodded and was relieved to find that Scotch was good for more than just a buzz. It worked as a numbing agent as well. "Something we can agree on then, because that does happen to me. Sex, then hurt. Every time so far, actually."

He turned his head, his eyes reflecting regret and sorrow. "Ali—"

Not wanting sympathy, she grabbed the Scotch and toasted him. "To . . ." She broke off and considered. "Not having any more mind-blowing sex." She took another sip. This one didn't burn nearly as badly. In fact, it went down smoothly, and a delicious warmth began to spread within her.

Luke let out a low laugh and took the bottle back from her.

"You think I'm funny?" she asked.

"No. I think you're dangerous as hell. And sexy as hell. And smart as hell, smarter than me." He toasted her now. "To you, Ali."

"For what? Driving you crazy?"

"Well, you are *very* good at it," he said.

Now she laughed, and tried to reach for the bottle again, but she missed. *Huh.* And that's when she noticed that her vision was blurry. She blinked, but it didn't help, so she used both hands to try to make a double-fisted grab for the bottle and *still* missed.

He grinned. "You're wrecked."

"Am not." Little bit . . . "So what's the pity party about?"

"Not a pity party." The alcohol hadn't seemed to affect him all that greatly, though the way he was easily slouched back on the dock was evidence he was feeling pretty damn relaxed.

"All alone on the dock with a bottle of booze feels like a pity party," she said. "What's the matter?"

He looked at her for a minute and then shook his head. "What the hell, you're not going to remember this anyway."

"I'm not *that* drunk."

"Yeah you are. You're a lightweight."

She'd have attempted to dispute that, but her tongue wasn't cooperating. "Tell me."

"It's Thursday."

"All day," she agreed with a nod. In truth, she couldn't remember *what* day it was.

"I have to go to San Francisco by this weekend," Luke said.

"To visit?"

"No. I'm visiting here. I'm going back to stay."

Her smile faded. "Oh," she said softly, "right." She'd almost forgotten there for a minute.

He tossed back another shot.

She grabbed the bottle and did the same, and then went to set it down—or at least that's what she meant to do, but she missed the dock and it fell into the water below.

She stared down at the black, choppy water swirling beneath them. "Whoops."

He stared at the water too. "I wasn't done with that."

"I'm so sorry!" She turned to fully face him, surprised to find her world spinning good now. Apparently she *was* a lightweight. "Want to go in after it?"

"Hell no. That water is damn cold tonight."

She looked up into his face, taking in the square, scruffy jaw, the mouth that could be both firm and soft, the eyes that missed nothing, and felt her breath catch.

He was leaving.

And her mom and Edward were right. She *was* in love with him. "Luke?"

"Yeah?"

"You're so pretty."

He smiled. It was an uninhibited smile. A wolf smile. And it made her nipples get very perky. "I think I'm indicated."

"Intoxicated?"

"Yeah, that."

His smile widened.

Oh my, she thought, heart fluttering at the sight. Trying to be cool, she leaned back and ended up going the same way as the Scotch—ass over kettle backward into the waves.

Luke was right, she thought with a gasp that filled her mouth with water. The ocean was damn cold tonight.

Chapter 19

"Shit," Luke said, rising to his feet as Ali surfaced, sputtered, and went back under. "Shit," he said again, and dove into the water after her.

The shock of the cold water sucked the air from his lungs as he hauled Ali into his arms, treading water for the both of them.

She was shivering, but not hurt or scared—or so he assumed by the way she laughed with abandon and wrapped her arms around his neck.

"You didn't have to come in," she said. "I can swim."

Except she wasn't. Still laughing, she was holding onto him, making no attempt to keep herself afloat. Her sundress clung to her skin, and her hair lay in dark tendrils on her shoulders.

And his.

"You weren't kidding about the water," she said. Clueless to the fact that he was the only thing holding her up, she wrapped herself around him like Saran Wrap. "Are you okay?" she asked.

"I'll let you know when my balls defrost."

This set her off laughing again, and she dropped her head to his chest.

Shaking his head and smiling in spite of

himself, he gathered her in close and got them both to the shore. When he dragged her out of the water, she dropped to her knees.

"That was fun," she said. "Let's do it again."

He took in her grinning face. Her eyes were shining as bright as the stars, and just looking at her was a kick in the gut.

He was leaving.

How was he going to leave her?

And why did it matter so much? They'd known each other for a blink in time. But already she was a tie, binding him here to this place he loved so much. He felt his mouth curve in genuine amusement when she stared at him. "Whoa," she said, "you're making my world spin."

"Pretty sure that's the Scotch," he said, but he dropped to his knees next to her.

She leaned into him, letting out a soft, dreamy sigh. "I'm pretty sure it's you," she said softly. Then she cupped his face, pulled it to hers, and kissed him, long and hot and wet.

He let himself get lost in her for a deliciously long moment, then pulled free. "You're toasted."

"Mmm . . . toast," she purred. "I really like peanut butter toast. When I first moved out on my own, I used to eat peanut butter for dinner 'cuz it was cheap. I'd stick a spoon in the jar and lick it slowly, like a lollipop, to make it last."

He felt his heart clench again, hard. And utterly unable to help himself, he tugged her back in and kissed her again. She tasted of Scotch and warm, sweet Ali. And something else.

She tasted like his.

"You know," she said very seriously, "you're all wet."

He laughed.

She grinned up at him, clearly pleased at the sound. She spread her arms and lay back, eyeing the sky. "You don't see this many stars in White Center, you know. Too many lights. Plus going outside at night was a huge, big, no-no. My cousin Lacey went outside at night once, to get her schoolbooks out of her mom's car, and never came back."

"Jesus," he said, all amusement fading. "What happened?"

With a sigh, she closed her eyes. "They found her body two days later in the river."

He leaned over her, stroking the wet hair from her face. He wanted to erase all the bad in her world and leave only the good, but as he was a part of the bad, he had no idea how to do that. "Tell me they caught the guy," he said.

"It was her boyfriend. Turned out, he'd won a big pile of cash at the slots that day, and she'd stolen it from him." She sighed again, maybe thinking about the money she was accused of stealing. "Can I have another shot?"

"It's gone." He stroked the wet hair from her face. "And besides, that's not what you need."

"No?"

"No," he said, and picked her up into his arms.

"Oh," she said, clutching at him. "Are you taking me in, Officer?"

"Yes."

"Are you gonna interrogate me?"

"No, you're going to exercise your right to be silent." He carried her into the house, set her down by her bed and stared at her sundress, which was clinging to her like a second skin.

A *sheer* skin, and there were no buttons or zipper on the front.

"I don't do silent so well," she said.

No shit.

"Maybe you should get out your cuffs," she said kinda hopefully.

His body went from zero to sixty at the image of her cuffed to his bed, begging him to take her however he wanted.

And he wanted. He wanted her in every possible way. With a hand to her hips, he turned her away from him and finally located a zipper. He slid it down and gulped.

No bra.

Thong panties.

Close your eyes, asshole, he told himself as he peeled the drenched and clinging dress down her curvy bod.

But he didn't close his eyes.

Biting back the groan at the perfection in front of him, he reached past her, pulled the blankets down, and poured her into the bed.

"Can't go to bed with wet hair," she said, rolling to her back, exposing her breasts. "It'll get crazy."

He wasn't sure how she could tell the difference, but he loved her crazy hair. "It's good," he said, stroking it from her face.

"Really?"

"Really." Her nipples were hard, two perfect gumdrops, and his mouth watered. He yanked the covers up to her chin. *There.* He was sweating, and feeling like he should be awarded a medal for being a saint.

Ali made a soft, disagreeable sound and kicked the blankets off, revealing her glorious body again. And then, before he could stop her, she grabbed his hand and tugged until he fell on top of her.

Well, okay, so he *could* have stopped her, but he didn't, and he didn't really want to think about that, because then she wrapped her arms and legs around him, holding him there.

"Mmm," she said dreamily.

He let out a low laugh against her temple and tried to extricate himself, but every time he freed a limb, she tightened another. She was silent through this, eyes closed. Then suddenly she opened them and looked right into his. "You haven't left yet."

Sucker punched right in the gut because he knew she didn't mean right this moment. She meant that the men in her life left her. All of them. "It's my house," he teased, not in any shape to have this conversation.

But she didn't laugh, and that took him aback. He stopped trying to free himself. "Ali," he said, low. Desperate. "I'm trying to do the right thing here."

"Well, don't." She rocked up into him and moaned.

The sound gave him a rush. "You're going to sleep," he said firmly.

"Who will keep my feet warm?"

"I'll get you an extra blanket."

"A stick in the mud," she muttered. "Who'd have thought that the hot, sexy Luke Hanover's nothing but a stick in the mud?"

"You'll thank me in the morning." Again he pulled the blanket up to her chin, firmly tucking her in so that he wasn't tempted to do anything stupid.

"My panties are wet."

He dropped his forehead to hers.

"And my shoes are still on."

He sat back on his heels. Again she kicked the covers off and lifted her foot for him to remove her sandal.

He pressed her foot to his chest and went to work on the buckle over her ankle, doing his damnedest not to notice that her panties were as sheer as her dress had been.

A white lace thong that barely covered her mound.

She smiled up at him, her eyes soft and dreamy and glazed over. He felt the helpless smile curve his mouth in return. "You're trouble," he said. "You know that?"

"I've been told."

An innocent response, but it reminded him of exactly how often she'd been disappointed and hurt. He was *not* going to be one of those men. Ever.

"I also tend to drive people crazy," she said. "Especially men. I drove all my mom's men right off. She'd say 'Oh, Ali-gator, there goes another one.' I'm pretty good at doing it to my own men too, driving them off." She sat up and tried to pile her hair on top of her head using the hair band she'd had around her wrist, but she was having some coordination issues. And then the thing got stuck in her hair, so there she sat, in her barely there panties, arms up over her head, hands entangled in her hair, looking like a walking/talking wet dream.

"Luke?"

Deciding it was safest to leave her hands restrained, he ignored her, the same way he was trying to ignore the unintentionally gut-wrenching tales of her life, as he fought her sandal off.

"Hey," she said, tugging on her hair.

"Hey, yourself." When he finally got her sandals off, he leaned in carefully to take over the hair fiasco. He managed some sort of bun, though it was lopsided.

She smiled at him in gratitude, all flushed, a little damp, and looking hotter than anything he could possibly imagine. "Kiss me, Luke."

A demanding drunk, he thought, amused, and gave her a short, sweet smackeroo.

But he'd greatly underestimated her determination.

"Mmm," she said, wrapping him up tight in her arms, deepening the kiss, drawing him into her nefarious plans like a moth to the flame. He let her have her way—hell, who was he kidding, he probably wanted it even more than she did—but when she slid her hands beneath his shirt and then paused, he sucked in a breath. A few moments ago he'd been trying to extract himself but now all he could think was: *Up or down, Ali?*

She chose up first, brushing his nipples, tugging a low groan from him. Then down, over his abs and farther, her fingers playing with the tie on his board shorts.

When she tugged, he caught her hands and pinned them above her head. He had no idea where the hell he found the strength, but he couldn't let her do this. He kept trying not to get sucked in by her.

And kept failing. But she had the singular ability to both break his heart and make him yearn and burn.

He'd told Sara she was work, but she wasn't work at all. Nor was she a vacation diversion.

She was . . . real. The first real thing in his life in far too long.

Ali fought a hand free and touched his face. "You're a good man, Luke, you know that?"

With a groan, he tried to concentrate on anything besides the sexy, warm woman beneath him. Her curves were pressed up against him, chest to chest, hips to hips, thighs to thighs.

But that's not what was grabbing him by the throat and holding on. As always, it was her eyes. And all the things he could see there, which was everything, every single thing, including the fact that she cared about him.

Far more than he deserved.

He dropped his head to the pillow beside hers, thinking here she was, all sweet and sleepy, snuggling up to him. And here *he* was, wanting to fuck her until she screamed his name.

Some good guy.

"Ali." She didn't answer.

He lifted his head to kiss her goodnight because he *was* leaving.

Right now.

But caressing her hair from her face, he had to laugh softly. Her eyes were closed, her mouth slightly open, her limbs loose and relaxed.

She was fast asleep.

And he hurt just looking at her. Pressing his lips to her temple, he breathed her in. "You're perfect," he whispered, "just the way you are."

Chapter 20

Lucky Harbor was a town of hearty souls, and they rose early, whether for work or play. Ali had always been one of those early risers too, but this morning, she tried to get up and could only groan in misery.

"Yeah. Thought you might be having trouble."

Along with Luke's dry tone came the scent of coffee. Ali whimpered in gratitude and cracked open an eye. "Why is the world spinning?"

"Because alcohol is a finicky bitch." Luke set a cup of coffee on the nightstand. "You going to live?"

Not at all certain, she sat up, clutching the covers to herself as it all came back. Last night. The Scotch. Falling into the water . . . She took a peek beneath the covers. Just a thong. "Oh God, I'm naked."

"Not quite," Luke said. "And not for lack of trying either."

She stared up at him, remembering everything but completely unable to get a read on his mood. He was dressed for paddleboarding, looking like a Greek god. "You didn't want me."

"Wrong. I just prefer my women conscious."

His board shorts were lifeguard red today, down to his knees and frayed at the hem. "You were a lifeguard?" she asked.

"Yeah, with Jack and Ben. But only because we got to sit on the beach and look at girls in bikinis all day. It was a no-brainer."

He could still fit into a bathing suit from ten years ago, which was a good reason to hate him. That, and the fact that he didn't appear to be the slightest bit hungover. Where was the justice in that? "Who got the most girls?"

"Ben. He had his dad's truck and a black Lab pup named Ketchup. Both Ketchup and the truck were babe magnets."

"You should have gotten a dog."

He smiled sexily, as if the memories were that good. "I did okay."

She bet.

"I have news," he said.

Uh-oh. "Good or bad?"

"I wanted to tell you last night, but you fell asleep on me," he said without answering her question. "There's nothing on the surveillance tapes."

She absorbed the hit of it and shook her head. "I'm not going to get lucky today in bed or out of it, is that what you're saying?"

At the look of regret on his face, she blew out her breath. "Forget it. I know, you're leaving and you don't want anyone to get hurt, blah, blah,

blah. And anyway, I might be getting arrested today, so it doesn't matter. I hope Zach isn't in L.A." Not wanting to face him, or the fact that her heart had tightened painfully, she plopped to her back and covered her head.

"Ali, we're going to figure this out."

She felt her heart squeeze at the "we." She knew he believed that, but she wasn't sure she did.

"Ali."

She closed her eyes. "I'd like to be alone," she said softly. She needed to get used to that.

"Ali—"

"Please, Luke." And whether it was the threat of tears in her voice or something else, she heard him go. She rolled over and fell back into a fitful sleep, and this time when she woke up, the sun was a little higher and she felt a little more human.

She was also alone. She staggered out of bed, and as she got ready for work, there was only one call from a reporter. Progress.

She drove to the flower shop. It was locked up and dark, which was odd since it'd been Russell's one morning a week to open.

But Russell was still sitting in his car, sipping from a to-go coffee mug, staring pensively at the shop. Ali slid into his passenger seat, making him jerk in startled surprise and spill his coffee.

"Crap," he said, looking down at the stain spreading over his trousers.

"Go ahead." She handed him a napkin. "Just tell me."

"Tell you what?"

"That you're closing the shop."

Russell let out a long breath. "I'm sorry, Sweetkins. I should have told you, I know. But God, the thought of disappointing you . . ."

He'd done exactly that by keeping it from her, but she didn't add to his burden by saying so. "Are you sure about this?" she asked softly. "Really, really sure?"

He nodded solemnly, but his eyes were lit with excitement. "I leave in a few days. Paul's ecstatic, said he can't wait. He needs me."

And Russell needed out of Lucky Harbor. She understood. She really did. But she stared with longing at the building, which was exuding quirky charm and ambiance despite the dark windows that broke her heart. She'd give just about anything to be in a position to take over the flower shop.

"Heard there's probably going to be an arrest soon," Russell said quietly.

"Yeah."

"Want to talk about it?"

There was something in his voice, and she turned her head to his, a funny feeling in her stomach. "I didn't do it."

"Of course not, Kitten."

She swallowed the hurt, because that's what

she did. When she fell down, she picked herself up without waiting for a helping hand. And though she now had the new panic of being unemployed burning a hole in her esophagus, she eyed the notebook on the dash.

The. Notebook.

Russell was a complete technophobe. He had his entire client base in that notebook, not to mention his bookkeeping records handwritten in purple ink in his bold scrawl.

And it was all right there . . . "Russell, I have a question."

He tensed a little. "Okay."

He looked worried, like maybe she was going to ask him to help her hide the damn money. She bit back the frustration and the urge to spill his coffee again. "What if I wanted to buy the flower shop?"

"I don't own the actual store, you know that. I lease the spot. And I got out of the lease last night. I talked to the owner; Mr. Lyons was a hard-ass about it, but . . ."

Ali stared at him. "Mr. Lyons owns the building? *My* Mr. Lyons, from the senior center?"

"Honey, he owns half this street. He's also Aubrey's great uncle. You didn't know?"

"No . . ." Ali's mind started racing. "And I didn't mean I wanted to buy the physical space . . ." Though if she could, she'd love to lease it. "I meant your book."

He sucked in a breath and put a hand to his chest as if she'd shot him. "My book?"

"Well, that and the rest of your records. The business. If I took it over . . ."

"Sweetkins, the shop is done. There's just no money in it."

She didn't want to hurt his feelings, so she picked her words carefully. "I think I could make a go of it."

Russell studied her for a long moment, then smiled. "You know what? I think you're right."

"So how much?"

"I'll have to think about it. I need start-up money for the new salon Paul and I want to run in Vegas."

Ali tried not to think too much on her way home. But it really started to hit her. She was thoroughly unemployed. "But you haven't been arrested," she told herself in the rearview mirror. Her reflection didn't smile. It wasn't funny. In fact, panic gnawed at her gut, but it was beaten back by the sight of a man in Luke's driveway. He was aiming his phone at her as she parked, clearly trying to take a picture.

"Hey!" she yelled at him. "Stop that."

He didn't stop. He clicked a series of shots. "I'm looking for Luke Hanover," he said as he kept snapping pictures. "I'd like to get him as well."

"You're trespassing," she told him, fresh out

of patience, calm, or anything nice. "Go away."

He didn't, so Ali put the truck in neutral and revved her engine, intending to intimidate. But her engine coughed like a weenie, and her gas gauge jerked toward empty. Dammit. Understanding the phrase "going postal," she put the truck into gear, and this time the guy lowered his phone and took off running.

Satisfied, Ali shoved the truck into park, but before she could open her door, Luke was right there, offering her a hand, mouth curved into a barely there smile. "Nice job, Tex."

"He was looking for you," she said. "He wanted a picture. Not going to happen on my watch."

He cocked his head, his gaze running over her features, which she carefully schooled into a blank expression. "Yeah, I'm getting that," he said slowly. "You okay?"

"One hundred percent."

"Were you really going to run him over?"

"I was going to flatten him like a pancake."

He nodded. "You're fierce as hell, you know that? Remind me to never get on your bad side."

"Not that that's a real worry, since you're leaving. Right?"

He looked at her for another long beat. "Ali—"

"Nope." She shook her head and started inside the house. "Sorry, I've gotta—"

He caught her hand and pulled her back around.

"Look," she said, "you're the lone wolf. I get it.

And also, I'm sorry if I hit on you last night."
She grimaced. "*And* all the time. I know how
awkward it must be to have to constantly fight
me off."

His sharp, blue eyes never wavered from her
face. "Not what I was going to say."

"No?"

"No. And I'm not fighting you off. What I'm
fighting off is my urge to toss you down to the
grass right here and show you who wants who."

Her girlie parts perked right up. *Stupid girlie
parts.*

Tightening his grip on her, he reeled her in.
"Now tell me what's wrong."

She let out a shaky breath. "Russell closed the
shop. I'm unemployed."

"Aw, hell." He gathered her in against him. She
resisted for about two seconds, and then caved
like a cheap suitcase, because there was nothing
better than a Luke Hanover full-body hug.

"I'm sorry," he said, kissing her forehead.

Closing her eyes, she just breathed him in,
unable to respond. As big a blow as the closing
of the shop was, not to mention Russell's moving
away, having Luke exit her life was going to be
the biggest loss of all.

Luke walked Ali inside, wishing like hell he
knew how to make this better for her. He'd always
been careful to go into any given situation know-

ing the rules; in his job, his dating life, everything.

But from the moment Ali had come into his life, he hadn't understood a damn thing. Feeling helpless, he stood there in the center of the kitchen. "You hungry?"

She gave him a small smile. "You don't cook."

"No, but I'm an expert at take-out—"

A horn honked out front at the same time that Luke's phone rang. He pulled it from his pocket: Jack.

"Get your ass out here," Jack said. "Your grandpa's on his way to the ER. Chest pains. I'll drive."

Luke looked around for his keys but gave up. He grabbed Ali's hand and pulled her with him out the front door. "Come on."

"What's wrong?"

He was moving fast, forcing her to run to keep up. "It's Edward—"

They both stopped short at the sight of the Lucky Harbor Dial-A-Ride white van in the driveway. Jack rolled down the window and waved for them to hurry. The side door was open.

"What the—" Luke stared at the other passengers: Mr. Lyons, Mr. Elroy, and Mr. Wykowski.

"Everyone wanted to go," Jack said. "You coming today or tomorrow?"

Luke shook his head and gestured Ali in. He'd barely snapped his seatbelt when Jack hit the gas. "How bad?" he asked.

"He was conscious and responsive when he was loaded at the senior center," Jack said.

"He'd just driven us back from bingo," Mr. Lyons said. "We were talking about the new rec center, and the ground-breaking ceremony tomorrow, and how nice it was to build new things. He was talking about Fay, and his son—your dad, of course—and also you kids. You and Sara. He said something about how old things need to be respected too. Old things like family ties. And then he clutched at his damn heart . . ." Mr. Lyons's voice broke. Tightening his lips, he turned his head and stared resolutely out the window.

Luke glanced at Ali, who stared back at him, her eyes shimmering with unshed tears as she reached out and clasped his hand. He stared down at their entangled fingers and thought *if that old fart dies before I get there, I'll kill him* . . . "I've got to call Sara," he said.

"Done," Jack said.

"You called her first?"

"I like her better." Jack met Luke's eyes in the rearview mirror. "And I came for you in person. That has to count for something."

"You called her first," Luke repeated in disbelief.

Jack blew out a sigh. "Okay, yeah. I called her first. A couple of years ago, she made me promise that if anything ever happened to him, I'd call her immediately."

"Before me."

"*You* didn't make me promise," Jack pointed out. "And anyway, everyone knows chicks are better at this shit, man. She's getting on a flight. We need her here. *You* need her."

They made it to the ER and sat in the waiting room, waiting on news. Several hours later, Sara ran in.

Tall, athletically lean, with her blue eyes filled with worry, she walked right into Luke's arms.

"Nothing yet," he told her. "We're waiting on tests. They haven't let us see him."

Sara nodded and sniffed, wiping her nose on his shirt. He let that one go and introduced her to Ali.

"Sorry," Sara said, swiping beneath her eyes. "I see Luke, and I always cry. It's a silly reaction, but I just always know that when he's in charge, it's all going to be okay, you know?"

"It *is* going to be okay," Luke said.

Sara gave Ali a soggy smile. "See?"

A few minutes later, the doctor came out. "Intestinal distress," Dr. Josh Scott said.

They all just stared at him.

"I'm sorry," Luke said. "What?"

"He didn't have a heart attack," he said. "He ate two pastrami on rye sandwiches, three large dill pickles, and an entire bag of spicy Cheetos. He had indigestion."

Sara grinned broadly. "Sounds like grandpa."

Dr. Scott shook his head. "He has dangerously

high cholesterol, and we're setting him up with a dietician. But otherwise he's as healthy as an ox."

Luke was the first to go in to see him. Edward was propped up on his hospital bed eating Jell-O.

"You've got to be kidding me," Luke said.

Edward frowned. "Don't take that tone with me. I could have died today."

"You had gas."

Edward pointed the spoon at him. "But you didn't know that. Were you worried?"

"No."

Edward gave him a small, knowing smile. "Liar."

Since Luke's legs were suddenly wobbling from relief, he sank to the side of his grandpa's bed and scrubbed his hands over his face. "You scared the shit out of me."

"Why, because you nearly let me die without fulfilling your promise to Sara?"

Luke dropped his hands from his face. "What promise?"

"To give me a hug."

"You want a *hug*," Luke said with disbelief.

"You deaf, boy?"

Luke stared at him. "If I hug you, do you promise not to die on me?"

Edward's smirk faded, and he set the Jell-O down. "I promise not to die today. How's that?"

"Good enough," Luke said, and hugged him tight.

Chapter 21

That night Sara stayed in Lucky Harbor at Luke's house. Ali made omelets while watching brother and sister, fascinated by their relationship.

Sara was at the table, flipping through one of Fay's old photo albums. "Jeez," she said to Luke, "here's one of you up in a pine tree on the bluffs. What were you, Luke, ten? Grandma had just told you not to climb any, remember? So of course, Ben dared you, and you climbed a damn tree. You got up about forty feet and then froze. We had to call the fire department, and Jack's dad had to come with his ladder truck and save you. You were such an idiot."

"Thanks," Luke said.

He'd been quiet, very quiet, and Ali knew that the worry about his grandfather had left him exhausted.

"Here's another one," Sara said, pointing to the next page. "You tried to windglide from the roof straight into the water, you freakazoid. Look, remember that? You broke an arm and a leg. You're lucky you didn't crack your skull." She paused. "Probably because your head's too thick to break."

Luke gave a small, distracted shake of his "thick" head but didn't say anything.

Sara gave him a worried glance before flipping through the pages some more, and Ali realized Luke's sister wasn't trying to bait him for the hell of it, she was trying to coax him out of his mood. Her heart melting for both of them, Ali brought over two plates with omelets. She stroked a hand over Luke's shoulders and felt the tight knot of taut muscles, so she stopped to rub his neck.

With a grateful sigh, he dropped his head forward to give her room to work, eyes closed, silent.

Sara stood up. "Be right back." Two minutes later, she came back in with two stacks of files—one large, one small—and plopped them down onto the table.

"What's this?" Luke asked.

"I didn't want to tell you, but I stopped in to see Craig."

Luke narrowed his eyes. "You stopped in on my commander?"

"No, I stopped in on my ex-boyfriend," Sara said. "I knew him first, if you'll remember, and he wasn't your commander back then. I borrowed these from him." She pointed to the first stack of files, which was a foot thicker than the other stack. "Know what those are?"

"Your criminal records?"

"Funny, har-har," Sara said. "They're the cases

you've closed. The cases you solved. The cases filled with scores and scores of people whose lives you changed for the better."

She pointed to the much, *much* smaller stack. "Those you can pout about. Those are your supposed failures. Without that stack, without you being good at your job, this stack—" She tapped the big one, "—these people's lives would be destroyed. So take a good, hard look, Luke, and tell me that you don't always do your absolute best. That you didn't give each and every one of your cases a little piece of your heart and soul."

She paused, and when she spoke further, her voice was softer and very, very gentle. "You didn't fail grandma. You certainly have never failed me. And you didn't kill Isabel Reyes. Say it. Say that you know you're a good man, the best man I know. That there's still enough heart and soul left inside you to go on. Because if you've given up, Luke, I don't know what I'll do. I'll . . ." Her voice broke.

Looking pained, Luke reached for her.

She curled into him. "*Tell me,* Luke."

"I'm okay," he said gruffly.

Sara lifted her head and searched his gaze. "Really?"

"Really."

"Okay." She nodded and sniffed. Then she stood up and gathered the files quickly, but Luke caught her before she could run off. "The files," he said. "They're not from Craig. He'd never have given them to you."

"Of course not," she said.

He shook his head. "What did you fill them with?"

She bit her lower lip. "An empty ream of paper from your printer."

"You're a nut," he said.

And then they ate omelets.

The next day at the ground-breaking ceremony, Luke watched the crowd, wondering if the thief was also watching. Just about everyone in Lucky Harbor was at the building site, where the early afternoon sun beat down on the empty lot and the masses, who were held back by a wide, yellow ribbon.

Ali was next to him, and they were off to one side, trying to lie low. On the other side of the ribbon, up on a makeshift platform of plywood, stood Tony and Bree Medina. The mayor and his wife were both holding shovels and smiling into the cameras. Near them were Ted Marshall and a handful of town council members. Bree was telling one of the council members about a show she'd recently seen, and Ali suddenly tensed.

"What?" Luke asked.

She sneezed. "That show," she whispered. "The one Bree's talking about? I found two ticket stubs to it in the key pot the night Teddy moved out." She sneezed again. "Sorry, it's her perfume. It gets me every"—sneeze—"time."

He squeezed her in close, pressing her face to his chest. She breathed in deeply and let out a soft, little "mmm," which shouldn't have done anything to him, but completely did. She was always trying to inhale him, as if the scent of him was the best thing she'd ever smelled. He felt the same about her. "You okay?"

She set her head on his shoulder. "I was going to ask you the same thing."

"I'm fine." She'd been incredibly gentle with him since yesterday, when they'd rushed to the hospital for his grandfather. Quiet, warm . . . a solid presence in his life.

But now the clock was ticking down.

He knew he'd been quiet and withdrawn. Knew, too, that Ali thought it was because of his grandfather. And it was.

Some of it.

The rest was because he was trying to wrap his brain around the fact that he was leaving . . . and didn't want to be.

He scanned the crowd and then eyed the platform again, watching Marshall wave at the crowd, charming everyone in his path. Tony and Bree moved across the stage, both of them soaking up the crowd's attention. And suddenly his eyes locked in on a most interesting thing.

Unable to believe it, he turned to Ali, who tore her gaze off Bree and met his gaze, her own wide.

She'd seen it too.

Bree was beautiful and always very carefully made-up, complete with designer clothes and torture devices on her feet masquerading as high-heeled sandals. Her toes were easily visible, as was the very clear tan line across her second right one. She'd worn a ring there, recently, and long enough for it to leave a definite impression.

"Oh my God," Ali whispered. "It's her!"

"It's as circumstantial as the bill band being in your possession," he warned her.

She was smiling. "Yes, but . . ."

He smiled back. "Yeah. *But.*" It was good. Really good. Bree was blonde. Bree would have had access to the back door the night of the auction. She would have parked in the back, in employee parking, and not gone out the front door. And the coup de grace—she had clearly been wearing a toe ring and wasn't now.

They escaped through the crowd and went back to the house. Luke went straight to his computer and his magic search programs.

Ali leaned over his shoulder, her hand resting on his bicep. He resisted the urge to flex like a caveman and toss her over his shoulder and drag her to his bedroom. Instead he typed in Bree Medina and then stared at the screen. "Well, hello."

"What?"

"She filed divorce papers two months ago."

"Divorce?"

"Yeah, and then . . ." He scrolled down. "She withdrew it. She withdrew the papers on . . ." He let out a slow whistle.

Ali leaned in closer. A strand of her hair caught on his jaw. She smelled great.

"Wow," she said. "She withdrew the divorce two days after the money went missing." Turning her head, she stared at him. "What does that mean?"

"Something made her want to leave the mayor," he said, "and then something changed her mind. Maybe she thought she'd found someone better."

"Better than the mayor?"

"Tony Medina's a good guy," Luke said, "but look at Bree. She keeps herself up. She's forty-five and looks twenty-five. Tony's a balding, paunchy, fifty-year-old who works twenty-four seven." He met Ali's gaze. "Maybe Bree got lonely or bored. And then maybe she also got distracted by a younger man, a walk on the wild side, someone who gave her something Tony's money couldn't—the feeling of being young and alive."

Like you do for me . . .

"You're thinking she was also fooled by Teddy."

"You said Aubrey thought *she* was Marshall's one and only," he said. "But what if Bree thought so too? What if Bree thought it was the real

302

deal? So she files for divorce, and then she discovers Marshall's screwing other women and gets ticked."

"And then tries to frame him for taking the money."

"It's a lot of maybes," Luke warned. "And I'm just thinking out loud here, but I bet I'm in the ballpark."

Ali was looking revved up and ready to kick some ass. Loving that fight in her, he tugged her into his lap and nuzzled the sweet spot on her neck, the one that made her purr like a kitten.

"Mmm," she said in a soft, sexy moan, tilting her head to give him better access. Which he took, sucking on the soft skin just beneath her ear before working his way south. He *loved* the southlands . . .

Breathing heavily, she slid her fingers into his hair and arched into him. "We weren't going to do this again . . ."

"I know." Damn, he really did know. It'd been his idea. Stupidest idea he'd ever had. "Ali . . ."

She squirmed off his lap, and he felt the disappointment in every inch of his body. Some inches more than others.

But then Ali dropped to her knees between his sprawled legs and sent a slow smile up at him, stopping his heart. "Sometimes," she murmured, opening his jeans and reaching inside, "rules are made to be broken."

• • •

Much later, Ali lay on the kitchen table, a little sweaty and a whole lot delirious from pleasure. It took her five full minutes to catch her breath and roll onto her side to eyeball Luke.

He was still flat on his back on the table, too, eyes closed. He wore only his jeans, still opened, indecently low on his hips. He was sprawled out like a decadent dessert, the kind that was totally fattening, but was so good that you couldn't regret the calories. She ran a finger down the center of his chest to his abs, which contracted at her touch.

Eyes still closed, he groaned. "Okay, but you've got to feed me first. I'm a growing boy."

She stared at his erection. "I can see that . . ."

Snorting, he moved unexpectedly, and quick as lightning, he rolled onto her, pinning her to the table.

She pushed at his chest. "Hold on a second."

Pushing up to his elbow, he took his weight off of her and gave her a "what's up?" gaze from heavy-lidded eyes—his bedroom eyes.

"I've been thinking," she said. "I bet Bree hid the money at Teddy's place."

"You've been thinking? When? When could you have been thinking?"

"Earlier. But it makes sense, don't you think?" she pressed. "If her goal was to frame him, she'd want to—"

"Earlier? You mean earlier when I was buried so deep inside you that I could feel your tonsils as you screamed my name and—"

She covered his mouth and laughed. "I did not scream. Exactly. And what? Is my mind supposed to turn off?"

Looking a little bit out of sorts, he rolled off of her, and it made her laugh again.

"Sorry," she said, "women's brains are different."

"No shit."

They sat up, and she began pulling her clothes back on. "At this point, all we have is circumstantial. I heard that tomorrow Teddy and some of the town council members are going off for a team-bonding fishing overnighter. I'm going to wait until after I get back from my mom's birthday party and then go check out his place for the money."

"No," Luke said. "Hell, no. It's too dangerous. If you find the money there, everyone's going to think you planted it."

She warmed at his concern, but reminded herself not to get used to it. He hadn't said word one about seeing her after he left, and hell if she'd beg for crumbs. "I have nothing to lose. Everyone already thinks I stole the money. And I'll be careful, trust me." She shoved her feet into her sandals.

"Where are you going?" he asked.

"I want to talk to Aubrey."

"Wait for me." He pulled up his jeans and looked around, probably for his keys, which seemed to elude him daily, even though they were right there on the counter in the new key bowl she'd made.

"Can't wait," she said. "I'm on a tight schedule to stay out of jail."

He choked out a laugh. "You weren't on a tight schedule a few minutes ago."

"Well that was different. I got distracted by an orgasm."

He let out a very male smile of satisfaction. "*Three* orgasms. Pretty good for someone who was 'thinking.'" Leaning in, he kissed her. "You want to do this alone."

She needed to get used to alone. She met his gaze, wondering if he was going to even discuss it. His leaving. What might happen between them after he did.

But he said nothing.

"Yes," she said, "I need to do this. Alone."

"You don't have to."

"You're leaving, remember?"

His jaw tightened. "I'm not likely to forget."

She let out a breath. *Stay strong.* "Aubrey'll be far more likely to talk to me if I'm by myself."

Looking like he got it but didn't necessarily like it, he nodded. "Call Zach. Tell him about Bree. I'll call Sawyer."

"I will," she said, "since jail doesn't work in my

plans very well. Hard to be a self-sufficient, well-rounded, contributing member of society from behind bars. Plus I don't think I could learn how to paddleboard there either." She was doing her best to sound positive and upbeat. This was the trick to denial. Sound positive and upbeat and maybe you'll buy it.

"Paddleboard?" he asked.

"Yeah. I've been watching you, and I've decided it's on my bucket list."

"A bucket list is for someone who's dying."

"Well," she said as lightly as she could, turning away from him on the pretense of checking her reflection in the small mirror above the foyer table. "I don't see myself living through a prison sentence," she quipped.

Two hands gripped her by the shoulders and turned her back around. He stared into her eyes, and she could tell by the grim set of his jaw that he could see her fears. "You're not going to jail."

She nodded, but she must not have looked convinced, because he dipped down a little to look into her eyes, his own fierce. "You're *not*."

Someone knocked on the kitchen door, and Ali jumped. She turned and peeked out the window over the sink and saw the broad-shouldered Jack standing there. "Oh my God," she whispered. "If he'd shown up five minutes ago, he'd have heard us!"

"Us?" Luke inquired, amused, giving her a look that had her blushing to her roots.

Right. *She* was the noisy one. She couldn't help it, not with him.

At her embarrassment, his eyes softened, filling with affection. "I love the noises you make," he said huskily. "Sexy as hell." He pulled open the door.

"Hey," Jack said, "I'm not interrupting, am I?" And before they could answer, he pushed his way in. "Need to borrow a paddleboard."

"It's in the shed, not the house," Luke said.

"Need a wetsuit too."

"It's June," Luke said. "Only pussies need wetsuits in June."

"I've got a date later. Can't risk shrinkage."

Luke started to shove him out, but Jack planted his feet. "Not going anywhere until you give me your wetsuit. I can stand here all day. You know I can."

Luke muttered an oath and turned to the door himself. "There's one in the garage somewhere. Hold on."

When he was gone, Jack turned to Ali and flashed her a smile. "You can feel the love between me and him, right?"

Ali laughed. He was absurdly handsome and even more absurdly charming. "I can absolutely feel it."

"Luke's the son of two doctors," Jack said, "so

it's probably not his fault that he's such an ass. Or that he thinks he's always right."

"Is he? Always right?"

"Yeah, but don't tell him that. It'll go straight to his head. He's got that classic hero complex thing going. It's why shit hits him so hard. He likes to blame himself."

"Thanks, Dr. Phil," Luke said dryly, coming back into the room, tossing a wetsuit at him. "You can leave now."

"Sure. Oh," Jack said, turning back, "I'm supposed to tell you, Joe Wykowski wants you to figure out who's stealing the reclaimed lumber he has stacked on the side of his house. It's worth a fortune. He suspects it's his ex-wife's boy-friend's son, who's a carpenter, if that helps."

"If he knows who it is . . ." Luke started.

"The guy carries his nail gun on his hip like he's Dirty Harry," Jack said. "They need you and your badass attitude. And *real* gun."

Luke stared at him. "So I'm what, the new geriatric private detective of Lucky Harbor?"

"Hey, I'm not the one who found Mr. Schmidt's GTO," Jack said. "On shift last night, I had to rescue Mrs. Myers's cat out of a tree, and she was telling her entire bridge club about you. Apparently they all have various problems that they need the *local investigator stud muffin* to solve—*their* words, by the way. Not that you're not a total stud muffin; you're just not my type."

Ali laughed.

Luke manhandled Jack out the front door and then turned to Ali. At his expression, her heart squeezed. She'd watched him pretend not to care about anything, even as the opposite was true. He'd helped his sister get on her feet and stay there. In his job, he did whatever was needed. He'd fixed up the house he'd neglected.

And then there was her. He'd given her a place to stay, a friendship . . . and more.

They'd grown up so differently. His parents had expected a lot out of him, looking to him to pretty much raise himself and his sister too. As a result, Luke stood up for himself and others too weak to do so.

Ali admired that, so much.

"About earlier . . ." Luke said.

She took in his expression. "It's okay, Luke," she said softly. "You don't have to give me the speech."

"The speech?"

"The one where you rationalize how we got naked again, and how it's the *last* time, yadda, yadda."

A ghost of a smile curved his lips. "I thought it was blah, blah, blah."

"Look, you're right to hold back with me," she said. "Historically I've made some bad decisions, and—"

He snagged her and hauled her in close.

"There's *nothing* wrong with you," he said with quiet steel. "Not one thing. You're perfect."

"Well—"

"Say it," he said.

She softened and cupped his face. "Luke, I—"

"Say it, Ali. Say you're fucking perfect."

She stared up at the fierce look of protectiveness in his features and felt her heart clutch. She needed to lighten this mood of his and fast, or she wasn't going to be responsible for jumping him. "I'm fucking perfect," she said.

It worked. He flashed a smile. "I really like it when you say 'fuck.'"

Chapter 22

Ali found Aubrey at her desk in Town Hall, typing away on her computer, her brow furrowed.

"Does everyone always work on the weekends?" Ali asked.

"Just the lucky ones." Aubrey looked up and took in Ali's hair with assessing eyes. "You're supposed to use that anti-frizz every day."

Ali ran a hand down her hair and grimaced. "I forgot today. Listen, I have a question."

"No, I'm not still doing my boss."

"I actually wasn't going to ask that. Although I'm kinda wondering why you still work for him."

It was Aubrey's turn to grimace. "It's a good job," she said. "And I can resist him." Though she didn't really look one hundred percent sure. "Listen, I'm pretty busy, so . . ."

"Is there anyone else?"

"Excuse me?"

Ali moved closer and leaned in. "I'm wondering if there's anyone else that Teddy's seeing. Other than you and Melissa."

Aubrey looked at her for a long time. "You have someone particular in mind?"

"Maybe."

Aubrey arched a perfectly waxed brow and looked like she might have something to say, but Gus walked by with a mop.

Aubrey and Ali remained quiet until the hallway was empty again.

"We can't talk here," Aubrey said.

"I know. Just tell me you know something."

"Not concrete."

"Would you be willing to call me if that changes?"

"You mean if the couch gets put into use again, something like that?" Aubrey asked.

"Yeah."

Aubrey went pensive, then sighed. "Damn, I really liked this job."

Luke drove into town and found Sawyer at his desk, head down on his arms. "Bad day?"

"Some high school punks drove all the way up to Mt. Hood—three hours each way—loaded up fifteen truckloads of snow, drove it all the way back into town, and packed in all the doors to the school last night. Not yesterday afternoon. Not after dinner. At three a.m. Summer school detention had to be cancelled today."

"Could be worse," Luke said.

Sawyer lifted his head and blinked bleary-eyed at Luke. "I'm afraid to ask."

"I think Bree Medina stole the fifty grand."

Sawyer stared at him and then silently handed Luke his empty coffee mug.

Luke took it, walked down the hall to the service table, filled it with straight, hair-raising black, and brought it back to Sawyer's office.

Sawyer drank, winced, and then drank some more. Eyes far more sharp now, he looked at Luke. "What the fuck?"

Luke opened his mouth, but Sawyer stood up. "No, wait. Not here."

They headed out in Sawyer's utility vehicle while Luke gave him the rundown.

"Jesus," Sawyer said and called the mayor. "Hey, Tony. Yeah, we did get a great turnout at the ground-breaking ceremony earlier. Listen, what's Bree up to? She busy?" he paused, listening. "I just wanted to talk to her about redecorating my office . . . I understand. Tell her I hope her mom's feeling better real soon." He slid his phone away. "Bree's gone to her mom's place in Ocean Shores for a few days."

"Ocean Shores," Luke repeated. "Her mom lives in Ocean Shores. Where the next closest nail salon is. We should . . ."

Sawyer pulled over and used his smartphone to find the number and make the call. When he hung up, he looked at Luke. "Bree is a client there, and they said she has gotten blue, starred nail tips before." He pulled back onto the street, made a few turns, and stopped about halfway down a street, pointing to a duplex on the corner. "Marshall's new place."

There was no activity.

Sawyer turned off his vehicle. "Marshall cancelled a meeting with me, said he wasn't feeling good. Think that's a coincidence?"

"I don't believe in coincidences," Luke said.

"Me either."

"So what are we doing?" Luke asked.

"You forget what a stakeout looks like?"

"No." Luke slouched in his seat. "But a heads up would've been nice. We don't have any food."

Sawyer leaned forward and opened his glove box. Inside was a treasure trove of candy bars and other crap food.

"Nice," Luke said, helping himself.

Half an hour later, the mail carrier worked her way down the street. Two minutes after that, Marshall's front door opened. Teddy appeared in boxers and an opened bathrobe.

"He's dressed like he's sick," Sawyer said.

Or like someone who'd just gotten laid. "Only pussies wear bathrobes."

"I have a bathrobe. The wife bought it for me."

Luke looked at him. "Chloe bought you a bathrobe?"

"It's from her day spa."

"You ever wear it?"

"Hell no."

"I stand by my point."

Teddy stepped outside. Before he got anywhere, a man's necktie came around his neck from behind.

In Sawyer's vehicle, both he and Luke tensed for action, but then the shadowy figure behind Ted materialized into the shape of a woman. She wore a black leather bustier, matching thong, and thigh-high, stiletto boots.

Bree Medina, the mayor's wife, the one supposedly visiting her sick mom. She slapped Teddy's ass and then pulled him back inside by the tie.

The door slammed shut.

"Jesus," Sawyer said, rubbing a hand over his eyes. "I don't think I can unsee that . . ."

That evening, Ali stood at the work table in the garage, completely lost in the cool, wet clay. In the zone, she worked and shaped, using her sensory skills instead of her brain so she could just be.

She heard the truck pull into the driveway, so when someone came up behind her, she knew it was Luke. He didn't touch her, but she doubted a piece of paper could fit between them. "You want to play *Ghost*?" she murmured.

He stepped into her, brushing up against her so that she could feel his erection. "Do I feel like a ghost to you?" he softly asked.

She faced him and felt her heart tug at the sight

of him soaking up the sight of her. "I need a shower," she said, gesturing to the front of her, which was a mess.

"Funny, so do I."

Don't get sidetracked by his hunkiness, she told herself. He was hiding it pretty well, but he was pissed at something. Her gut tightened a little bit, and maybe her heart too. He let her see the real man, something she knew he shared with few others. "You okay?"

"I was with Sawyer. We saw Bree at Marshall's new place."

She could tell that there was a whole lot more to this story. "And?"

"And it was a . . . compromising situation."

"Compromising how?" she asked.

"Compromising."

She looked up into his face. "Just tell me, Luke. Were they naked, rolling around on fifty thousand dollars in cash?"

"Not quite naked, and no cash. But Bree was . . . taking charge. I'm pretty sure Marshall is tied up with his own necktie about now."

Her jaw dropped. "Seriously?"

He lifted a hand, like *Boy Scout's honor.* Except there was no way Luke Hanover had ever been a Boy Scout.

She drew a breath. "So we've linked the mayor's wife and the town clerk to an illicit— and what might or might not be a BDSM—

317

affair." She shuddered. "It has a high ick factor, but it's not necessarily illegal."

"True," he agreed. "We've got to smoke out the money."

"How?"

"If she's got it," Luke said, "she's hiding it somewhere. Not in a bank account, but somewhere accessible. Holding it over Marshall's head." He stepped close, crowding her. "All we have to do is catch her with it."

"Oh, well, if that's all."

He gently pulled her in.

"Careful," she warned, "I'm covered in clay."

"Ali, the police are going to announce there's an arrest imminent."

She went still even as her heart began to pound. "They've already done that," she said.

"Yes, except this time they're going to leak that it *isn't* you."

She let out a breath. "Okay. I like the sound of that. Keep going."

"Bree's under surveillance," he said.

"You think she's going to move the money."

"I know it," he said. "It's what I would do if I'd just gone from scot-free and in the clear to guilty as hell. I'd get rid of the evidence." He stroked the hair back from her eyes, letting his fingers linger on her.

Yesterday, she would have been touched by the sweet gesture. But right now, sad and aching for him, it just hurt—hurt and pissed her off. He'd stood by her, believed in her when others hadn't, let her stay when all he wanted was to be alone— and yet he was leaving tomorrow. And as attentive and wonderful as he'd been, he hadn't said one word about seeing her again. In sudden overload, she poked his chest with a clay-covered finger.

"Hey," he said.

She did it again, getting clay on his white T-shirt.

"Stop that."

She didn't.

"Ali." He caught her wrist when she went to poke him a third time. *"Stop."*

"Right. I'll just stop. Stop caring about you . . ." *Stop wanting you, stop loving you.* Except she couldn't seem to manage any of that. Once again, she was going down with the sinking ship that was her heart.

But she wasn't going down quietly. Nope, not this time. With her free hand, she scooped up a fingerful of the soft clay on the table and streaked it across his chest.

He stared at her, easily catching her other hand as well. "What the hell's gotten into you?"

"You said you like to keep things real, but you don't," she said. "You wear your cynicism better than you do your badge. I get that you do it to keep your heart protected from whatever's going on, but what's going on is that we're falling for each other."

She couldn't blame him for staring at her like she'd just announced she had two heads. She hadn't meant to let that slip, but it was out there now and she couldn't, wouldn't, take it back.

"Ali," he said quietly. "I told you—"

"Yeah, yeah, you told me." She was tired of his calm steadiness. Did he ever lose it? Why wasn't he losing it like she was? He was still holding her, and instead of trying to pull away, she stepped into him. Her sole intent was to cover him with more clay until she felt better, a plan that utterly backfired because it put her up against him.

Which she liked *way* too much, and which of course was the problem. "Yes," she said, "you told me. You told me plenty. I guess I don't listen very well. It's a Winters trait, you know. Denial. And I'm damn good at it."

"I don't want to ever hurt you, Ali."

"You're hurting me now."

He let out a long breath, released her hands, and then made the mistake of closing his eyes.

Ali slapped some more clay on his chest, with both hands this time, and turned back for more clay.

"What the hell are you doing?"

"Fighting dirty—unlike you. You won't fight at all. You play clean and safe."

"You think I play clean and safe?" he asked, his voice deadly calm. Not his eyes, though. His eyes were fired up as he grabbed two fistfuls of clay.

Gulp.

"You know what?" she asked quickly, raising her hands. *"Uncle."*

"Too late." He stalked her slowly, surely, on legs far more steady than hers, and then hooked her leg so fast she never saw it coming. She fell right onto his grandma's sheet-covered beanbag chair.

Before she could scramble free, he was on her, pinning her down, running his hands from her throat to her ankles, spreading clay all over her body.

"I can't believe you did that!"

He rose in one fluid motion, satisfaction unmistakable on his face. He took a step back, slipped in a puddle of water she'd spilled earlier while softening the clay, and went down on his ass.

She scrambled to her knees and crawled to him. "God. God, Luke. Are you okay?"

"No. I think I broke my ego."

Relief making her giddy, she dropped her head to his chest and laughed.

His hands came up and possessively gripped her butt. "I'm not playing clean or safe, Ali. Not with you. And that's the problem. I'm feeling things I shouldn't be feeling." And then he rolled them, tucking her beneath him.

"There's something else you're feeling," she said.

"No kidding." He rocked into her, eyes intense and glittering with heat, a forearm on either side of her head. The overhead light caressed the tough, sinewy lines of his body, emphasizing the flexed muscles of his shoulders and biceps.

Around them the air felt charged. There was a soft vibration just beneath her skin, the hum of anticipation that spread warmth through her, settling into her good spots. She let her eyes drift over his face, let the hunger for him show. And her need . . .

Whispering her name, he lowered his head, brushing his mouth along her jaw to her ear. "You kill me. You know that, right?"

Wrapping her legs around him so that he was settled between her thighs, she arched up. This was it, she realized. Their last night . . . "It's a good way to go," she murmured.

Choking out a low laugh, he cradled her head in his hands, his fingers entangling in her hair. "Not on the floor." He rose, and pulled her up.

"Okay," she said, and looked pointedly at the workbench. She was assessing it for sturdiness when he choked out a low laugh and pressed up against her back. "Still killing me," he said, pulling her back around so that now the smooth steel of the table hit her at the lowest curve of her butt. "Like this. I want to watch you come." He hoisted her up so she was seated on the table. His hands ran up her legs, settling on her inner thighs before slowly pressing them open so he could step between.

Lowering his head, he concentrated on removing her apron, swearing when he had trouble with the knot. "This wasn't my intent tonight," he said, and giving up on the string, he tore it with his hands, giving her a little thrill deep in her belly.

"It's not your fault," she murmured. "Clay is sexy."

He laughed low and rough. "I'm pretty sure it's you, Ali."

She took in a deep, slow breath, smelling the wet clay and the scent of clean, heated male, and experienced a wave of desire that had her quivering.

When Luke finally freed her of the apron, he tossed it over his shoulder. Her sundress followed shortly, and then her bra. "Christ, you're beautiful." He snagged her bikini panties and slid them down her legs, leaving her in nothing but mud boots.

And a lot of clay.

A ragged groan rumbled from his chest. "My favorite look on you," he said, taking her in from his prime position between her dangling legs, which were spread and held open by his lean hips. "It's like a feast." He bent over her, a hand on either side of her hips. "And I am starving." He kissed first one breast and then the other, lingering to nuzzle.

His jeans were rubbing against her inner thighs and between, and she shivered. There was something incredibly erotic and completely sinful about being naked and sprawled out for him while he was still fully dressed. Even more so when he dropped to his knees on the garage floor and used his tongue. She might have come right off the table, but Luke caught her hips in his big hands, holding her in place so he could devastate her with slow, purposeful care. It took an embarrassingly little amount of time for her to completely fly apart. Even less the second time.

And then he was inside her. Wrapping his arms around her, he lifted her so that they were chest to chest, and began a slow, delicious glide in and out of her body.

"How?" she managed, breathless. "How is this better every single time? Is it because we don't want it to be?"

Latching his lips onto her throat, he shook his head. The gentle tugs of his mouth sent shock waves straight through her, and she cried out and clutched at him, tightening around him.

"Oh fuck, Ali . . ." he growled, tightening his grip. "Not going to last if you keep that up."

She did it again. In retaliation, he nipped at her shoulder, her collarbone, the swell of her breast, wrenching a moan from her as heat and pleasure spiraled. Somehow she managed to open her eyes and watch the intensity on his face as he moved inside her, which proved to be her undoing.

He came with her this time, hard, shuddering as he buried his face in the crook of her neck. She trembled, little aftershocks of pure pleasure, and Luke tightened his grip in a soothing, protective embrace. His heat seeped through her, consuming her until she felt like she might burst again as he breathed her in, nuzzling, kissing, nibbling her throat and jaw and ear.

Loving her.

Not that he'd admit it. Unable to help herself, she clung for a few minutes, trying to remember everything about this moment. Everything.

He let her cling for long moments, as if he felt the same. Finally he raised his head and met her gaze. She knew he was checking to see if she was okay, so she reached up, brought his face back to hers, and kissed him.

Because she wasn't okay.

He was leaving.

Chapter 23

The next morning, Ali woke up entangled with a big, warm, hard body.

Luke.

After their garage foray, they'd eaten, and then he'd taken her to bed.

His.

He was still deeply asleep on his back, one arm bent with his hand beneath his head, the other gripping her butt like he owned it.

She took a good, long last look at him, ignored the ache in her heart, and she slid out of the bed.

He mumbled something and rolled over, burying his head beneath his pillow. The rest of him was bared to the world, that strong back, those mile-long legs, and the best ass she'd ever had the pleasure of viewing. With a sigh, she slipped out of his bedroom.

He was leaving today, and her sadness had nothing to do with the distance between San Francisco and Lucky Harbor. It was that there'd been no mention of continuing this. Whatever this was. So really, the distance was irrelevant.

But she refused to watch him go.

She drove to Eat Me and had the now-famous

Grace's chocolate chip pancakes. Lucille was there with her blue-haired posse. She came over to Ali and gave her a hug. "Heard Detective Lieutenant Stud Muffin is leaving," she said. "Thought you could use some TLC."

"I'm fine."

"Good. Because men don't make the world go around. Although," she said, eying Mr. Wykowski as he entered the café, "they do make it more interesting."

To say the least.

"Been meaning to ask you about your ceramics," Lucille said. "A little birdie told me that Russell isn't interested in selling your stuff in his shop."

"A little birdie?"

Lucille grinned. "Okay, Leah. And the truth is, I covet your ceramics. I thought you might be interested in having a show at my gallery. If we price things right, you might even be able to pay that fancy attorney of yours."

"You'd do that?" Ali asked.

"Of course. You're good."

Ali smiled. "And if I wasn't?"

"Well, then, this conversation would have stopped at Detective Lieutenant Stud Muffin."

Ali's phone rang. Russell wanted to see her, so she headed to the flower shop. It wasn't open. It wouldn't ever be open again, at least in this version. Russell had boxed everything up and was standing at the front counter. He didn't look as sad as she felt. He didn't look sad at all. He was happy.

And she was very happy for him. And devastated for herself.

Russell smiled and pulled her in for a hug. Then he handed her . . . the book.

She stared down at it. The thing was ancient and frayed at the edges, with notes and pieces of paper sticking out everywhere. "Your business?"

"Yep. Lucky Harbor Flowers is yours, what there is of it. All you need is a place."

"But I don't have money to pay you," she said.

"Consider it severance."

She hugged the book, then thrust it back. "I can't take it, Russell. It wouldn't be right."

He didn't take the book. "Then pay me when you get the shop open and in the black."

She lifted her gaze to his. "How do you know I'll get to open a shop?"

"I know," he said, confident. "Of course, you'd have to stay in Lucky Harbor for that book to have any value . . ."

Ali looked down the street. It was very early. The strings of white lights were still on, twinkling like Christmas in June on the pine trees lining the walk. Until the theft of the money, she'd loved it here. Loved the people, the way it felt like home. And her three S's were here: stability, security, and safety.

So hell if she'd let herself run off with her tail between her legs when she'd done nothing wrong. "Yes," she said quietly. "I'm staying."

Russell smiled and hugged her again. "Keep in touch."

She would. And someday soon, although she had no idea how, she would open the flower shop. *Her* flower shop. It was what she wanted, with all her heart.

There were other things she wanted too. She wanted the money mystery solved. She wanted people to know she wasn't a thief. She wanted her mom and sister to be safe and happy.

She wanted . . .

Luke.

She drove home.

Home.

She parked and stared at the big, old, beautiful house. Granted, she was a sucker for a place with character but . . . home?

This wasn't her home. It was Luke's.

Yet there was no denying that she'd fallen for the place and the man, despite knowing better. Luke didn't want her to feel this way, except that particular message wasn't exactly sticking to her brain. The thing was, actions spoke far more loudly than words, and Luke's actions were telling her a very different story than his words.

His truck was still here.

She walked through the house toward the

kitchen, needing something for her suddenly dry throat. Scotch was her first choice, but she'd proven incapable of handling that. She poured herself a glass of iced tea, and with her gut saying that Luke would be on the water, she stepped out onto the back deck. Hearing voices, she moved so that she could see the dock below. Edward was sitting there with his usual cigar, though she was hoping it was unlit, since she knew his doctor had told him to quit.

Luke had just pulled himself and his board out of the ocean. Water sluiced off the body she knew she'd never get tired of looking at.

It'd only been a couple of weeks, but he'd gotten a hold of her heart. Maybe some things took no time at all, but the fact was, he'd proven that he was a man she could believe in. A man unlike any other man in her entire life.

She was still thinking about that when the men's words floated up the stairs to reach her.

"Don't be an asshole," Edward said. "Not to her. You're living with her, falling for her, letting her think it's okay to fall for you." He jabbed his cigar at Luke. "You telling me when you leave here today that you're not going to ever look back?"

Luke set his board against the dock and ignored his grandfather.

"You telling me you can just walk away *again?* Because let me tell you, boy-o, being alone? *Not* all it's cracked up to be. Now that I've looked death right in the face—"

Luke snorted. "You had gas—"

Edward jabbed with the cigar again. "Say it one more time and I swear I'll stroke out on you right here, right now, just to spite you."

It was a distance but Ali was pretty sure Luke rolled his eyes as he leaned back on the railing, arms crossed over his chest.

"All I want," Edward said, "is for you to learn from other people's mistakes. *My* mistakes."

"I'm not you," Luke said quietly. "Ali and I both know what's going on here, and what isn't."

Edward stared at him. "You want me to believe you're just helping her, that she's just a job to you?"

Ali held her breath for the answer, and when the quiet "yes" came, the blood roared in her ears. The first time he'd referred to her as a job had been to his sister, and he'd had a handy excuse for it then. This time the quiet conviction in his voice overrode any excuse.

Looking disgusted, Edward shook his head.

Ali tried to absorb the terrible, wrenchingly painful truth of it all, telling herself that this was not new information. But it still knocked her back a step. And then another.

And then she'd whirled and escaped into the house. She grabbed her purse and shoved a few things inside.

She had to go.

Still, she slowed long enough to leave a note hastily scrawled on a napkin, because leaving without a word was rude. Mimi had taught her better than that. Taping it to the fridge, she took one last look around, at the kitchen, out the window at the two men on the dock, one who'd been like a surrogate grandfather to her, the other who'd been . . .

Everything.

Her eyes were too blurry to see clearly, but she snatched the keys out of the ceramic bowl by the door and then stopped and eyed the bowl.

She thought of what had happened to the pencil pot she'd left Teddy, how it'd been shoved in a drawer. She couldn't leave this one to that fate, so she snatched it as well. She'd have to come back for her other things, of course, but later. Much later.

Like after Luke was gone.

She opened the front door and then faltered for a beat, but she didn't stop. Because for the first time in her life, she was going to leave first.

Luke turned from his grandfather and entered the house. He'd woken up alone. After paddleboarding and the run-in with his grandfather, he was hoping Ali was back. He needed to get on the road, but he wanted to . . .

Hell. He didn't *want* to say goodbye.

But it was Sunday. He'd pushed his luck as far as he could with his job. The review was in the morning. He needed to go or face the consequences.

Edward had come in behind him. "Feels quiet in here."

Yeah, it did. And Luke's gaze snagged on the napkin taped to the fridge.

Dear Luke,

Thank you for letting me stay when you wanted to be alone. For helping me when you were on a break from doing just that.

For saving me.

Ali.

Luke stared at Ali's words, dread spreading through him like wildfire. He hadn't saved her.

She'd saved him.

Why would she leave a note like this? What had happened that would make her write it? His mind raced in reverse, back to a few minutes ago, to what he and his grandpa had been discussing on the dock. Shit. It wasn't what chased her off, but who. *He* was why she'd run.

And his grandfather was right—without her, the house was quiet. He finally got what he'd wanted, to be alone. Except that wasn't what he wanted at all. Whipping around, he went in immediate search of his keys. Naturally, he hadn't left them on the counter. Or anywhere that he could see.

"What the hell are you looking for?" Edward asked.

"Keys," Luke grated out, moving into the living room to look there.

"She's got that key bowl, you know. You should try using it sometime. She made me one. It works like a charm."

The key bowl. He'd put his keys in the key bowl. He strode back into the kitchen, but the thing wasn't on the counter. Where the hell was it?

"Now what?" Edward asked.

Luke shook his head. "I have no idea where the stupid bowl is, but I have to go after her. I . . . fucked up."

"Well then why are you still standing here?"

"Because I still can't find my keys."

Edward shook his head. "Your grandma, she used to smack me upside the head whenever I'd lose my keys. Always worked too. I'd always find my keys right after she did it. Come closer, let's try it."

"You were married for like twenty minutes," Luke said. "When did you have time to lose your keys?"

Edward leaned in and smacked him on the back of the head.

"Ow. Jesus!"

"Two *years*," Edward said. "We were married for two years. And it'd have been a helluva lot longer if I'd gotten my shit together sooner." He fished deep in his own pocket and came up with a set of keys. "Connect the dots, you idiot. Be smarter than me."

Luke stared at the keys. "Tell me those aren't for the Dial-A-Ride."

"What, you have a problem with it? 'Cuz you can always just walk. Maybe you'll even catch Ali too. Sometime next year."

Luke sighed and took the keys.

Ali didn't let herself cry on the road to her mom's house. No, that'd be dangerous and stupid, and she tried really hard not to do anything dangerous and stupid.

So she did the responsible thing—she pulled over to the side of the road to sob her heart out. Right in the middle of it, Zach called her.

"What's wrong?" he asked immediately, obviously hearing the emotion in her voice.

"Nothing—oh my God. You're calling because I crossed the county lines without even thinking about it, right? They called you."

"Who?" he asked.

This stumped her. "The crossing-the-county-lines police?"

Zach laughed. "Relax, no one's going to arrest you for visiting your mom. I got your message about Bree. Are you sure?"

"Yes, but they haven't found the money."

"Luke'll sniff it out. He's not the type to let something he cares about go."

And yet he let *her* go . . .

She and Zach hung up, and Ali went on to what she was exceptionally good at—picking herself up and telling herself things would be okay. She blew her nose, slid on her dark aviator Oakley knockoffs, and got back on the road.

She arrived in time to sit at her mom's table and chop veggies.

"No one ever eats the veggies," Mimi said, sitting on the counter with a mirror in one hand and her eyeliner in the other. "But it seems classy to have them out, you know? *You get the beer?*" she yelled to Harper in the back of the old, tiny, narrow house.

"Mama, this is a damn surprise party," Harper yelled back. *"Stop asking questions about it and practice your surprised look!"*

Mimi grinned and practiced in the mirror. "How about this, honey?" she asked Ali. "Do I look surprised?"

"Yes," Ali said without looking. She munched on a piece of celery and wondered if Luke would eat celery. It was green, which probably put it on his taboo list.

"Did I tell you I'm learning how to do taxes?" Mimi asked. "It's going to change everything, honey. You'll see."

She was eternally optimistic in spite of the fact

that life had never handed Mimi Winters a single thing, including a break.

But the thing was, Mimi believed wholeheartedly that everything could change, and up until recently, so had Ali. All along she'd thought all she had to do was leave White Center and that would *change everything*. All she had to do was become the best damn florist in Lucky Harbor and that would *change everything*. All she had to do was love Luke and that would *change everything*.

But if wishes and dreams were sure things, the world would be a whole different ball game. And deep down, she'd always known that. And, she had a feeling, so did Mimi. But that had never once stopped her mom from trying to impart hope into both of her daughters' hearts. Ali's chest tightened a little bit. "I love you, Mom."

Mimi looked up, surprised, then smiled softly. "Aw, baby. I love you too. What time's Luke coming?"

"He isn't."

Her mother set down the mirror, her expression of surprise a real one this time. "Why not?"

"Because we're not together. I've been telling you that. Besides, he'd be on his way back to San Francisco by now." Ali closed her eyes and dropped her head to the table. "And I messed things up."

"Oh, Ali-gator." Mimi hopped down from the

counter and sat next to Ali, hugging her close. "It happens. Listen, we'll go to the Victoria's Secret outlet store. We'll get you something pretty, and you can make it up to him—"

"No." But that did squeeze a laugh out of her. "It's not like that. I messed up by falling for him."

"Well how's that messing up?"

"Because he didn't fall back."

"Oh honey. What man wouldn't fall for you? You're strong and smart, and so pretty. Although you should smile more. You've got those nice white teeth—"

Ali pushed to her feet. "I'm going to go see if Harper needs any help outside decorating. You keep working on your surprise expression, okay?"

Two hours later, the party was in full swing. Ali had been sent to the store—twice—and was back in the tiny, cramped, hot kitchen, her mom's cake in one hand, a knife in the other. She'd come inside to put the cake away, but now she was thinking she needed a third piece.

Problem was, a third piece would put her at about a million calories for the day, so she cut off a bite-sized portion. She ate right off the knife, because everyone knew that the calories eaten right off the knife didn't count. She was leaning over the cake stuffing her face, when she heard footsteps behind her. She turned, then nearly fell over in surprise at the man standing in the doorway.

"Luke?"

His shoulders nearly brushed the jamb on either side of him, making him look far too big for the place. He was wearing a T-shirt, faded Levi's, and battered athletic shoes. The casual wear should have had him fitting right in, but he didn't really. Maybe he had the hard-edge and see-all eyes it took to survive in this neighborhood, but his badassness came from being a cop, not from worrying about having a job and putting food on the table or whether it was safe to walk to his car.

"What are you doing here?" she asked, surreptitiously swiping her face, hoping she didn't have chocolate all over it. "Why aren't you gone?"

"I wanted to see you before I left."

White Center wasn't exactly en route to San Francisco. He'd gone pretty far out of his way to talk, but she needed to protect herself. And get over him. Getting over him would be supremely helpful. "I'm pretty busy here, Luke."

He slid a glance at the cake in her hands. "Yeah, I can see that. Should I give you two a moment alone?"

"No. *Yes.*" She noted that she sounded peeved, which was good. It hid the hurt. And she *was* hurt. So damn hurt, with no one to blame but herself.

He came forward and took the knife out of her hands, setting it far out of her reach. Then he very gently took the cake as well.

"How did you find me?" she asked. "And why are you even here?"

Mimi stepped into the kitchen and said in a horrified voice, *"Ali Anne Louise Winters,* how is that a way to talk to your man?" She put a hand on Luke's arm and smiled up at him. "You made really good time from Lucky Harbor, honey."

"I did," he said, and dipped down to kiss her on the cheek. "Happy birthday."

Mimi fawned over that. "Oh my, aren't you the charmer." She smiled at Ali. "Isn't he, Ali?"

"Yes," Ali agreed tightly. "He's quite the charmer. But he's not my man, Mom. We've discussed this."

Mimi sighed, and Ali braced herself for the lecture. *A man is everything, Ali. Don't disappoint him, ever. Be what he needs you to be . . .*

But Mimi said none of that. She simply stepped around Luke, cupped her daughter's face, and smiled gently. "Just talk to him, baby."

"Mom—"

"I know you've been let down. And I also know that's more my fault than any man's."

Ali sighed and brought her hands up to her mom's wrists. "Oh, Mom. That's not true."

Mimi smiled sadly. "You always were the sweet one. My miracle," she said to Luke. "So willing to see only the best in me." She turned back to Ali. "But honey, maybe you could try to see the best in him too." Then she kissed both of Ali's cheeks, patted them gently, and left the two of them alone.

Chapter 24

Luke didn't touch Ali. God knew he wanted to. She was standing there, arms wrapped around herself, the don't-touch vibes coming off of her like lightning bolts.

He'd caused that. Instead of keeping his mouth shut and saying goodbye to her, he'd ruined what they'd shared during their short time together. Worse, he'd hurt her. "I called you," he said quietly. She hadn't picked up. He'd called her again, and Mimi had answered, saying that Ali had gone to the store and left her phone. Mimi had invited him to her party.

Luke had been on his way regardless, but the invite had been nice.

"My mom's dying of curiosity about you," Ali said.

"She's protective of you."

That brought her gaze to his. In all this time, she'd been an open book. But she'd closed herself off now, shuttering everything from him.

His own doing. "She wanted me to know you were upset," he said.

Ali made a sound and closed her eyes, and he stepped closer. "I told her it was my fault,"

x

341

he said, "and that I wanted to come see you."

"Well, you're seeing me now."

"Ah . . ." he said helplessly, "we need to talk."

"Not here." And with that, she walked outside.

He drew a deep breath and followed.

They didn't go around to the back, where the party was ramping up, if the raucous laughter and loud music meant anything. Instead, she started walking down the street.

Luke went with her. "Ali—"

"Not here either."

He decided to shut it and let her lead.

But she stopped so short at the sight of the white Lucky Harbor Dial-A-Ride van, he nearly plowed her over.

She swiveled her head and looked at him in disbelief.

He shrugged.

"You drove the Dial-A-Ride here?"

"Someone took the key bowl," he said, "with my keys in it."

She stared up at him. "Oh my God. That was me. I took the bowl." She smacked herself on the forehead. "I've *got* to stop doing that."

He smiled, and they walked in silence a few blocks.

Weeds poked through the cracks in the beat-up asphalt in front of the houses that had seen better days decades ago. Some had bars in the windows, and others had flowers in pots on their porches.

"We lived on that corner once," Ali said, pointing to a place on the right, where there was a skeleton of a Chevy up on blocks. "We also lived across the street."

"Where does that loan shark asshole live?" he asked. "The one who threatened to sell you?"

She took a look at his face. "You want to beat the shit out of some guy who scared me fifteen years ago?"

"Badly," he said.

She shook her head again, but there was the very smallest of smiles on her face.

"Ali."

"I still don't want to talk."

Fine. He'd give her a few more minutes, but that was it because then he *was* going to talk.

And she would listen.

Hopefully. Because, actually, he hadn't had a whole lot of luck in getting Ali to do anything that she didn't want to do.

They walked another few streets, and then she pointed to a house just like all the others, this one pale yellow and nearly falling off its axis. "That one," she said. "That's where we lived with The Pincher."

His chest squeezed hard, like maybe his heart was swelling and bumping up against his ribs. "I'd like a moment with him too," he said grimly.

A minute later, they came to a deserted elementary school. Ali slipped in between a small gap in the linked fence, like she'd done it a hundred times.

Luke eyed the gap. Not nearly wide enough for his shoulders, even if he squeezed in sideways. With a sigh, he climbed the fence.

Ali had claimed a swing and was watching him. There was something new in her face now. She was more than just closed off to him. She was closed off *period,* disassociated from their surroundings. He'd seen this all too often on the job, so he knew exactly what it meant. It meant that being here had brought her memories that were hard—if not impossible—for her to deal with. "Talk to me, Ali."

"Well . . ." Her gaze tipped upward to the corner of the structure supporting her swing. "There's that web right there, and I'm wondering where the owner of it is."

"Long gone," Luke promised.

"And then there's the fossilized dog poo just behind you. Don't step in it."

"Ali."

"I love getting to see my mom," she said quietly. "And my sister." She shook her head and kicked off gently to swing. "I just hate being here."

He moved behind her and gave her a big push.

She sighed as she flew through the air, leaning back into the motion of the swing as if to savor the motion and the sun on her face.

"You went to school here," he said, staying behind her, continuing to push her.

"I went to school here, yes. I also used to run away here. And hid away here too, when it was necessary."

He'd stayed in back of her so that she wouldn't have to look at him when she talked, sensing that she needed that. But now he was glad that she couldn't see his face, because although he was good at hiding his feelings, he couldn't seem to do it with her.

"I left here," she said. "I wanted to go somewhere new and be smart and independent. I wanted people to like me. I wanted a new life. I wanted to be happy."

He stopped her motion, and from behind her, pressed his cheek to the top of her head. "You are all of those things," he said, "and more. Smart and sweet and caring." He twisted the swing so that she faced him. Squatting before her, he took the steel chains in his hands, caging her in between his arms. "I'm going to talk now," he said.

She opened her mouth, but he leaned in and kissed her to shut her up. "What you heard me say to Edward," he said, moving back just enough to speak, "I shouldn't have said."

"I shouldn't have stood there as long as I did," she said. "When I heard you two talking, I should've gone back inside."

"Lots of should haves. But you overheard me

talking out my ass, Ali. You're not a job to me. Not even close."

She leveled him with those big, hazel eyes. "Then why did you say it? *Twice?*"

He blew out a breath and tried to put it into words. "I guess I was just coming to grips with what's going on between us and I wasn't ready to discuss it." He let out a low, pained laugh. "Hell, Ali, I'm not good at talking about this stuff, even when I *am* ready."

"And you're not," she said, eyes on his. "Ready?"

It was a question, not a statement. And a fair one. "I didn't think so," he admitted. "And the thought of being yet another man who's disappointed you or let you down—"

She pulled back a little more at that. "I'm not your responsibility, Luke. I *won't* be your responsibility."

"I know that. But I care about you."

She nodded, and yet her face was still closed off. Luke knew she felt off balance. Their location wasn't helping much, but that wasn't the number-one problem. The number-one problem was him. Him and the stupid, idiotic words that he'd thrown out there to get his grandpa off his back. "You're not just someone who needed help," he said to her, leaning in so that her knees touched his chest. "I don't think of you like that."

She was looking at him but through him, and

worse, she was tensed for flight. He was already losing her. He could feel it. He was losing her before he'd even realized the miracle that he'd had.

Because like Mimi had said—*she* was a miracle. His miracle.

She'd brought him back to life. He wasn't sure how, or what he was going to do about it, but he knew that he had to figure his shit out fast before it was too late.

"I don't *need* help," she said.

"I know. *I'm* the one who needs it."

This brought him a very small smile. It would seem she agreed that yes, he needed help. "I love your determination," he said. "You're tough and resilient, Ali. And amazing." And he wanted her. More than he'd wanted anyone before. That alone was enough to terrify him, but he was willing to put the terror aside to make this right between them.

"You've got to go," she said. "It's late. And your job's on the line. You're going to have to drive all night to make it for your review."

He didn't move, and she closed her eyes. "Please don't look at me like that," she whispered.

"Like what?"

"Like you love me."

His heart stopped. Just stopped. "I think I do," he said.

He instantly knew his mistake. It was one of those big, life-altering bonehead moments that he couldn't take back.

"You *think* you do," Ali repeated softly. She sucked in some air, then shook her head with a low laugh. "You think . . . No. No, Luke, I'm here to tell you that you don't. Because if you did love me, we'd have discussed like rational adults what would happen after you go back to San Francisco. Instead, we're here, with you about to toss your cookies because you think it *might* be true that you feel something for me. God, the horror."

"Ali—"

"Oh, no. I'm not done." She poked him in the chest. "The fact is, Luke, you don't do love. You don't because that would mean *feeling,* and you don't like to do that either. I get it though. I really do. You think you let other people down, and now you've got it all mixed up in your head somehow, and you think you're unworthy of love. And that's just bullshit."

He scrubbed a hand over his face. "Ali—"

"You've closed yourself off to receiving love, which sucks, especially because that means you can't give it either. I get that too. You're a detective because you're good at it and because it allows you to stand back and observe. And the biggie—you get to stay distant. Which, by the way? You're freaking fantastic at."

He wished like hell he wasn't holding onto the chains of the swing so he could touch her. But if he let go, she'd spin.

And then she would walk.

He'd faced bullets and bad guys in his work, and yet he was still a coward. Ali Winters, floral designer and pottery artist, was the brave one. She was so brave that she was going to walk right out of his life because she knew she deserved better.

And indeed, she rose to her feet, bumped him back, and walked away.

Chapter 25

Ali was still in White Center with her mom and sister at ten that night when she got a phone call from Aubrey.

"She's gone off the deep end," Aubrey said.

"Who?" Ali asked.

"You Know Who," Aubrey said cryptically. Like it was *She Who Shall Not Be Named.* "I was working late, and she tried to sneak into Ted's office. We scared the crap out of each other. She got irritated at me and left. I don't know why I'm calling you with this."

"Because even though you have perfect hair—which is annoying—you're a good person." Ali chewed on her lower lip, trying to imagine what Bree had wanted to do in Teddy's office. Except she didn't have to imagine. She *knew.*

Bree was going to put the money back. "Did she say where she was going next?" she asked Aubrey.

"No."

"Is Teddy still at his team-building fishing trip?"

"Yes. You think I should call him?"

"What would you say?"

There was a pause. "Good point," Aubrey said.

"I'm going home now. I put in my resignation today. I realize it's a Sunday night, but the powers that be will get it in the morning."

"Wait—what?"

"Yeah. I'm switching gears. I don't know what gear yet, but I'll get there."

"Wow," Ali said. "Well, thanks for the call."

"Yeah, and by the way, we're even now."

"Oh, not hardly," Ali said.

"Really? How's your hair?"

Ali looked in the mirror over her mom's faux antique table. Smooth. Shiny. "Good," she admitted.

"We're *completely* even," Aubrey said, and hung up.

Ali kissed her mom and sister goodbye and headed back to Lucky Harbor.

Bree was on the move with the money.

Ali was going on the move too, to catch her.

The highway was narrow and windy and took a lot of concentration to drive at night. This was good because it gave her no time to think about Luke. Or that he'd come to see her.

Or dropped the L-bomb.

Except he hadn't.

She had. She wanted to thunk her head onto the steering wheel, but the road was badly rutted, and she was upset, not suicidal.

So she occupied herself by replaying the conversation with Aubrey in her head. She'd have liked to call Luke, but he was long gone by now. And because that gave her a quick stab to the chest, she called Leah.

"Hey," Leah said, sounding worried. "It's late, you okay?"

"To be determined later."

"Uh-oh," Leah said.

"Yeah. Listen, are you up for a little . . ." Ali grimaced. "B and E?"

"Always." Leah laughed, then she got serious. "Wait. I thought you were kidding, but . . . are you? Kidding?"

"No." Ali filled her in on Aubrey's call and how she intended to go search Teddy's place for the money.

"Aren't you dating a certain hot detective?" Leah asked.

"No."

"No?"

"Long story," Ali said. "You in or not?"

Leah blew out a breath. "What the hell. There's nothing on TV. You don't think Bree will go back to the office now that Aubrey left?"

"No, I don't think she'll risk it again. I think she's going to go to Teddy's to dump the money. It's just a feeling."

They arranged to meet at eleven thirty. Ali turned her phone over so she didn't have to look at the lit-up screen that revealed no missed texts or phone calls.

Her own doing, of course. But though she'd managed to get her heart broken, she refused to have her spirit broken too. Hell no. She was on a mission to fix her crazy life.

She'd worry about her heart later.

She parked, turning to look as Leah slipped into her truck and handed her a brown bag.

Ali peeked in the bag. "What are these?"

"B and E clothes. All black."

Ali pulled out black jeans and a long-sleeved black T-shirt and then eyed the taller, leaner Leah doubtfully. "I hope these are your fat jeans."

"Just strip. I've got an hour before I have to get back to give grandma her meds."

Ali pulled off her clothes and shimmied into the ones Leah had brought, which wasn't so easy behind the steering wheel.

"Cute undies," Leah said.

"Stop looking."

"Hard to miss the neon-pink boy shorts and demi bra. Victoria's Secret?"

"Fifty-percent-off sale."

"Nice," Leah said. "The bra makes your boobs look perky."

Yeah, well, that was a complete waste given how her day had gone.

Or how her love life was going.

"So what's the plan here?" Leah asked.

"We wait for Bree," Ali said. "I think she's going to come here to his house." And hopefully not in black leather. "It'll feel safer to her than risking the office again."

Leah eyed Teddy's dark house. "Maybe she's already been, or she's there right now. We should call her, except I don't know her number."

Ali had an "aha" moment and tore through her purse for the book from Russell.

"You're going to read?" Leah asked. "Now?"

"No, I think I have her number." *Come on, Russell, come through for me . . .* Ali flipped through the pages, hoping and praying.

As an interior designer, Bree had ordered lots of flowers from Lucky Harbor Flowers, and indeed, she had her own page with preferences and contact information. Ali pulled out her cell phone and punched in Bree's cell number.

"What are you going to do if she answers?" Leah asked.

Ali wasn't quite sure until indeed, Bree answered.

"Hello? Who's this?"

"Ali Winters. I was just calling to see if you really wanted this delivery at midnight."

"What the hell are you talking about?"

"Well, Russell left me directions to make a delivery for you." At the lie, Ali looked at Leah.

Leah covered her mouth with her hand to hold back her horrified laughter.

"I don't have a delivery on order right now," Bree said, sounding like she was on the move.

Ali strained her ear to the phone. Had that been a horn she'd heard? "Are you sure?" she asked. "Where are you right now, because I can bring it by and—"

"It's late," Bree said.

Definitely in a car, Ali thought. There was a radio playing softly and an engine running. "Oh. Right," she said. "Well, okay, then. So . . . how about a drink? Or a late-night brownie at Eat Me?"

Click.

Ali winced and slid her phone away. "She didn't want to talk. Nor did she mention where she was. But I'd bet my last dollar she was in her car."

"Maybe she's on her way."

"Or she's on her way back to the office," Ali said. "Hey . . ." she peered out the window, looking down the street to the Lexus parked in front of Teddy's place. "That's Teddy's car. He must have gotten a ride with the other guys to their fishing thing." She turned to Leah. "Let's peek inside."

"You have his keys?"

"I know his code." They got out into the dark night in their black B&E gear and sneaked up on the car. Ali punched in the code. "I'm getting into the back," she said, eyeing the gym bag on the seat. She opened the back passenger door and quickly turned off the dome light to avoid highlighting her activities to any neighbors who might still be up.

Leah got into the front seat and shut her door. Ali didn't shut hers, because she wanted to be able to hear someone coming up on them. "I've got his gym bag," she said. "I bet my iPod's in here. He stole it."

"Seriously?"

"I had better music, and he was always borrowing it for workouts. I want it back."

Leah flicked on a penlight and twisted to shine it so that Ali could see.

"Nice," Ali said.

"I like to be prepared."

"You have any candy in there? You know, in the name of preparation?"

Leah handed her a lollipop.

"I love you," Ali said. She popped the lollipop in her mouth and unzipped the gym bag. In unison, they both wrinkled their noses and jerked back from the odor of stinky guy emitting from the bag.

"Ew," Leah said. "Guys are disgusting."

Ali pulled the lollipop out of her mouth and stared into the bag. How badly did she want her iPod? Enough to move the stinky clothes around?

"Just do it," Leah said.

"You sound like a Nike commercial. I need more light."

Leah leaned closer with the light. "Hey," she said.

"What?" Ali instinctively checked out the windows to see if anyone was coming. "What's wrong?"

"You tell me. You've been crying."

Ali sighed. "Forget it."

"Oh, crap," Leah said. "What did he do?"

"Who?"

"Luke."

That Leah assumed Luke had blown it brought a warm fuzzy to Ali's heart, even as she laughed without much mirth. "It was me," she admitted. "He's got this way of making me feel like the prettiest, smartest, most wonderful woman on earth," she said.

"That bastard."

"No, you don't understand." Ali hesitated. "I fell for him. And it'd never work between us."

"Why not?"

"Why not?" Ali stared at her. "Have you seen him? He's totally out of my league."

"Bullshit," Leah said.

"And he's law enforcement."

"So, hot guy with a gun." Leah shrugged. "Still not seeing the problem here."

"My people don't go out with law enforcement," Ali said, "it just isn't done."

Leah laughed. "Your people? You mean women? Because, honey, women in general melt over guys like Luke Hanover."

"Yes," Ali said, diving into the unpleasant

task at hand to search Teddy's bag. "But you can't make him melt back, now can you?"

Leah paused. "He doesn't feel the same as you?" she asked, sounding quite up in arms over this possibility.

"Actually, I'm pretty sure he does," Ali said, "but he told me right up front, he wasn't going to get involved. I wasn't going to get involved either, so there's no one to blame here but my inability to follow my own decree."

"Men suck."

"I am in complete agreement. And look." Ali pulled her iPod from a side pocket of Teddy's gym bag.

"Wow. He's perfect for politics. He's got that lying, cheating, stealing thing down."

"Are you keeping a lookout?"

"Yeah—oh shit."

This was immediately followed by the back door opening, and a big body sliding in next to Ali. "Yeah, oh shit," said a low male voice. A low, unbearably familiar voice, and both Ali and Leah squeaked.

"Luke," Ali breathed, a hand to her chest.

"I need the both of you to go back to your vehicles and drive away," he said in his cop voice.

Ali blinked. "What's going on?"

Luke slid a look at Leah. "Give us a second?"

"No," Leah said.

"Excuse me?" he asked, voice still low and authoritative but with a hint of disbelief.

Women probably didn't tell him "no" very often.

"No," Leah said again, "I'm not deserting Ali."

He softened slightly. "You aren't deserting her," he said. "You wouldn't. But I need a moment with her, alone."

Leah looked at Ali questioningly. Ali nodded, and Leah started to get out of the Lexus, but then whirled back and put a finger right in Luke's face. "I'm watching you," she said.

Luke didn't laugh. He didn't get pissed off. Instead he nodded seriously and touched the tip of his finger to Leah's. "I'm watching me too. It's okay, Leah. It's going to be okay."

Leah stared at him for another moment, then nodded. "See that it is."

Ali had no idea what to make of that exchange, but apparently Leah didn't have the same problem. She flashed Luke a small, but much warmer, smile and then vanished into the night.

In the dark interior of the car, Ali closed her eyes. "You didn't go. Why didn't you go?"

"I couldn't leave you."

Oh. Oh damn, that was good. "Luke—"

"What are *you* doing here?"

"Aubrey called. Bree's gone off the deep end. I think she'll come here."

"I told you she was under surveillance."

He *had* told her that. Why hadn't she remembered that?

"Listen to me, Ali," he said, all cop again. "Teddy's car, house, and office are under surveillance too. Half the police department is staking out Town Hall. Bree's already been there. Aubrey finally left work for the night, and Sawyer's covering all the bases. We've got someone in place in Teddy's backyard. No one's home that we can see."

"So . . . you want me to go."

"I want you out of here, yes. I want you safe. Bree's moving the money tonight. We're sure of it. She needs to get rid of it since the word is out about an arrest first thing in the morning."

Ali nodded. She understood all that, but she didn't move. She couldn't take her gaze off his face. "I really thought you were gone," she said softly. "Oh, Luke. Your job. Your review—"

"It'll have to wait." He paused. "Or not. Ali," he said very seriously, "I know that the men in your life have fucked you over. I promised myself that I wouldn't do that to you. I didn't want to get involved."

She tried not to react to that blow. "I know."

"But things change."

She tried to see his expression, but with little to no ambient light in the backseat, she couldn't see it clearly. "Your job, your *life,* is in San Francisco."

"As it turns out, only the job," he said. "And it also turns out that I'm not just the job."

She wasn't sure what that meant, whether to accept the odd surge of hope that suddenly blocked her throat or go with the panic licking at her gut. She worked at getting herself calm and wasn't entirely there yet when she said, "I'm sorry I said you're distant and that you don't feel. I shouldn't have. I picked a fight because I was hurt."

"I know. But you did mean it, and that's okay. It's true. And I want you to say what you mean, always. I can take it." He paused. "*We* can take it. We're tougher than words, the two of us."

Ali's heart stopped and then started again in staccato beat. "Luke—"

The front passenger door jerked open. Cool night air rushed in and so did a figure.

A female figure, but not Leah.

Luke squeezed Ali's thigh, but she didn't need the warning to be quiet.

There was a fiddling in the front seat and a very small beam of light. The woman had a flashlight.

Bree.

"Shit," she muttered when she couldn't get the glove compartment open. "Shit, shit, shit . . ." Then the thing suddenly opened and some stuff fell out.

"God, he is such a slob," she said, dumping everything in the glove box to the floorboards. Then she began to stuff something back in there from the duffel bag in her lap.

Money.

Chapter 26

Ali couldn't believe it. Bree was working on getting money—and lots of it—into the glove compartment. But then she couldn't get it closed, no matter how much she pushed and shoved and swore. Bills were sticking out, and Bree swore at them too. Finally, she used the heel of her very wicked-looking boot to kick it closed.

Luke was doing something with his phone. Ali was working really hard on holding her breath, because Bree's perfume was getting to her. She was running out of air . . .

And then it escaped, a very loud, unladylike sneeze.

With a startled shriek, Bree whirled around, penlight in her mouth.

And a gun in her hand.

"Oh for God's sake," she muttered when she saw who it was. "Could this get any worse? Hands up," she ordered, swinging the gun back and forth between Ali and Luke like a pendulum.

Ali raised her hands, but Luke was slow to respond.

"Now," Bree warned him.

"You need to put the gun down, Bree," he said calmly.

She didn't. "What the hell are you two doing here?" she asked. "Especially *you*," she said to Ali.

"Me? What about *you*?"

"I'm having a fucked-up day, obviously!" Bree yelled. She blew a strand of hair out of her face, which was damp. In fact, she was uncharacteristically ruffled from head to badass-boot-covered toe.

"Put the gun down, Bree," Luke said again.

"Well, I can't now!" She glanced at Ali. "You screwed everything up. *Everything,*" she said. "You and your stupid, sweet, easy-going, artsy-fartsy ways. This is all your fault, you know that? Teddy was *mine*. And then you fell for him, and he couldn't resist you, another sweet little thing who thought he walked on water. He was mine first, dammit!"

"But"—Ali stopped to sneeze again, twice in a row—"you're married to the mayor."

"Yeah. And he's also a financial planner, don't forget. I can't, because he's always working. He's a workaholic whose lover is his job. And the great thing for him is his lover doesn't care that he stopped working out and snores."

Ali just stared at her. "So you started sleeping with the town clerk?"

"Teddy fell in love with *me*," Bree said, jabbing the gun near Ali's face. "Said he needed a *seasoned* woman, one who knew what to do with a man. He said that no one else could keep up with him. Well *I* managed to keep up with him just fine. I gave him whatever he wanted."

Ali didn't want to think about what that meant. She sneezed again.

"Stop that!" Bree yelled.

"It's your perfume. And you're making me nervous. Why do you even have a gun?"

"We live in Washington. Everyone has a gun." Her eyes were dialed to straight-up, bat-shit crazy. She was flushed, and her hair was sticking to her face. "Is it hot in here? It feels hot in here. Fucking hot flashes. It's the twenty-first century, and we can't cure hot flashes."

"I wasn't the only one Teddy was with," Ali said. "You know that, right? He was cheating on *all* of us, Bree, not just you."

"He told me you two were just roommates," Bree said. "And I didn't know about Melissa until the night of the auction, that skinny, young, taut-skinned bitch. I wanted to kill him, but he told me that it didn't mean anything, that I was still his one and only."

"So you forgave him by stealing the money?" Luke asked.

"Hey, sometimes a woman snaps, okay?" She swiped her forehead with her free hand. "My God. Someone open a fucking window!"

"Put down the gun, and I'll open all the windows," Luke said.

She jabbed the gun at him again. "Listen,

smartass, you might be sexy as hell, but I'll shoot you if I have to. Dammit!" She fanned her face. "This is out of control. All I wanted was to *be in a position* to frame Teddy so he'd straighten up. But *you!*" She whipped the gun back to Ali. "You went into his office and blew it."

"Hey, half the town was in his office that night."

"But *you* took the pot, the one I'd put the bill wrapper into," Bree said. "To frame *him,* not you."

"Yeah," Ali muttered, "I've really got to stop doing that."

"Marshall's not worth this, Bree," Luke said. "It's not too late to stop. Give me the gun."

Bree's face crumbled a bit, but she kept the gun level at his face. "The heart wants what it wants," she said. "And I wanted Teddy. Only he turned out to be as big an ass as the rest of them. Hell, look at his life. He's sleeping with half the women in town, and no one even knows. I tried to frame him, and he walks. Shit just doesn't stick to him. And the bastard never breaks a sweat. He's like the Energizer Bunny; he can keep going and going. A girl can't do that. We get bladder infections." Bree swiped her forehead again. "Tonight was the night that his luck was going to change. I put the money in here, and I was going to call the police."

Luke had been slowly lowering his hands. Ali

was going to trust that he knew what the hell he was doing, because she could scarcely draw air into her lungs. It was the gun. Every few seconds, it swung from Luke to her, back and forth. It was one thing to see it happen on TV, it was another entirely to be faced with the reality of it.

"Stop moving," Bree screeched, and Ali went still. Except then she realized Bree was talking to Luke. "I told you, hands up."

Luke ignored her directive, leaving one hand half raised, the other dropping to scratch his chest. "You never said—how did you get the money in the first place?"

"After we did it on his couch, I found a red silk bra behind a cushion. Melissa's, of course, as I learned later. So when he left the office to get rid of the condom—he thought he was being clever by doing that in the hallway bathroom so that no one would ever find out about us—I took the money from his bottom drawer and dumped it into my briefcase. I left one of the money wrappers in his stupid pencil holder so he'd have evidence on him."

"And he didn't notice any of this when he got back from the bathroom?" Luke asked.

"No. He suggested I leave first so that we weren't seen together, which worked for me. I wanted him to be the last in the office—not realizing, of course, that Miss Perfect over here was going to fuck that all up. *Twice.*"

Ali blinked. "You think I'm perfect?"

Luke hadn't taken his eyes off of Bree. "You're losing it, Bree."

"You *think?*" She jabbed the gun in his direction. "And for the last time, I said *hands up.* I mean it." The gun shifted back to Ali. "I'll shoot her, Luke. And I really don't want to do that."

Luke pressed his knee into Ali's. For comfort, she thought, and glanced down. His phone in his pocket was glowing.

He'd gotten it on somehow. He'd been a busy guy, because he'd also tugged up his pant leg, revealing an ankle holster and the gun he had there.

Oh, God. Did he really expect her to grab it? She glanced at him and found his eyes on hers, steady and sure. Yes. He did. Because he believed in her.

I've got you.

His words, he'd said them to her several times now. She hadn't been in a place to fully believe him before, but by now, she absolutely believed him.

He nudged her again.

Right. The gun. She didn't have to fake the next sneeze, but she added a dramatic head toss to go with it, bending forward with the momentum. She was wrapping her fingers around Luke's gun when Bree yelled *"Hey!"*

Luke, apparently tiring of waiting for Ali to get

the gun, made his move without her. Lunging forward, he reached over the back of the seat to grab Bree's wrists and shoved upward.

Bree's gun went off, blowing a hole in the car's roof.

"Ali," Luke said, "get out of the car, take cover. Can you do that?"

Ears ringing from the close-range gunshot, Ali stared at him still strong-arming Bree's hands above their heads with the back of the seat between them. "Y-yes."

"Excellent," he said calmly. "Do it now, Ali."

Oh, God, she couldn't leave him. Wouldn't leave him. He was in an awkward position trying to control Bree from the backseat. And then she realized he was holding back, waiting for her to get to safety so that a stray bullet couldn't hit her.

Reaching behind her, she opened the car door and stumbled out, still holding Luke's gun. She couldn't use it. She had no idea how, plus she couldn't see in the dark to aim. She crouched behind the back rear tire, her fingers shaking so badly it took three tries to pull out her phone.

She knew Leah would have called the police by now, and surely the cops in Teddy's backyard would be coming any second, but she still hit 9-1-1.

From the inside of the Lexus, the gun went off. Oh, God . . .

"9-1-1 emergency dispatch," a disembodied voice said in her ear. "What is your emergency?

"Sh-shots fired," Ali said through chattering teeth. "Off-duty officer and a crazy woman with a gun."

"Location?"

Ali gave the street name and the Lexus's license plate. *"Hurry,"* she said, and peeked around the back of the car.

No one had emerged.

She crawled to the open back door, using the light from her phone to see with one hand, pointing the gun with the other.

Luke was still sitting in the backseat, sprawled out now with Bree's gun in his right hand pointed at her.

The streetlight shined into the interior of the car, highlighting Bree in bold relief. She was still in the front seat on her knees facing Luke, hands raised. Her hair was crazy, her makeup smeared, her eyes shiny with unshed tears.

No gunshot holes.

The streetlight didn't light up the backseat, so Ali couldn't see Luke's face at all, but there was a stillness to him that terrified her. "Luke?"

"It's okay," he said evenly, holding Bree's gun. "Bree's done now. Right, Bree?"

Bree bobbed her head. A sob escaped her, and she covered her mouth with one hand, leaving the other in the air.

Ali didn't want to blind Luke, so she very carefully lifted her phone just high enough to see his body. And her heart stopped, just stopped dead in her chest. "You were hit."

"I didn't mean to," Bree whispered. "I just wanted to put the money in here. I just wanted Teddy to get what he has coming to him. That's all."

Ali shoved the gun into the back of her waistband to free up her hands. She had no idea why, but she'd seen it done in the movies. Then she crawled into the backseat, leaned over Luke, and tore open his shirt.

"I love it when you get rough," he said.

"Shut up a minute." The bullet had gone into the meaty part of his shoulder but it looked terrifyingly close to his chest. She could hear the sirens now and sagged in relief. She peeled Luke's shirt down his arm and pulled him forward just enough to see that the bullet had also exited his body. She pulled off her own shirt and pressed it to his front to try to staunch the bleeding.

He grimaced in pain. "Ali."

She leaned over him. "Right here."

"Take the gun."

She took Bree's gun from his fingers. This put her in the possession of two guns. *I Love Lucy* does *Criminal Minds*.

"Keep an eye on her," Luke said.

Since Bree had collapsed on the front seat and was quietly crying into her hands, this wasn't difficult. Ali twisted to keep her in sight. "Done."

"Good," Luke said. "I'm going to pass out now. Nice bra though . . . isn't this how we met, with you in your underwear?"

And then his eyes closed.

Raw fear nearly choked her. Still holding the gun on Bree, she sank to his side. "Go ahead," she told him, her tears falling onto his face. "I've got you."

The street had come alive with police. The first ones to the car were two cops, both with guns pointed right at her.

That's when she realized she was still holding a gun on Bree. "No," she said, shaking her head as it occurred to her that they probably thought *she* was the one she'd called 9-1-1 about, the crazy woman with a gun. "Oh, no. It's not what you think—"

"Ma'am, put the gun down."

"Okay, dropping the gun now." She dropped it at her feet and then was unceremoniously yanked out of the car and away from Luke.

That's when the other gun fell out of her pants and hit the ground. "Okay," she said. "I know this looks bad, but—"

But nothing. She was quickly and perfunctorily searched for more weapons and pulled clear of the scene. She craned her neck trying to see Luke around the officer dragging her away, but all she could see was a sea of uniforms. There were voices yelling out medical jargon with a sense of urgency that shriveled her soul. She couldn't hear over the rush of the blood roaring in her ears. She couldn't see. "I need to—"

"You need to relax, ma'am."

"Those weren't my guns."

"They were in your possession."

"Yes, because I was holding them for Luke. That's Bree Medina in there, the mayor's wife. She stole the money from town. The fifty thousand? We caught her trying to put it in Teddy's car to frame him. You'll see it in the glove box." He wasn't listening to her rant, she could tell. "Please," she said, "I just want to make sure Luke gets to the hospital."

"He's on his way."

And indeed, just then the ambulance pulled out, heading down the street, lights and siren going.

And then Ali was once again taken to the police station.

Chapter 27

The slow, annoying beeping broke into Luke's consciousness first. And then an antiseptic smell. Ah, *shit*.

A hospital.

He drew in a breath, and pain shot straight through his shoulder and chest, clogging the air in his lungs. Getting shot hurt like a bitch, but oddly enough, he felt a heavy pressure on his *good* side. He opened his eyes and blinked the room into focus.

The pressure was Ali, asleep in the chair at his bedside, her head pillowed on his good arm, wearing . . . a firefighter shirt.

On the other side of his bed sat Jack. He was leaning back, booted feet up on the bed, hands casually linked on his belly, all relaxed, as if he were watching a ball game. He wore his firefighter uniform—minus the shirt.

"Morning, Sleeping Beauty," Jack said.

"What the fuck?"

Jack smiled grimly. "You caught Bree with the stolen dough, got her confession recorded on your phone, got shot, had surgery—you're one lucky son of a bitch, by the way—and you're about to get the girl."

Luke looked at Ali. Her hair was wild and crazy and in her face. Her mouth was open a little, and she was drooling on his forearm. He'd never seen her look more beautiful.

"Don't wake her," Jack said. "She had a rough night."

Luke's heart kicked, and one of his monitors beeped a warning.

Jack leaned forward. "Relax, man, she's fine. It's just that when the cavalry showed up, she was holding a gun. The call had gone out about a crazy lady with a gun so . . ."

"Jesus." Luke wished she wasn't on his good arm so that he could touch her. "Did they—"

"Drag her off you kicking and screaming? Yes. And took Ali downtown." Jack lifted a hand. "She's okay. Your phone made a great witness, and Bree herself confessed everything. I came here first, saw you into surgery, then went down to the station to see what I could do, but Ali was already being released. I brought her here, where we've been ever since."

"So it's over?"

"The hard way, but yeah. You saved the day, man."

"Ali did," Luke said.

Jack shook his head. "I'm pretty sure it was you—"

"No, she saved me," Luke said. "She . . ." He

couldn't tear his gaze off her. "I've been pushing her away since the beginning."

"Tried, you mean."

Luke let out a low laugh, then sucked in a breath of pain. "Oh, Christ, don't make me laugh." He inhaled very carefully, then let it back out again. "I did try. And she let me think I was getting away with it too."

"She loves you."

Luke's gaze touched over Ali again. "Yeah." *His own miracle.* "Go figure."

"With all that bad 'tude and surly grumpiness," Jack said, "what's not to love?" He paused. "You love her back?"

"More than my own life."

"Which became pretty clear when you put your body between mine and a bullet," Ali said groggily, lifting her head. Her eyes locked on Luke's, searching.

He could see the worry, the strain, the fear in every line of her face. "I'm okay," he said, and then turned to Jack. "Right?"

"Well, your MLB pitching career is over, and PT is going to be a bitch," Jack said, "but your arm and shoulder will eventually be okay. As for your psyche, that's a whole different ball game. Oh and some other good news—Ben's coming back. Unlike you, he's all in one piece, no bullet holes." He rose, stretched, and then bumped his fist very gently to Luke's hand sticking out of the bandages. Walking around the bed, he kissed Ali on the top of her head before walking out of the room.

Ali never took her eyes off of Luke. The night had been the longest of her entire life—being held at the station while Luke had been here, then sitting in that OR waiting room with Jack, pacing through the hours.

If Luke had gone to San Francisco when he'd planned on going, this wouldn't have happened. But he'd stayed to help straighten out her life, and it had nearly cost him his.

"Stop," he said, voice gravelly. Tired. His eyes were knowing. "Stop blaming yourself."

Her throat burned so much that she couldn't speak. "You took a damn bullet for me, Luke."

He lifted his good hand and cupped her face. "I'd do anything for you, Ali."

That was becoming quite clear, and she leaned over him, very, very serious. "Anything?"

"Anything."

"Then love me," she whispered.

He slid his fingers into her hair, stroking it from her face. "Done," he said softly.

She was quite certain her heart couldn't swell any more without bursting a rib. "I want one more thing."

He let out a small smile. "You mean other than my life and also my heart and soul?"

She didn't return the smile, couldn't. "Let me love you back."

His smile faded. "Ali—"

"I don't care that you'll be in San Francisco. I don't. Hell, I'd move there if you wanted me too. I love you, Luke. I have from that very first moment you looked at me like I was a crazy, naked woman in your house."

"You *were* a crazy, naked woman in my house." He stroked a finger over her temple, down her jaw. "You need to think about this, Ali. Loving me isn't a day in the park. I'm stubborn and like to be right. I rarely make my bed. I can never find my fucking keys. And last but not least, I love you so hard it hurts. I might die of it, actually, which makes me a short-term bet at best."

With her heart in her throat, she had to both laugh and cry as she dropped her hand to his good shoulder. "I already know you're stubborn as a mule. And I can let you be right—half the time."

She felt his smile and lifted her head. "And an unmade bed works for me," she said softly, "because then we can just get back into it whenever we want without worrying about messing it up."

She felt his hand fist on the back of her shirt, holding her close. "You're the best thing that's ever happened to me," he said fiercely. "The very best." Then he nudged her in closer for a kiss—

"Ahem."

Ali broke away from Luke and turned. In the open doorway, peeking around the curtain, was Sawyer and the mayor.

"Luke," Sawyer said, nodding. "Ali."

The mayor, somber, greeted them as well.

Ali had seen both men briefly in the station last night, though neither had spoken to her. Sawyer had had his hands full with the night's activities. Tony—no doubt called when Bree had been brought in, still sobbing about how she'd been framed by her "own stupid life"—had looked exhausted and solemn.

Which was how they both looked now.

"Wanted to make sure you were still kicking," Sawyer said to Luke.

A very small smile curved Luke's lips. "Been through worse."

"I imagine you have. Couldn't have figured this one out so fast without you."

"It was Ali," Luke said.

Sawyer nodded. "I know. I also know you missed your review. I called Commander O'Neil. They're proceeding without you, but your job's safe and intact." He met Ali's gaze then. "You're a social media sensation this morning."

Oh boy. "You mean like *Hapless Florist Nearly Screws Up Investigation?*"

He smiled. "I believe they said something

about Calamity Jane meets Annie Oakley . . ."

Ali groaned. Luke tried to laugh but choked it off with a sound of pain that had Ali whipping back to him.

"We'll make this short," the mayor said. "Obviously, I'm horrified at the part Bree played in this."

He was careful not to claim her as his *wife,* Ali couldn't help but notice. Probably Bree's days with that title were severely numbered.

Tony looked at Ali. "I wanted to do this right away." He pulled out his phone and accessed a video.

It was the senior center, the room Ali used as a classroom. All the seniors were there, crowded close to the screen, a sea of wrinkled, anxious faces.

"We never should have doubted you, Ali," Mr. Wykowski said.

"And we love and admire you," Lucille said.

"Stay," Mr. Elroy said.

"Please," Mr. Lyons said.

Mrs. Burland was sitting there tight lipped. Lucille smacked her in the arm. Mrs. Burland glared at her, and then into the camera she said, "I know you're smarter than to let a bunch of nosy-bodies chase you away, Ali Winters."

Edward's face appeared. "You're special," he said. "Special and amazing."

"So special and amazing that I'm gifting you

the first and last month's lease money for the shop Russell vacated," Mr. Lyons said. "And now for the reward money . . ."

The video pulled back to get all of them in the same shot. They held a huge mock-up of a check in the amount of five thousand dollars, written to . . . her.

Ali gaped.

Tony slid his phone away and pulled out a piece of paper.

Her check.

"The reward money," Tony said.

"Oh," she breathed, stunned. She looked up at the mayor. "But I can't accept this. Luke—"

"It's all yours," Luke said.

Ali stared down at the check in shock. "It's so pretty," she whispered reverently.

Sawyer laughed, and both he and the mayor left.

"Wow," Ali said with a shake of her head. "I feel like I won the lottery."

"That's not all you won," Luke said.

She leaned in and kissed him. "A trip to Disneyland?" she teased.

"If you want," he said seriously, "but not what I was thinking."

"Some lease money for my flower shop?" she asked, waving the check.

"Most definitely, but still not quite it. Keep going, Ali. You're getting warmer."

"Luke—"

"Need a hint?"

"Please," she said.

He tightened his grip on her. "Me. Us." He kissed her. *"This."*

She couldn't breathe again, but this time it was because hope and love and affection were tangled in her throat, vying for space. "We're an us?"

"Yes," he said, "which is a much better deal for me than you, so be sure—"

She put a finger against his lips. "I'm sure. In fact, I've never been so sure of anything in my life."

Epilogue

Two weeks later, Ali picked up a tray of tea and coffee with hands that weren't quite steady. "I'm so nervous."

Luke, still wearing a sling but getting more and more movement back every day, leaned in and kissed her. "You'll nail this."

"Like she did you," Leah quipped. She picked up the second tray, filled with the pastry goodies she'd made for the grand opening of the new flower shop.

Ali's Blooms.

She'd signed the lease and was officially in the space next to the bakery again.

It was all she'd ever wanted.

Half the town was here for the opening party, and the other half was on their way.

"She can nail me any time," Luke said, and snatched a custard puff from Leah's tray and stuffed it in his mouth. He gave Ali one more quick kiss, tasting like vanilla.

She hummed her pleasure. Just looking up in his warm, blue eyes quelled her nerves. He was her rock.